PENGUIN BOOKS

WAKING GODS

Sylvain Neuvel was born in Quebec and dropped out of school when he was fifteen. Since then he has sold ice cream in California, peddled furniture across Canada, and taught Linguistics in India. He has also worked as a software engineer, journalist, certified translator and received a PhD in Linguistics from the University of Chicago.

He is an amateur robotics enthusiast and life-long fan of all things science fiction. *Sleeping Giants*, his debut novel and first in the Themis Files series, was published in 2016. *Waking Gods* was his second novel and *Only Human* is his third.

BY THE SAME AUTHOR
Sleeping Giants
Waking Gods

WAKING GODS

BOOK TWO OF THE THEMIS FILES

SYLVAIN NEUVEL

PENGUIN BOOKS

PENGUIN BOOKS

UK | USA | Canada | Ireland | Australia
India | New Zealand | South Africa

Penguin Books is part of the Penguin Random House group of companies
whose addresses can be found at global.penguinrandomhouse.com

Penguin
Random House
UK

First published in the United States of America by Del Rey 2017
Published in Great Britain by Michael Joseph 2017
Published in Penguin Books 2018
001

Printed in Great Britain by Clays Ltd, St Ives plc

A CIP catalogue record for this book is available from the British Library

ISBN: 978–1–405–92191–6

www.greenpenguin.co.uk

MIX
Paper from
responsible sources
FSC® C018179

Penguin Random House is committed to a
sustainable future for our business, our readers
and our planet. This book is made from Forest
Stewardship Council® certified paper.

To Barbara and Han Solo.
Look, Bara, you're my rock, my everything,
but Han died! You don't mind sharing, do you?

WAKING GODS

PROLOGUE

PERSONAL JOURNAL ENTRY—EVA REYES

Melissa made fun of me at school today. She's all about boys now. Enzo and his friends started calling me La Evita Loca again and she joined in. She said: "Look! Crazy Eva's gonna cry!" I hate her.

She was my last good friend. Angie goes to Baldwin now and I hardly ever hear from her. Essie moved to Bayamón. They were the only ones I saw outside of school. Mom keeps telling me to get out more but there's no one to play with. We used to look for rocks by Rio Piedras. Essie loves rocks, especially those blue ones. I think they're called kyanite. I went by myself the other day and I found tons of them. I told her I'd bring them when I visit, but I don't know when Mom will let me go. She says I have to get better first.

I'm seeing that psychiatrist again tonight. He thinks I'm crazy, like everyone else. They keep telling me it's normal to have bad dreams. But I know they're not dreams. I have them when I'm awake now. I saw it again today at school, and I started screaming. It's the same one I've been having for months. Everyone's dead. There are thousands of them, dead on the streets, a whole city filled with corpses. I see my parents lying in blood inside our house. I haven't told them that part. Today there was something new. I saw a robot, like Themis, a big metal woman falling into the clouds.

PART ONE

KITH AND KIN

FILE NO. 1398

NEWS REPORT—JACOB LAWSON, BBC LONDON
Location: Regent's Park, London, England

A twenty-story-tall metallic figure appeared in the middle of Regent's Park this morning. Caretakers at the London Zoo were the first to notice it at around 4 A.M. Standing on one of the Hub's football pitches at the north end of the park, the figure, or robot, bears a resemblance, in both size and shape, to the UN robot we now know as Themis. This new giant, however, appears to be a man, or shall I say is made in the image of a man. It is much more muscular than the slender feminine titan that visited London less than a year ago, perhaps taller as well. Its colour is also different, a lighter grey than the UN robot, and it is striated with yellow light, in contrast to the turquoise-veined Themis.

According to early witnesses, the robot appeared out of thin air in the middle of the park. "It wasn't there, then it was," said one of the zookeepers. Fortunately, the football pitches at the Hub were deserted at this hour, and not a single casualty has been reported. It is unknown, of course, whether this early appearance was deliberate, as we do not know where this robot came from or who sent it. If this is indeed a robot like Themis, and if it is controlled in the same manner as she is, there could be pilots aboard. If pilots there are, are they Russian, Japanese, or Chinese? Or are they from somewhere else entirely? We can only speculate at this juncture. There might be no one at all in this giant structure. In the four hours it has been standing here, it has not moved an inch.

The Earth Defense Corps (EDC) has yet to issue an official statement. Dr. Rose Franklin, head of the scientific division, was reached in Geneva, where she was to give a speech later this morning. She would not speculate as to the origin of this second robot but has assured us that it is not part of the UN planetary defence. If true, this would suggest that either a second alien robot has been discovered on Earth and kept from us or that this one does not come from our planet. In New York, the EDC has scheduled a press conference for three o'clock London time.

The Earth Defense Corps, which was founded nine years ago by the United Nations following the American discovery of the Themis robot, is tasked with extracting new technologies from the alien artifact for the benefit of mankind and to protect this planet against extraterrestrial threats. Only time will tell if we are facing such a threat today.

No word yet from His Majesty's Government, but sources say the Prime Minister will address the nation within the hour. The British people will not have to wait to hear from the other side of the aisle. The official opposition was quick to issue a statement earlier today, immediately calling for the Prime Minister to offer some reassurances. Opposition leader Amanda Webb took to the air about an hour ago, saying: "There is an alien device with potentially devastating power standing in the middle of London and all the Prime Minister has seen fit to do is to restrict access to one city park. Can he tell the thirteen million people who live in the Greater London Area that they are safe? If he can, he owes the British people an explanation, and if he can't, I for one would like to know why we aren't talking about evacuation." The former Foreign Secretary went on to suggest that Central London be evacuated first, something that, by her calculation, could be accomplished in an orderly manner in less than forty-eight hours.

Londoners, for their part, appear in no hurry to go anywhere. Perhaps as surprising as the robot's appearance is the utter nonchalance the population has displayed since. The towering figure is visible from most of London, and while one might expect civic unrest, or a massive exodus from the city, Londoners, for the most part, have gone about their business; many have even made their way towards

Regent's Park to see this new titan up close. The police have closed off the area south of Prince Albert and north of A501 between A41 and Albany Street, but some have managed to escape their attention and found their way into the park. The police even had to evacuate a family that was preparing for a picnic, a mere few steps from the giant metallic feet of the intruder.

It's hard to blame Londoners for seeing a creature similar to Themis as a friendly figure. They have been told that a race of aliens left her on Earth for our protection. Her metal face and backwards legs are on the telly almost every day and have made the front page of every red top for nearly a decade. There are Themis tee shirts for sale on every corner, and young Londoners have grown up playing with Themis action figures. Themis is a star. Her visit to another one of London's Royal Parks a year ago felt more like a rock concert than first contact with something from an alien world.

This is a defining moment in the short history of the EDC. The fruit of a very fragile coalition, the organization has been called a public-relations stunt by its detractors. Many have argued that a single robot, no matter how powerful, could not defend a planet against an invader. By adding a second robot to its arsenal, or forging a formal alliance with another race, the EDC would come a long way in silencing its critics.

FILE NO. 1399

PERSONAL JOURNAL ENTRY—
DR. ROSE FRANKLIN, HEAD OF SCIENCE
DIVISION, EARTH DEFENSE CORPS

I had a cat. For some reason, no one remembers my having a cat. I've been picturing her curled into a ball on the kitchen floor, slowly starving to death while waiting for me to come home. I keep forgetting that Rose Franklin came home that night, that she—the other me—never left. I'm glad my cat didn't starve, but part of me wishes she'd waited for me by the door. I miss her. My apartment feels incredibly empty without her small presence.

Maybe she died. She wasn't that old, though. Maybe I got rid of her when my job became too demanding. Maybe she didn't recognize the person who came home that night pretending to be me and ran away. I wish. She'd probably be afraid of me if she were still around. If there's a "real" Rose Franklin, chances are I'm not it.

Thirteen years ago, I got into a traffic accident on my way to work. Strangers pulled me out of my car and I woke up on the side of the road, in Ireland, four years later. I hadn't aged a day.

How is that possible? Did I travel to the future? Was I . . . frozen, cryogenized for four years? I'll probably never know. I can live with that. What I'm having a hard time dealing with is that I wasn't really gone for those four years. I—someone like me, anyway—was here. Rose Franklin went to work the next day. She did a whole bunch of things during those years. Somehow, she ended up studying the giant metal hand I had fallen onto as a child. She became convinced that there were more giant body parts lying around and devised a method for unearthing them. She pieced together a giant alien robot called Themis. Then she died.

It was a busy four years.

I don't remember any of it, of course. I wasn't there. Whoever did all those things died. I know for a fact it wasn't *me* me. Rose Franklin was twenty-eight when she was put in charge of the research team studying the hand. She died at thirty. A year later, they found me. I was twenty-seven.

Themis ended up with the United Nations. They created a planetary defense branch, called the EDC, with the robot as its main asset. I wasn't there for that either. One of me had died. The other hadn't been found yet. They put me in charge of the EDC research team about a month after I reappeared. The other Rose must have made quite an impression because I was probably the least qualified person for the job. I had never even *seen* Themis. As far as I was concerned, the last time I had seen any part of her was on my eleventh birthday. They didn't seem to care. Neither did I. I really wanted the job. I've been at it for nine years. Nine years. One would think that would be enough time to get over what happened to me. It's not. I had four years of catching up to do, and that kept my mind busy for a while. But as I settled into some sort of routine, got more comfortable with my new job, my new life, I became more and more obsessed with who and what I am.

I realize that if I did travel through time, I probably don't have the knowledge to fully understand it, but there shouldn't have been two of us. Move an object from point A to point B, logic dictates you won't find it at point A anymore. Am I a clone? A copy? I can live without knowing what happened to me, but I have to know if I'm . . . me. That's an awful thing to doubt.

I know I don't belong here, now. I'm . . . out of sync. It's a familiar feeling, now that I think about it. Every so often—maybe two or three times a year—I would get this anxiety rush. I'd usually be really tired, maybe had too much coffee, and I'd start feeling . . . I never knew how to describe it. Every second that goes by feels like nails on a chalkboard. It usually lasts a minute or two but it feels like you're just a tiny bit—half a second or so—out of sync with the universe. I was never able to really explain it, so I don't know if I'm the only one who ever felt this. I suppose not, but that's how I feel every minute of every day now, only that half second is getting longer and longer.

I have no real friends, no real relationships. The ones I have are based on experiences I didn't share, and the ones I lost have been damaged by events I didn't live through. My mother still calls me every other night. She doesn't understand that we hadn't spoken in over a year when I came back. How could she? She's calling that other person, the one who isn't still dealing with her father's loss, the one who everyone liked. The one who died. I haven't talked to any of my old friends from school, from home. They were at my funeral. That's such a perfect ending to a relationship, I wouldn't want to spoil that.

Kara and Vincent are the closest thing I have to friends now, but even after nine years, I'm somewhat . . . ashamed of our friendship. I'm an impostor. Their affection for me is based on a lie. They've told me what we supposedly went through together and we all pretend that we would have shared the same experiences had the circumstances been different. We keep pretending I'm that other person, and they like me for it.

I don't know what I am, but I know I'm not . . . her. I'm trying to be. Desperately trying. I know that if I could just be her, everything would be all right. But I don't know her. I have gone over every page of her notes a thousand times, and I still can't see the world as she did. I see glimpses of myself in some of her journal entries, but those fleeting moments aren't enough to bring us any closer. She was clever, though; I'm not certain I could do what she did if we were looking for giant body parts today. She must have found some research I don't know about, probably something that was published while I was "away." Maybe I'm an imperfect copy. Maybe she was just smarter.

She certainly was more optimistic. She believed—was utterly convinced—that Themis was left here as a gift for us to find in due time, a coming-of-age present left to an adolescent race by a benevolent father figure. Yet they buried all the pieces in the far corners of the Earth, in the most remote of places, even under the ice. I can see why I might get excited by a treasure hunt, but I can't find a good reason for the added hurdles. My gut tells me these things were hidden . . . well, just that. Hidden, as in not to be found.

More than anything, I can't imagine why anyone, however advanced, would leave behind a robot that, in all likelihood, we wouldn't be able to use. Anyone with the technology to build one of these things, and to travel light-years to bring it here, would have had the power to adapt the controls to our anatomy. They would have had a mechanic aboard, someone who could fix the robot, or at least Mac-Gyver their way out of small problems. All it would really take is their version of a screwdriver to turn the knee braces around so we could use them. They couldn't have expected us to mutilate ourselves in order to pilot this thing.

I'm a scientist, and I have no proof for any of this, but neither did the other Rose when she assumed the opposite. Without evidence, even Occam's razor should never have led me in that direction.

The irony is that they built this entire program based on my findings. If I had told them how scared I am of what will come, they never would have given me the freedom to do what I'm doing now. The lab is the only place I find comfort in and I'm grateful for that. I'm grateful for Themis, to be in her company every day. I feel drawn to her. She isn't of this world either. She doesn't belong here any more than I do. We're both out of place and out of time, and the more I learn about her, the closer I feel to understanding what really happened to me.

I know everyone is worried about me. My mother told me she would pray for me. You don't do that for someone who's doing great. I didn't want to upset her, so I said thank you. My faith has never been really strong, but even if it were, I know there's no God coming to help me. There's no redemption for what I've done. I should be dead. I died. I was brought back by what I assume is advanced technology, but you might as well call it witchcraft. Not too long ago, the Church would have burned someone like me.

I may believe in God, but I'm at war with Him. I'm a scientist, I try to answer questions, one at a time, so there's a little less room for Him as the answer. I plant my flag, and inch by inch, I take away His kingdom. It's odd, but none of this has ever occurred to me before. I never even saw a real contradiction between science and religion. I see it now, I see it clear as day.

I've crossed that line we're not supposed to cross. I died. And I'm still here. I cheated death. I took away God's power.

I killed God and I feel empty inside.

FILE NO. 1408

INTERVIEW WITH BRIGADIER GENERAL EUGENE GOVENDER, COMMANDER, EARTH DEFENSE CORPS

Location: Waldorf Astoria Hotel, New York, NY

—You should hurry, Eugene.

—How long have we known each other?

—Fourteen years this September.

—Fourteen years. And in all that time, have I ever, once, given you permission to call me Eugene?

—"General" seems . . . inappropriate after what we have been through.

—It does, doesn't it? Imagine how it feels to have absolutely nothing to call you.

—Not that I do not enjoy hearing you ramble endlessly about my anonymity, but you are addressing the United Nations General Assembly in less than one hour. I know how much you loathe speeches, so if you require my help, now would be a good time.

—Then why don't *you* give the address? You're the one who got me into this mess in the first place.

—Let me hear your opening.

—Where's that damn piece of paper? Oh, here it is. Have you seen my—

—**They are on the nightstand.**

—Thank you. It goes like this: "I know many of you are afraid. I know you want answers."

—**I meant what is the beginning of your speech?**

—That *is* the beginning of my damn speech.

—**Eugene, you are not talking to cadets at the academy. This is the UN General Assembly. There is protocol. You normally begin by naming everyone. Mr. President, Mr. Secretary General, members of the General Assembly, ladies and gentlemen.**

—Fine. I'll start with that, then I'll say "I know many of you are afraid. I know you want answers."

—**No, you have to say something profound first, something inspiring.**

—Something inspiring? There's a giant goddamn robot in the middle of London. What people want is for me to get rid of it. There's nothing profound about that.

—**Then say something completely unrelated but profound. The last address I heard in person was from a US President. He said something like: "We come together at a crossroads between war and peace; between disorder and integration; between fear and hope."**

—Very well then. Mr. President, Mr. Secretary General, members of the General Assembly, ladies and gentlemen. Those of you who know me know I am a man of few words. Those who know me well also know how much I loathe speeches. So with your permission, I will steal my opening remarks from a former president of the United States. He said: "We come together at a crossroads between war and peace; between disorder and integration; between fear and hope."

—**That is—**

—I was joking. I *have* a quote from another fellow who had a better way with words, I can just move it up. After that, you'll have to settle for some words of my own. His name is Thomas Henry Huxley. He was a scientist in the early days of modern biology. He said: "The known is finite, the unknown infinite; intellectually we stand on an islet in the midst of an illimitable ocean of inexplicability. Our business in every generation is to reclaim a little more land." Almost a decade ago, when Themis was revealed to the world, we realized that ocean was a lot bigger than we thought, and what transpired this morning in London has made our islet of certainty feel so small that we may wonder if we even have enough room to stand on.

Now can I say it?

—I know many of you are afraid.

—Don't make fun of me.

I know many of you are afraid. I know you want answers. Let me be blunt, I don't have the answers you're looking for. Not today. I also have a confession to make. I . . . am also afraid. I'm afraid because I don't know what that thing is, or what it wants. I don't know if there are more coming and I really don't know if we could do anything about it if there were. There is a lot we don't know. A little bit of fear is only healthy if you ask me.

—How reassuring. I feel better already.

—We can't let fear stop us from doing what we must do. We also can't let fear dictate our actions. We *must* exercise patience. What we've got here—

—What are you trying to say?

—That everyone should wait before doing something really stupid.

—Such as?

—You know that there are those in England who want a show of force. I also know that NATO is considering military action of its own. I want everyone in that room to use their influence. I want them to use every means at their disposal to make sure that doesn't happen.

—Why?

—You know why! This second robot is probably even more powerful than Themis. It's doubtful that British ground forces could put a scratch on it. And this is London. In an urban environment, there is simply no way to concentrate enough firepower with a ground assault. An all-out air strike has more potential, but we'd need a joint operation between our biggest air forces. We'd also level the city of

London. If that doesn't bring the robot down, a high-yield nuclear bomb would be our best, and last, option, though it would mean relocating most of England's population after the fact. Is that clear enough for you?

—**If that is what you want people to leave with, then you should say it like that, in those words. Make them understand there is no "best-case scenario" if they attack, that they cannot "bluff" their way out of this.**

—You don't think it's a little rough? You asked for profound and inspiring.

—**You open with profound and inspiring so that, twenty years from now, people can feel clever quoting you around the dinner table. If there is something you want people to understand today, say it like you are addressing your grandchildren. Half the people in that room will hear you through an interpreter, and most have the attention span of a five-year-old. When they leave the room, these people will call home. They will probably talk to their defense ministers, their top generals, their chiefs of staff, people with an army at their disposal who are itching to use it. You are asking them to trust a group of scientists before their own military advisors. Make sure the reason for that is not lost in translation.**

—I had another paragraph that made me sound reasonably intelligent.

—**Let me hear it.**

—What we've got here is not a London problem. It is not a British or a European problem. It's certainly not a NATO problem. What we've got here is an Earth problem. It's a problem for all of us, for every nation represented in this room, and we must find a solution to it, together. This institution was founded in the wake of the most devastating war in human history, to promote peace by allowing nations to resolve their disputes here, in this room, and not on the battlefield. It was also created so that we could pool our knowledge and resources and achieve great things none of us could dream of achieving on our own. Today we have a chance to do both: prevent war on a level we've never imagined and bring humanity to a whole new frontier. If there has ever been a time for the United Nations, it is now. If there has ever been a reason for the EDC, this is it.

—Put that at the end for when they have stopped paying attention. For now, you should talk about your military career so they can relate.

—I say a few words somewhere . . . Here . . . I also know many of you have doubts. The decision to create the EDC was not a unanimous one. Why should you trust the EDC and not your own military? That is probably the only question I can answer today. I'm a military man, have been for over forty years. I can tell you this: Military people need intelligence . . .

—You need to say more than that. Tell them about how many wars you have been in, how many people you killed. Make them see the blood. Make them think of you as a warmonger who would drop a bomb on London at the first excuse. Only then will they believe you when you tell them they should not.

—What can I say? I am a Brigadier General in the South African Army and Commander of a UN military force. In South Africa, I was in charge of the Army Armour Formation, that's a hard-to-pronounce way of saying lots of tanks. I fought in a segregated unit during the Border Wars, I have been part of peacekeeping operations in Sudan, I have led forces for the UN Intervention Brigade in the Democratic Republic of Congo. I have been in one army or the other for all of my adult life—

—Perfect.

— . . . and I can tell you this: Military people—people like me—need intelligence to be useful. We need to know what's going on. Without intelligence, take my word for it, you do not want your fate in the hands of the military. We *do not* improvise. We're like an elephant in a china shop, we can make a big mess of things if you have us chasing our tail.

I am also the Commander of the Earth Defense Corps, technically another military force with a single, gigantic weapon. As Commander, I have two soldiers under my command. Make that one soldier. The other is technically a Canadian consultant. I also have sixty-eight scientists working for me. They didn't exactly phrase it like that when they offered me the job because they know I don't like scientists. Scientists are like children: They always want to know everything, they all ask too many questions, and they never follow orders to the letter.

That, people, is the EDC. A big robot, one soldier, a linguist, and a whole lot of disobedient children. What we need, what the world needs right now, is them, my insubordinate kids. They know more about alien technology than anyone on Earth and they're learning more every day. That is what they do, they learn things, constantly. They claim land for our little island of knowledge so that we can have room to breathe.

—Touching.

—I remembered the speech you gave me when you tried to sell me this job the first time around.

—You said no.

—I did, but it was a good speech. Then I have a few paragraphs about what we know, mostly about what we don't know.

—What do we know?

—Not much. Here's what I have.

We've only had a few hours to look at the data that's available, and our people haven't been onsite yet, so this is what we know. The figure in London is roughly ten feet taller than Themis, and about 10 percent more massive. We're calling it Kronos. That's it. The rest is conjecture.

There might be no one in that big metal man. It might be remote-controlled, it might not even be a robot; it hasn't moved since it arrived. We feel this is rather unlikely, but it's not something we can blindly discard as an option. There might also be humans in there. That would mean another robot was buried somewhere and was discovered by one of the nations represented here today. That also seems unlikely but not impossible.

Given what we know about Themis, the most probable scenario is that there are two or more alien pilots on board, and since the figure in London looks a hell of a lot like Themis, our working assumption at this point is that it was built by the same race. That doesn't necessarily mean that we are dealing with the people who built Themis. They left one giant robot on this planet, it stands to reason they could have done the same thing on another inhabited planet, and it might be *these* people visiting us. Like I said, we don't know much.

Assuming we are in fact dealing with aliens, they might be friendly. They didn't come out guns blazing—that's usually a good sign—and our current theory about Themis is that she was left here for us to defend ourselves. Their intent might very well be hostile. It would be odd for a foe to give us this much time to prepare, but its presence might be a prelude to a full-scale invasion or attack. Another very reasonable explanation, the one we're leaning towards, is that they're still trying to figure us out. They would have no way to know whether we mean them any harm or how we'll react to their presence.

But enough speculation. All I can offer you right now is a lot of ifs and maybes. I was asked to come here and make a recommendation. For now, it's a very simple one: Send Themis to England, that will take seven or eight days. Let my kids do their job for another week and we'll reconvene. In the meantime, I will ask, implore all of you to exercise restraint and let this process take its course. This is not the time for impulsive action, no matter how tempting it might be.

That's it. That's my speech. Is that long enough?

—It will do just fine.

—Of course, it didn't help that I had to write a whole new one for the press corps after Rose lost her goddamn mind.

—What did she do?

—You missed that? She went on television and told the whole world we shouldn't be involved.

—Who is we?

—The EDC. She said sending Themis would be our biggest mistake. I know you like her, but you know she hasn't been thinking straight. That girl is hanging on by a really thin thread.

—She has been through some . . . unsettling events.

—I get that. What I don't get is why you put her in charge. She could have been on the team without running the show, you know. She doesn't like me because I'm the big bad military, but what she's doing really isn't helping. Sending Themis over there is the only way I can buy some time. Without that, there'll be troops in Regent's Park by morning, and we both know how that'll end.

—Let me hear it.

—What?

—**What you prepared for the press corps.**

—Fine. You may have heard the Head of our Science Division, Dr. Rose Franklin, speak to the media this morning. She had a lot to say, but, to summarize, Dr. Franklin believes we should do nothing, send no one, not even the EDC, and hope that the robot eventually leaves of its own accord. Dr. Franklin is a brilliant scientist and she is certainly entitled to her opinion, even if she doesn't speak for the EDC. As you may know, Dr. Franklin was almost killed in an accident involving Themis in Colorado, and I believe the incident has left her unnecessarily cautious. While I disagree with her conclusion, she did say a lot more than "we shouldn't send the EDC." She made a few good points this morning.

We're making first contact with an alien species. No matter how it goes, this will be a defining moment in human history. We should all stop for a minute and realize how significant and far-reaching these events are.

With that in mind, Dr. Franklin pointed out that sending an armored division and a few thousand armed soldiers is probably not the best way to make a good first impression. I find it hard to disagree.

She did suggest that sending Themis would be an even bigger mistake. Tanks and foot soldiers might be perceived as a sign of aggression, but they would most likely pose no serious threat to the robot if it's anything like ours. Themis, on the other hand, could possibly give 'em a run for their money. I believe that showing the aliens a familiar face might be a good way to open a dialogue, but there is an argument to be made that sending the only thing on this Earth that could hurt these guys might not be such a great idea.

—**Concise. Decisive, yet supportive. I like it. Grab your jacket. It is time to go.**

—Do you remember what you told me the second time around to get me to take this job?

—**I do.**

—You said: "I found you a military post where you'll never have to kill anyone ever again."

—**I know. I still intend to keep that promise.**

FILE NO. 1416

INTERVIEW WITH CAPTAIN KARA RESNIK, EARTH DEFENSE CORPS

Location: Somewhere in the Atlantic

—**Good morning, Ms. Resnik. I hope I did not wake you.**

—Holy shit! No! I just got out of the shower. I was running laps on top deck. Why does it feel like we haven't talked in a decade?

—**It has been eight years since our last conversation. Can you talk?**

—You mean can anyone hear me? I doubt it, Vincent's still asleep in his bunk.

—**I meant are you busy?**

—I missed this.

—**What?**

—This!

— . . .

—No, I'm not busy. I have time to talk.

—**Where are you?**

—In the middle of the Atlantic, but you know that already.

—I meant on the boat.

—In our quarters. We have a little . . . It's like a very, very small apartment. We have a couch, a TV, kitchenette.

—**I am pleased to hear that you are comfortable. I requested some amenities when the UN acquired your vessel. I know how much you disliked the previous one.**

—Oh, it's night and day, sir. The boat we took before was carrying grain, we were like stowaways. This one's been overhauled just for us. It doesn't do anything else. We still sleep in bunk beds though I'm not sure why that is. How've you been? I bet you're bored out of your mind without us.

—**Believe it or not, there are things in the world that do not revolve around you. Not many, but enough to keep me reasonably occupied.**

—I was just asking how you were. I haven't talked to you in eight years!

—**You were asking about my personal life?**

—God, I missed you! Why has it been this long, though? I know you talked to Dr. Franklin a bunch of times.

—**You and Mr. Couture appeared to be doing well. I did not see the need.**

—You could have said "Hi"!

—**Chitchat requires some form of reciprocity, which I cannot offer. But, as I said, I requested some amenities when the UN acquired your vessel.**

—You mean you thought of me . . . once. Some years ago.

—**Exactly. What was it you called me in Puerto Rico? All mush inside? How is Dr. Franklin doing?**

—Well, you know, you spoke to her. She's a little darker than she used to be. I thought it would go away after a while, but it's been nearly a decade, so I think that's the new her. We still get along great, me and her, though. She likes Vincent too. Everyone else, not so much.

—She has been through trauma. That is to be expected.

—You mean she died. I know; I was there. I killed her. Then she came back four years younger. She never told me how she came back. Does she know?

—She does not.

—Do you?

—I do not.

—You wouldn't tell me if you did.

—Probably not, but I really do not know. And to be accurate, she is only missing three years of her life. She was dead for the fourth one.

—Remind me never to come to you for reassurance. No wonder she's not coping well. I'm not the one who died and came back and I'm freaked-out. I mean, me and Vincent spent hours with her every day before she died. Who did we spend all that time with?

—Dr. Rose Franklin.

—Well, that Dr. Franklin died. The Rose Franklin we spend time with now doesn't remember any of it.

—I realize how confusing this is. I am as bewildered by the situation as you are. I will provide answers when I have them. May I inquire as to the status of your relationship with Mr. Couture?

—Have you been watching us these past few years?

—As far as I know, neither you nor Mr. Couture are under surveillance.

—How nice. I meant on TV. Do you even know what we've been doing? You weren't kidding when you said it would mostly be parades and photo ops. We spend a couple hours a day in the lab trying to learn more about Themis. That's ten, fifteen hours a week tops, and that's when we're in New York. When we're on tour, then there's no research whatsoever. The rest of the time is what you said it would be. There aren't many parades—the logistics are just insane, she destroys everything she steps on, even roads. There aren't many cities willing to deal with the expense and the security—but we sure take a lot of pictures. Human interest, mostly. We visit schools, hospitals; children's hospitals are the best. Vincent's great with kids. He does the knee thing, that helps, but he's really good with them. We're a circus act.

—You must hate every minute of it.

—You think I would, right? But I don't. It's a nice routine. We eat well, hotel rooms are great. Jenny takes good care of us.

—Who is Jenny?

—The tour manager. She handles our bookings, special requests. Like I said, we're an act. I thought I would quit after a month when we started, but I'm sort of enjoying it. I'm horrible at it, though. They have to record my interviews in advance or have someone ready to bleep half of what I say. Vincent does most of the talking now. I'm not very good with kids either. They have no sense of irony whatsoever. I made a sick kid cry once. She had leukemia, I think, and I made her cry.

—I fail to see what you find enjoyable.

—The P.R. part is bad. If it were just that, I . . . It's what comes with it. We work a few hours a day. Jenny thinks she's overworking us, but she doesn't know we used to pull sixteen-hour shifts in Denver. How do I put this? We travel together. We have lots of time to ourselves. We haven't tried to kill each other yet. I don't know. It feels . . .

—Normal?

—Yeah. That.

—Did you manage to keep Mr. Couture from proposing all this time?

—I guess I did. To be honest, I haven't really been trying the past couple years.

—What made you change your mind?

—Oh. I haven't changed my mind. I just didn't feel the need anymore. I think he's given up on me.

—Does it bother you?

—Maybe a little. I guess part of me was hoping I *would* change my mind. I know how much it matters to him. He should be with someone who wants kids as much as he does. I think he finally realized that's not me. Anyway, it doesn't matter now.

—What do you mean?

—I don't know. We're going over there to face that alien robot. We're . . . back. I'm back. That's how it feels anyway. Am I a horrible person for feeling that way?

—You are likely on your way to a quick death at the hands of a superior enemy, and this somehow makes you happy. *Horrible* is not the first word that comes to mind.

—Maybe not happy, more . . . alive. I feel more like myself than I have for a while is what I'm trying to say. Maybe normal isn't for me. Maybe I was trying to be something I'm not.

—I do not wish to impede your journey towards self-discovery, but I am reasonably certain that there are ways of being yourself that do not require a global crisis. Did you consider the possibility that you might simply be scared at the prospect of a family?

—Hmmm. Let me think . . . No. I haven't considered that. But enough about me. Let's talk about you . . . Good! Now, can you tell me anything new about that big alien fellow? Dr. Franklin told us he's bigger than our girl, but that's about all we know.

—I just left an EDC briefing. Dr. Franklin and her team are still gathering data. There is nothing new to report.

—Has it moved?

—It has not. Its light output is also stable. It does not appear to be receiving or emitting any signal.

—So what are we supposed to do? Just walk up to him and shake his big alien hand?

—It might be as simple as that. For now, you will land at the London Gateway Port and assemble in the clearing behind it. There you will await instructions. Hopefully, we will know more by then. I do not wish to appear pessimistic, but I would like to know more about your combat-readiness in the event a conflict should arise. Dr.

Franklin tells me you have discovered how to trigger an energy discharge and focus it?

—Yes, we knew we could trigger the discharge. That's how we destroyed the lab in Denver. We just had to figure out what buttons Vincent fell on. The rest we found by accident. Turns out if you release the burst with the sword on, it comes out of it. The bigger the sword, the more focused the beam is. In New York, we train on the shores near New Rochelle and shoot at the water. The blast makes a hole about the size of a city block, then it fills up again. It's pretty cool to watch. We also tried on something solid, made a fairly large rock disappear. I can't tell you if our weapon would work against that robot, but it'll wipe anything of this world off it.

You know Dr. Franklin thinks going to London is a bad idea.

—I do.

—Well . . . What she said made more sense to me than anything else I've heard. We assume we were supposed to find Themis, but say it wasn't the case. Say they came here to get it back, destroy it, whatever. More to the point, there's nothing you can put in front of that robot that would pose any serious threat to it, except maybe us. Do we really want to make first contact with an alien species by sending the only thing we have—which isn't even ours—that it could see as a menace? I'm just asking. I'm a soldier, so if they tell me to walk up behind it and kick it in the butt, I will. But if we can avoid the whole me and Vincent dying thing, you know . . . that'd be good.

—I sympathize. What you must understand is that the powers that be will not let that alien robot sit in the middle of the most populous city in the UK much longer without doing anything. At some point, human nature will take over and they will send something. If that something is not Themis—who, by the way, is also the only thing that might seem familiar to this new robot—it will be His Majesty's Armed Forces. If I have to choose between the two, I would rather send you.

—Isn't there anything we can send that doesn't have weapons attached to it? Something cute, and fuzzy. Send Barney, or a bunch of kittens. Did you see *Close Encounters of the Third Kind*? We can play keyboards to it, do a light show, teach these guys some sign language.

—The British Government is ahead of you on this one though your ideas are remarkably similar. They have initiated what they call first-contact protocol.

—Do I wanna know?

—They have installed screens around the park and are showing pictures of monuments, animal species, cities, some clips from old movies. They are playing music from the fifties and sixties on a speaker system.

—Why the old stuff? What's wrong with new music?

—I believe the rationale behind it is that any signals that made it far enough for an alien species to pick up would have left Earth a long time ago.

—So they won't be disappointed if they came here for Elvis?

—Creating familiarity is indeed the intent. It does feel a little improvised, but you have to understand that scientists believed that finding alien life would mean microbes, or an overly regular radio signal, nothing like what we are faced with today. I realize how futile this all may seem, but at the very least, it does not hinder our efforts and it makes it appear as if the government is doing *something*.

—So what's the best-case scenario here? They like the British light show, they exit the robot, and they stay for dinner?

—I believe that, secretly or not, everyone is hoping they will simply leave. If they do not, then we hope that they will be the ones to initiate a dialogue and dictate the terms of our mutual discovery. Given their obvious technological superiority, it would seem like the most logical and safest course of action.

—Why would they travel all this way only to leave after a couple days?

—Interestingly enough, it is probably what we would do. At least, it is what we would have done half a century ago. It might be an urban legend, but I was told that in the fifties, the US military started thinking about what it would do if we encountered sentient alien life. They came up with a seven-step procedure, starting with remote surveillance. We would then secretly visit the alien world, and if we felt our weaponry and technology to be more advanced than the aliens, we would begin a series of brief landings during which we would gather samples of plant and animal life, perhaps abducting an alien or two in the process. After that, we would make our existence known to as many aliens as possible, and if we were satisfied with their reaction, we would make contact.

—And if we felt the aliens were superior? What was the plan?

—Pray that they do not see us as food.

FILE NO. 1422

PERSONAL JOURNAL ENTRY—
DR. ROSE FRANKLIN, HEAD OF SCIENCE
DIVISION, EARTH DEFENSE CORPS

This is what I was afraid of. This is why I wish we . . . I . . . had never found Themis. They're here. Her family's here, now. Maybe they came to take her home. I wish they would. I wish they'd take me with them. Leave the world as it should be. Even if I stay behind, I do hope they simply leave because whatever they choose to do, there isn't anything we can do to stop them.

That robot—we named him Kronos—could be six thousand years more advanced than Themis. Assuming that our societies followed a similar evolutionary path, their technological capabilities would have increased exponentially as well. We invented more things in the last one hundred years than we did in the previous one thousand, and we're likely to invent more than that in the next ten years. Technology might plateau at some point and evolve more slowly, but I can't even begin to imagine what six thousand years of technological progress might mean for people this advanced. I mean that literally: I can't imagine it. To say that Themis might be antiquated is such an understatement. She might be the equivalent of a wooden toy for the robot in London. I'd like to keep her as far from there as I can for as long as I can. Unfortunately, that may not be very long. I suggested evacuating the area and waiting six months before we attempt anything. If these aliens want to make contact, let *them* do it. More importantly, don't force them to if that's not what they're here for. Eugene—he would kill me if he heard me call him by his first name—made it very clear to me that the British Government doesn't have that kind of patience. I like Eugene. He's a self-righteous sixty-year-old general with all the open-mindedness you'd expect from a self-righteous sixty-year-old general. But Eugene hates war. He's seen enough death for a dozen lifetimes, and I trust him to do the right thing.

The right thing might indeed be to send Themis if the alternative is the army. They may not speak any of our languages, but I'm sure they know the meaning of ten thousand men with guns. If there is one aspect of our report that should have been clear, it's the section on defensive capabilities. I can't fathom why they would even consider sending troops when the only thing we can say with some degree of certainty is that our weapons would have little or no effect on the robot. And since this robot is bound to be at least as powerful as Themis, it could obliterate any army in a few seconds. Why would anyone want to face that robot? They would at best simply be ignored, and at worst die a completely meaningless death before they ever realize what's happening.

I am curious, however, as to how that robot made it to London. Witnesses said it didn't even make a sound. Just appeared out of thin air. For years now, we've been looking for a propulsion system, in part because Alyssa thought there might be one, mostly because it would be really convenient. We always assumed it would be just that, a propulsion system, some sort of jet pack that Themis could use to fly. We didn't find anything, so we looked for commands that would resemble throttle, pitch, yaw, hoping some flames would come out of her feet. But what if it's not propulsion? If Themis can indeed travel long distances, she might do it in much the same way that robot made it to London. If she can just "beam" herself wherever she wants to go, the commands would look completely different. It might be as simple as entering a set of coordinates and punching go. Of course, I have no idea how such a coordinate system might work, but I'm sure Vincent will be excited to try to figure it out if he gets the chance.

I don't think Kara and Vincent would last very long against that machine, and if Themis is destroyed, it will surely be the beginning of the end for all of us.

I sincerely hope I'm wrong. I hope a hatch opens on that robot and lets out happy, oddly legged aliens who just want to hug everybody.

Everyone at the EDC is so excited about making first contact, I try my best to hide my pessimism. They already think I'm on the verge of depression; they'll start medicating me if I tell them how I truly feel.

But I can't shake the feeling that something horrible is about to happen.

Who knows? I might be in desperate need of medication. Believing you're the only person with their head on straight is usually not a sign of good mental health. Signs of post-traumatic stress disorder. That's what they said I should be looking for. I wish. That can be treated. I'm afraid there's only one cure for what I have.

FILE NO. 1427

HOUSE OF COMMONS DEBATES, PARLIAMENT OF THE UNITED KINGDOM

Wednesday 6 December

The House met at half past eleven o'clock

PRAYERS

[Mr. Speaker in the Chair]

Points of Order

6 Dec: Column 1325

Daniel Stewart (Rutland and Melton) (LD): On a point of order, Mr. Speaker. On Monday, in questions to the Prime Minister about municipal response to the alien occupation of Regent's Park, I described a certain London official in very unfavourable terms and made accusatory remarks that went well beyond my meaning. That city official and my right hon. friend the Member for Ealing, Southall (Sir Charles Duncan), in whose constituency the gentleman resides, have made fervent requests for a retraction. In my attempt to convey just how anxious and concerned I was, I clearly used language that was inappropriate and unfit. I wish to offer an apology and publicly withdraw those remarks.

Mr. Speaker: I thank the right hon. Member for this display of civility. The House is satisfied.

Sir Charles Duncan (Ealing, Southall) (Lab): Further to that point of order, Mr. Speaker, I am also grateful the right hon. Member for Rutland and Melton (Daniel Stewart) for his fulsome retraction.

Mr. Speaker: Honour is served.

6 Dec: Column 1326

Sir Robert Johnson (North East Hertfordshire) (Con): On a point of order, Mr. Speaker, I seek your guidance. Yesterday, at column 654 in Hansard, I intervened on the Secretary of State for Defence (Alex Dunne) to ask him to confirm NATO's position on our London predicament. He assured us that NATO was supportive of our nonintervention policy. Yet, in Paris that same afternoon, his French counterpart, Minister Poupart, said:

"Si Londres ne tient pas tête à cet envahisseur, la France, l'OTAN, ou le monde devra s'en charger."

Loosely translated: "If London does nothing to confront this invader, France, NATO, or the world will." Would the Defence Secretary like to amend his previous answer to put the record straight?

Mr. Speaker: I am grateful to the hon. and learned Gentleman for his translation, and equally impressed with his mastery of *la langue de Molière*. I am sure that the hon. and learned Gentleman has the best interests of this nation at heart, but I am asked whether the Defence Secretary would like to amend his answer based on the French Minister's comments. While it would be presumptuous of me to speak on behalf of the Secretary, I can say, with some certitude, that Minister Poupart does not speak for the North Atlantic Treaty Organization, and, with even more confidence, that he does not serve in any official capacity as representative of the world. As for France, the *Premier ministre*—loosely translated: the Prime Minister—said this morning that Minister Poupart's statement was a figure of speech meant to convey the Minister's disquietude, and that the French Government deferred to the sovereignty of the United Kingdom on the matter. The Defence Secretary should thus feel no need to amend his answer, as the record appears to be perfectly straight. Let us move on to the business at hand.

12.14 P.M.

Business of the House (Today)

6 Dec: Column 1327

London Evacuation and Safety

Motion for leave to bring in a Bill (Standing Order No. 23)

Deborah Horsbrugh (Lewisham Deptford) (Con): I beg to move,

That leave be given to bring in a Bill to require the Secretary of State for Defence to order the evacuation of the area surrounding Regent's Park and to deploy the Household Cavalry Regiment.

Tomorrow marks the anniversary of the Japanese attack on Pearl Harbor. The attack was both unprovoked and unannounced, which prompted President Roosevelt to call December 7 "a date which will live in infamy."

Unannounced. Attacks seldom come with a warning, as the attacker wishes to benefit from the element of surprise.

There will be no surprise in London. What we are facing today, what stands a mere two miles from this chamber, did not fire from the shadows. It did not sneak up on us in the middle of the night. It appeared in the centre of our city, at first light, and has been standing there, immobile, arrogant, for two days. If it were to attack London tomorrow, it would probably be the most telegraphed, the most well-announced attack in human history. And yet, we are totally unprepared for what may come. To this day, we have done absolutely nothing, made no preparations for what could be an imminent strike. Londoners living a few streets from the intruder are still in their homes, completely vulnerable. This building, this palace, which transformed over nearly a thousand years from royal residence to the home of a modern democracy, is defenceless. If we were the victims of an attack tomorrow, December 7 is a date which would live in idiocy, for we could not have been more warned.

6 Dec: Column 1328

Londoners, for the most part, have not fled as they should have. They have stayed in part out of carelessness, but mostly because for ten years now, they have been indoctrinated by the EDC, led to believe that we live in a safe and peaceful universe filled with amicable creatures by an organization more concerned with justifying its own existence than with the safety of the people it is meant to protect. This government has done more than turn a blind eye to this propaganda; it has been active in its dissemination, complicit in its formulation.

I bring in this Bill so that the government can do the right thing. Evacuate Central London. Bring in the Household Cavalry Regiment, so that Londoners, the good people of the United Kingdom, the world, and the aliens standing in the middle of our great city all know that our sovereignty is not something you can trample on with impunity. Let everyone know that we are still a great nation, a proud nation. To do nothing is simply un-British.

12.37 P.M.

Philip Davies (Shipley) (Lab): I rise to oppose the Bill, if only because the right hon. Member for Lewisham Deptford (Deborah Horsbrugh) introduces it on the basis of falsities. First, this building is not defenceless, nor is the city of London. There are nearly six thousand troops patrolling the streets. Last I checked, Combermere Barracks had not moved, and is still less than twenty-five miles from Central London. The Household Cavalry Regiment *is* on alert, and is less than forty minutes away. Second, I cannot stay silent while Londoners are called careless for not abandoning their homes. To the best of my knowledge, the right hon. Member from Lewisham Deptford still resides in London, which would make her careless herself, or a hypocrite. I will—[Interruption.]

Mr. Speaker: Order. I—[Interruption.] I will have order.

Dec: Column 1328

The Secretary of State for Defence (Alex Dunne): Mr. Speaker, if I may add a few words to those of my esteemed colleague, I would like to comment on this most ridiculous analogy with Pearl Harbor. The attack was both unprovoked and unannounced. It would be nice if the right hon. Member for Lewisham Deptford (Deborah Horsbrugh) would listen to her own words. *Unprovoked* seems to be the operative one in that sentence. History would look upon a Japanese attack very differently had the Pacific Fleet been deployed near Tokyo Bay the day before. I am not reluctant to commit to action, but I will not provoke beings we know little or nothing about for the sake of posturing. I will not send soldiers on a grand-sounding mission to oppose an enemy they cannot fight. I will not start a war. *That* would be un-British.

Question put (Standing Order No. 23) and agreed to.

Ordered,

That Deborah Horsbrugh and Harry Gilbert present the Bill.

Deborah Horsbrugh accordingly presented the Bill.

Bill read the First time; to be read a Second time on 12 December, and to be printed (Bill 116).

Oral Answers to questions the Prime Minister was asked—

6 Dec: Column 1329

Daniel Stewart (Rutland and Melton) (LD): The *Sunday Telegraph* carried a UK-wide poll which shows that 62 percent of the British people believe the government is not doing enough. Will the Prime Minister tell us what he plans to do to alleviate the fears of the population? Or will he stand before this assembly and tell us he will simply ignore two-thirds of the British people?

The Prime Minister (Frederick Canning): This is not a popularity contest. This is a time to do the right thing, and, sometimes, doing the right thing means being patient. We have to deal with the reality of the situation. Part of that reality is that the United Kingdom is part of a worldwide organization known as the United Nations. That organization has a branch whose sole purpose is to handle situations such as this one. We have a responsibility to the rest of the world not to engage in the kind of hasty action that would put the entire planet in jeopardy. Make no mistake, this situation concerns everyone, not just the people of London. What we do here, now, will define the relationship Earth has with an entire civilization. I will not take that lightly, and I will not put the population at risk by succumbing to public pressure.

Daniel Stewart (Rutland and Melton) (LD): I would like to remind the Prime Minister that this government survives because of Lib Dem votes. It would be imprudent for the Prime Minister of a minority government to brush aside our concerns if he wishes to continue governing. The Prime Minister thinks he can ignore the British people until the next election, but he cannot ignore *us,* or that election will happen much sooner. Liberal Democrats will not be silenced. I for one will give some serious thought to these issues before casting my vote next week.

FILE NO. 1429

INTERVIEW WITH MR. BURNS, OCCUPATION UNKNOWN

Location: New Dynasty Chinese Restaurant, Dupont Circle, Washington, DC

—Greetings, Mr. Burns. I took the liberty of ordering for you.

—Did you get the Indonesian rice?

—Kung pao chicken. It has been nine years after all.

—What if I'd been here yesterday? You know people *do* eat even when you're not around.

—Forgive me. I did not mean to be presumptuous. I assumed you had been away since I have been unable to reach you for nearly a decade. I have also had this restaurant under surveillance, and I know you have not eaten here since we last met.

—For nine years? I should be flattered.

—Only during business hours.

—Of course. I wouldn't want anyone to work overtime on my account. No sniper this time around?

—No. Not this time.

—Ahhh. I'm touched. How've you been?

—Occupied. Can you tell me why you disappeared?

—I didn't disappear! I was . . . occupied. And now I'm back!

—You are back, just as a giant alien robot materializes in the middle of London. That seems . . . convenient.

—I know! Can you believe I almost missed it?!

—Are these the people who built Themis?

—Oh, it's them all right.

—Can you tell us what their intentions are?

—I don't know. Right now—

—The robot is not moving at the moment.

—It may not be moving, but it's doing *something*. Right now, it's scanning everything and everyone around it.

—For what purpose?

—Maybe they're curious.

—What should we do?

—Now? We should eat!

—Please. We are in the midst of a pivotal moment in our history, one that could signal a new era of discovery, or put an end to us all. Whatever . . . personal conviction is stopping you from helping us must be weighed against the stakes at hand.

—You really haven't been listening to anything I say if you think I'm keeping things from you out of some misguided principles. That robot will do what it came here to do, whatever that is. There isn't anything you can do about that. For now it's scanning you, so be scanned.

—Is it here because of Themis?

—It could be. Does it really matter? It's here.

—My understanding of space travel is very limited, but if traveling from their home world to our planet takes several years, or decades, they might not be aware of what has transpired recently, or that we have discovered the robot they buried. This may sound stupid to you—

—No! Not at all. You're a little off. It takes about ten days to get from there to here. But you're absolutely right in that they're probably completely unaware of what happened during that time. If you did anything really bad last week, you might just get away with it.

—Making fun of my ignorance will not stop me from asking. I am trying to prevent a war. There must be something you can tell me that will increase the likelihood of a peaceful resolution.

—Do you like squirrels?

—I ask for your help in preventing a conflict of apocalyptic proportions and your answer is: "Do you like squirrels?"

—Yes. I have a good squirrel story.

—Of course. By all means.

—Squirrels can hide thousands of nuts every year. They—

—What species?

—Does it matter?

—There are several species. Some bury nuts individually in multiple locations, others will stockpile them aboveground.

—I don't know. The grey ones with the bushy tail. The ones in the parks. They bury thousands of nuts every fall and they look for them during winter when they get hungry. Squirrels have tiny brains, though. They can't remember where they hid them all, so—

—Studies suggest they recover about one-quarter of the nuts they bury, but—

—That's what I said. So they end up sniffing around everywhere and they find a lot of nuts that were buried by other squirrels.

—I was going to say that they do remember a significant number of cache locations. In a controlled environment, they have been shown to retrieve nuts from their own cache sites up to two-thirds of the time after delays of four to twelve days.

—Can you stop interrupting? It's a story. There's a fairy in it. No, I don't know what *species* of fairy.

—My apologies.

—...

—Please, continue.

—Too late. I'm curious now. How do you know so much about squirrels?

—Work. Squirrels do not simply hide nuts and dig them out when they get hungry, they will check on their cache sites to make sure they have not been pillaged, and will often ... reorganize their stock, rebury nuts in different locations. When a squirrel surveying its hiding sites encounters another squirrel looking for food, it will use various techniques—visiting empty sites, pretending to bury something—to deceive the predator and avoid revealing valuable nut-location information. I briefly monitored a research project hoping to mimic squirrel deceptive behavior in robots and automated drones. A robot designed to guard military supplies could, for example, alter its patrol route to lead an approaching enemy away from what it is trying to protect.

—Military squirrel applications.

—Indeed. Now, please continue with your story.

—Where was I? Oh yes, so the squirrels forget where they hid most of their nuts. One day, in a city park somewhere, a fairy shows up, and she sees this young squirrel digging aimlessly through the snow— the poor thing's all skin and bones, starving to death, all scuffed up from fighting other squirrels—and she feels her tiny fairy heart breaking. She blows a bit of magic dust at the creature and flies away with a smile on her face.

The squirrel sneezes to get the magic dust out of its tiny nose. As it clears its head, it suddenly remembers it hid an acorn at the base of a nearby tree. Oh, and one over there! And there! And there! The fairy gave the squirrel a photographic memory so that it could find all the food it painstakingly buried in the fall.

When spring comes, the fairy, still feeling pride over her good deed, visits the park again, hoping to see her squirrel thriving. She spots a young squirrel on a park bench, but hers had a scar on its tail. Another one is climbing a tree, no that's not the right one either. The fairy gets her hopes up about a hundred more times that day, all the while getting mad at herself for not making the squirrel pink, or something else that would make a squirrel easier to distinguish from a gazillion other squirrels. Come nightfall, the fairy's exhausted and a bit worried. She gets her magic dust out and makes the first squirrel she sees into a talking squirrel.

"Hello, little squirrel," she says. "Hell . . . Whoa! I can speak!" answers the squirrel. The fairy goes on to explain that she's given a perfect memory to a young starving rodent and that she's eager to find him. "You must mean Larry," the squirrel replies, uncomfortable. "He didn't make it."

Eager as she was to save the sickly squirrel, the fairy didn't think about all the other bushy-tailed gluttons in the park. Normal squirrels that they were, they had forgotten where they hid most of their loot about twenty minutes after they buried it. When hunger came a-knocking, they searched the park as best they could, digging just about everywhere to find something to eat. They found some of their own nuts, but they remembered wrong most of the time and ate a whole lot of nuts other squirrels had saved for winter, including Little Larry's.

With his supersized memory, Larry didn't make mistakes. He could pinpoint with perfect accuracy every tree, rock, bush, bump, trash can, and lamppost where he had buried a precious red-oak acorn. Unfortunately for Larry, the other squirrels had been digging all over the place and, knowingly or not, stole most of his reserve. Had he been as half-witted as the other animals, Larry would have found some of *their* nuts along the way, but Larry knew better, and he visited all the 3,683 spots where he had buried an acorn, one at a time, but the handful of nuts he recovered weren't enough to sustain him. Larry died a few weeks later.

The fairy is crushed by the news and flies away crying, leaving behind a talking squirrel. Being the only talking squirrel in the park, he lived a wretched life, scaring the living hell out of everyone.

—Is that the end?

—Yes! What do you think?

—I . . . I enjoy squirrel stories and found yours very entertaining. You conveyed the desperation of Little Larry really well and I was saddened by the news of his demise. With that in mind—and I hope you will not judge me too harshly for my lack of perspicacity— what could this possibly have to do with the aliens in London?

—Oh, it's got absolutely nothing to do with them; this one's about you!

—I am the squirrel?

—Yes, you're Little Larry. You see, I could tell you many things, fill your head with all sorts of information to help you come up with that "best course of action" you're looking for. Unfortunately, it's not you they came to see. They're curious about mankind right now, not you. If I told you anything, you'd try real hard to control the situation, but you can't. Inevitably, you'd fail, because you're not the only squirrel in the park. You might be able to stall NATO or London for a few days, but that won't last forever. People do what people do, and you'll be miserable in the end because you'll blame yourself for something you really have no power over. I like you. I don't want you to be miserable.

—How could you possibly know what NATO plans to do?

—A little bird told me. There are little birds everywhere. My point is you can't control every single person on this planet, no matter how much you'd like to.

—What would you have me do? I cannot simply sit back and do nothing.

—You're such a control freak! You just keep on doing what you're doing, and other people will do their thing.

—And then?

—How should I know? *Que sera, sera . . .*

— . . .

—You don't seem happy with my answer.

—I am not.

—Did I mention how much I like that suit? You look dashing today.

—Very well. I give up. I would, however, like to ask for your help on another matter, one I hope you will not be as reluctant to discuss. Dr. Franklin is deeply troubled. She is obsessed with the idea that she is not herself. As much as I would like to help her understand what happened to her, I cannot explain it, nor can I fathom what she is going through.

—What do you mean, not herself? Dr. Franklin is Dr. Franklin. If she weren't, then she would be someone else.

—Is she a clone?

—A clone? Of course not! Does she look like a ten-year-old? She would have been an infant when you found her. Do you really think I would have abandoned a newborn child on the side of the road?

—I meant a fully grown clone.

—Oh, movie clones! We don't do those. Clones are born. You can't just bake a grown person.

—That would suggest she has somehow traveled through time. To me, that sounds equally implausible. Truth be told, I am at a loss for an explanation that does not fall into the science-fiction category.

—Time travel! Yes, I drove up to her in a Delorean and asked her if she'd like to take a ride at eighty-eight miles per hour.

—Mock me all you want but something happened to her. If you did not send her zipping through time, what did you do?

—I'm sorry. I shouldn't have. Besides, I've been told it *is* possible, you know, time travel. But you can't move physical objects, you move information about objects, people, and you reconstruct them at a different time. We don't have the technology to do the time part, we just took what she was and made her, again.

—Four years younger?

—Four years before she reappeared, she got into a car accident on her way home from work. She rear-ended a van. Inside that van was a very powerful device that can . . . move things. It records an enormous amount of data about what you want to move, enough to reconstruct it somewhere. While she was unconscious, associates of mine took her inside the van and scanned her. Only they didn't move her, they stored her data in case anything was to happen to her, as it did. Like a backup, for your computer. Her backup was four years old when we used it, yes.

—Why were you following her?

—She rear-ended the van. So, technically, she was following *us*.

—Please answer my question.

—I told you! We wanted her data in case anything was to happen to her.

—But why her data and not—

—Yours? Maybe because she doesn't ask so many questions. What can I tell you? We like her. She's . . . special.

—So the person I met this morning is a copy.

—She is what she is. She's the same person, no more, no less.

—You just told me you re-created her using . . . backup data. That would make her a copy.

—We should really end this discussion here, it'll make you uncomfortable if we continue.

—I must confess, I am not entirely certain that I want to know more. I am, however, absolutely certain that Dr. Franklin needs to.

—Then down the rabbit hole we go. Universe 101. Everything in the universe, everything, is made from the same goo. Let's take something you can think of as discrete so it'll be easier for you to grasp. Atoms. Do you agree you're made of atoms?

—I did go to high school.

—That's not what I meant. Do you agree that you're made of atoms, just atoms? Not atoms plus some fantastic force that makes you somehow more important than everything else in the universe.

—I understand that my body is made of atoms.

—No you don't. People never do. I mean your memories about the neighbor's cat, the way you like your eggs in the morning, the things you never told your parents, what makes you, you. What do you think *you* are made of?

—Does the answer start with an "A"?

—Don't be a smart ass. I know you think you understand. I know you *want* to understand. The way you felt about your first love, the self-doubt you're feeling right now. You know it can all be described physically, but deep down you refuse to believe that's what you are because you don't think that's special enough, and you wanna be special. Everyone does. I do too!

—You are saying I do not have a soul.

—I don't mean to be rude, but if there were a Heaven, I doubt they'd throw you a parade.

—You misunderstood; I am not a religious person. I do not believe I will exist forever, nor would I want to.

—Then I guess it depends on your definition of a soul. I can see you haven't put much thought into this.

—What do you mean?

—Do you know what happens in your brain when you're thinking?

—Neurons fire electrical impulses.

—Good. Every thought you have is a physical process. We know this for a fact, we can see it happening. We also know that emotions can be described in similar terms. Obviously, what you see, hear, touch, taste, smell is tied to your body.

—Your point being?

—That I really don't get what you're clinging onto if this isn't about eternal life. Your *soul*, if you had one, the part of you that can't be summed up as a bunch of atoms, would have no physical presence, couldn't hear, smell, touch, or see anything. It would be incapable of thinking. No thoughts whatsoever, no sense of self. It wouldn't feel anything either. Your *soul* would be . . . a hole . . . emptiness. There's nothing special about that.

—You will forgive me if I choose to believe . . . if I continue to believe I am more than the sum of my parts.

—But you are! So much more! Most things are. As Wittgenstein said, when you talk about a broom, you're not making a statement about a stick and a brush. The universe is a marvelous place where just about everything is more than the sum of its parts. Take two hydrogens—they're everywhere—add an oxygen, and BAM! Water! Is water just oxygen and hydrogen? I don't think so. It's water! Does it have a soul?

—Can we leave my spiritual self alone for a moment and talk about Dr. Franklin?

—We are. What are you made of?

—... Atoms.

—Good man. Atoms, which are made of particles, which are made of other stuff. Matter. You're a very complex, awe-inspiring configuration of matter that is stable at room temperature.

—I do not mean to interrupt, but room temperature?

—More or less. The universe loves stability. That's why you don't fall apart into a quadrillion little parts or a puddle of goo. But you're only stable at this temperature. Raise it or lower it by a hundred degrees and you start falling apart.

—Heartwarming.

—It should be. Let me ask you this: Do you think your atoms are any different from those that make up the chair you're sitting on, the sun, or the kung pao chicken?

—Go on.

—Of course not. You got a lot of what you're made of from the food you ate. You have banana matter in you. Do you think that if I took two hydrogen atoms from the salt shaker and switched them up with two of yours, you'd be any different?

—No. I do not believe it would alter my essence.

—What if I switched more than two? How about all of them? You see what I'm getting at. If I grab a bunch of matter, anywhere, and I organize it in exactly the same way, I get . . . you. You, my friend, are a very complex, awe-inspiring configuration of matter. What you're made of isn't really important. Everything in the universe is made of the same thing. You're a configuration. Your *essence*, as you call it, is information. It doesn't matter where the material comes from. Do you think it matters *when* it comes from?

—I suppose not.

—So, as I said, Dr. Franklin is Dr. Franklin. If she weren't, then she would be something else.

—I must say, I find you particularly unhelpful today. I will do my best to replicate this conversation with her, but in all honesty, I would be astonished if Dr. Franklin found lasting comfort in atoms and banana matter.

—If it makes you feel better, I'll talk to her and I'll tell her exactly what we did. If you want me to, that is.

—Why not tell *me* so that I can relay the information?

—You haven't told her about me, have you?

—I have not.

—You should really talk to someone about your control issues.

—I have one question before we eat.

—I'm serious!

—So am I. I do have one question.

—You're hopeless, completely and utterly hopeless . . . What do you wanna know?

—Why take her to Ireland, of all places?

—The device was nearby. As I said, it is designed to move things, and the closer you move them, the easier it is to control where they reappear. We didn't want her to rematerialize in the middle of a lake or on a busy highway. This isn't as easy at it seems.

—It seems many things: inconceivable, far-fetched. It does not seem easy.

—Then it's just as hard as it seems. Maybe harder.

—I may regret asking, but how is what you did any different from traveling through time?

—You're right. For her, it would have seemed instantaneous, so from her perspective, it isn't different at all. From ours, well, I guess you could call this really, really slow time travel.

—I do not understand.

—The reason we can't send information zipping through time, as you said, is that we don't know where it will end up. How do I put this? Stuff moves fast. Really really fast! The Earth spins on itself a thousand miles an hour. It flies around the sun at sixty-six thousand miles an hour, while the sun is going about half a million miles an hour around the galaxy. Of course, the Milky Way is also moving in our cluster of galaxies, which is also moving, very very fast. And all of this is happening in a universe that's constantly expanding. Four years is a lot of mileage to keep track of. I'm sure there's a proper bullet analogy, but I can't think of any that would do this justice at the moment. The point is, we can't do it.

But her information did move through time. It was sitting in a drawer for four years. It took four years for it to travel four years into the future.

—So between the time of her death and her reappearance, Dr. Franklin did not exist, but information about her did, in a drawer, somewhere.

—I told you this conversation was a bad idea. Oh, thank God! Our food's here.

FILE NO. 1433

SURVEILLANCE LOG—WORKSTATION #3
Location: Earth Defense Corps Headquarters, New York, NY

[01:01] It's 6:00 A.M. London Time. Jamie MacKinnon at workstation #3. Continuing remote video surveillance of Regent's Park. Monitoring southeast cameras 1 through 5.

[01:03] Selecting camera 1. Overlaying image from . . . 5:00 A.M. Perfect match. No movement.

[01:08] Changing view modes. Toggle to infrared. No change in thermal readouts. Heat signature is uniform. Air temperature in London is . . . 8 degrees Celsius, 47 Fahrenheit. The robot registers at 10 degrees, 2 degrees warmer than ambient.

[01:21] Toggle back to visible light. Lea, did anyone check the EM readings?

[*Still nothing. That thing's like a rock.*]

Figures.

[01:31] Switching to camera 2. How'd we end up with the graveyard shift again?

[*Seniority*]

Oh! Come on! We've both been here longer than Nathan and I don't see him here. I think Dr. Doom just hates us.

[*Shhhh! She'll hear you!*]

She's still here? Does the woman ever sleep?

[*Just go back to work.*]

[01:43] What the hell? Lea, scoot over for a sec. Tell me what you see . . .

[*That's just a bird flying into the robot. Happens a lot.*]

No, let me zoom in if I can. Now, what do you see?

[*Shit!*]

Get Dr. Franklin now!

[1:49] [*What is it, Jamie?*]

Hello, Dr. Franklin. Sorry to bother you at this hour, but take a look at this. This is from camera 2 about ten minutes ago.

[*It's a bird.*]

Wait. Let me go back. Look closer.

[*Looks like it hit . . .*]

Yeah.

[*That's about what? A foot before the metal? Could just be an optical illusion. Can we get the same thing from camera 4?*]

Sure. Rewinding to 06 . . . 42. Should be about now.

[*Stop! Here it is. Damn! Play it again . . .*]

Should we wake up the General?

[*I'd rather have more than a bird . . . Let me think for a second.*]

Rain.

[*What?*]

It rained last night.

[*Oh. That's good, Jamie. Can you access it here?*]

Yep. Just give me one sec. Time index . . . Let's try three o'clock . . . No.

[*Earlier. Try one thirty.*]

Yep. It's raining.

[*We can't see anything. Switch to infrared.*]

Holy shit!

[*The rain isn't touching the robot at all, anywhere. Nice thinking, Jamie!*]

How'd we miss that?

[*We didn't detect anything so we forgot to look with our own eyes. Can you measure the field around the robot?*]

I get . . . 28 cm. Now, do we call the General?

[*I have to call Kara. They won't be able to defend themselves. Like a lamb to the slaughter.*]

FILE NO. 1439

INTERVIEW WITH VINCENT COUTURE, CONSULTANT, EARTH DEFENSE CORPS

Location: Somewhere in the Atlantic

—How long until you reach your destination, Mr. Couture?

—We'll be there by morning. It's a good thing too, I'm starting to get seasick. We've been hitting rough seas for the last couple days.

—I understand all too well. I do not fare well at sea.

—I'm glad you called. Kara just got off the phone with Dr. Franklin. What's this I hear about an energy field? They told us we didn't detect anything around that robot.

—We did not. We are still unable to detect anything. But I have seen the video footage and you can trust me when I say that nothing will come closer than eleven inches to that robot. Dr. Franklin also believes that, in the event of a fight, your energy weapon will not reach the alien robot, nor that it could vaporize it, as it does normal matter.

—That I figured out on my own.

—How?

—Made sense. The energy weapon we fire through the sword is just a focused version of the omnidirectional burst Themis releases when she's saturated with energy. If it were really harmful to her, we'd have obliterated ourselves when we destroyed Denver airport. So I know it won't vanish if we fire at it, but will our weapon do *anything*?

—Your weapon might not be completely ineffective. According to Dr. Franklin, it could have *some* effect on the alien device, like a push or a blow, if it reaches it. It most likely will not inflict significant damage.

—A push? You mean we were wasting our time training on that weapon? Kara's aim is getting pretty good.

—You were shooting at water.

—We blew a rock to kingdom come, once.

—Was it moving and shooting back?

—No. But it was a big rock. What about the sword and shield? That definitely has an effect. We left a ding on Themis's left foot with the shield during training. Is there any chance it could go through that energy field?

—We do not know. But even if it did, General Govender was quick to point out that you have had very little combat training, absolutely none against a real opponent.

—We're a little short on two-hundred-foot people to spar with. What about your friend? Can he help?

—I do not know which associate of mine you are referring to.

—You know who. The one who told you about Themis, about her name, Titans, aliens. You know, your friend.

—I . . . I can not—

—You're trying to come up with a way to tell me you learned all of this without anyone's help and you "can not" think of anything that doesn't sound completely preposterous. Am I close?

—In the vicinity. Suffice it to say that if such a "friend" did exist—

—I'm sorry, but your way out of this is a hypothetical?

—It has been a long day. As I was saying, if such a friend did exist, I would unfortunately be unable to secure his help.

—Then you need better friends. Why won't he help? He can't really wish us all dead.

—Perhaps he does not know how. He might also believe the outcome of this encounter to be predestined or unavoidable. Either way, I believe his intentions are good even if I do not fully comprehend his reluctance.

—Hypothetically . . . Sounds to me like he's holding something important from you. But what do I know? I never met the guy.

—I do not completely disagree.

—So, let me get this straight. No one will help. Our one long-range weapon won't work. The sword probably won't do anything either, and even if it did, we're terrible at it. Do you have anything nice to say?

—That is a fair assessment of the situation. You will understand when I say that we are hoping your presence will not be seen as a sign of aggression.

—You're hoping? I don't wanna sound pessimistic, but what if it's not happy to see us? How are we supposed to fight this thing if we can't even touch it?

—You are not. It would seem prudent to delay the introductions.

—Is that your opinion or the EDC's?

—Mine.

—I thought so. And how do you suggest we do that? We'll be in London and assembled in less than twelve hours. I don't suppose they'll let us sit there for very long before they send us.

—Then I would suggest postponing your arrival.

—Not sure the boat captain will listen to me.

—Probably not.

—Oh, no! We're not highjacking the boat. There's a, well, a boatload of soldiers aboard. Kara's good, but she's not that good.

—Do not sell yourself short, Mr. Couture. You have proven yourself quite capable as a soldier in the past. But I did not have an armed

assault in mind. A mutiny would be, shall we say, frowned upon, under the circumstances. I was thinking more along the lines of the European labor movement of the nineteenth century.

—Yes. We should unionize. That'll show them.

—In the late 1800s, the French anarchist Émile Pouget submitted a report at a labor congress in France in which he advocated for work slowdowns, a strategy that had proved successful in Britain. The British unionists referred to the slowdown policy as Ca'Canny, which did not translate directly into French. However, the French had long likened slow and clumsy work to that of a man wearing wooden shoes, or *sabots*, and Pouget, in his report, coined the term *sabotage*.

—You want me to break the boat?

—If done properly, it would delay your arrival and offer plausible deniability. Please accept my apology.

—For what?

—For giving French lessons to a French-speaking linguist.

—Oh, I didn't know. I never studied French etymology.

—I am aware of that. I still find it impolite to give anyone lessons in their field of specialty.

—You can make it up with some mechanical knowledge. There's a room called Engine Room so I can probably find the engine— engines?—in there, but I don't know anything about engines, let alone boat engines. I sure as hell don't know how to break one "properly."

—I will provide you with all the information you need. I can ask Ms. Resnik if you do not feel up to the task.

—I can do it. Now that I think of it, why didn't you? Ask Kara, I mean.

—I would like this operation to be handled as discreetly as possible. Ms. Resnik is more inclined towards impulsive decision making than you are.

—Hmmm. I'm not so sure. She's been . . . reasonable the past couple years. You might not recognize her.

—Do you? Recognize her?

—Yeah. She's in there. I'll catch a glimpse of her every now and then. It's not that I dislike the tame version of her—she's doing it for me. I'd have to be a real asshole to blame her for it—but sometimes I wonder if she's wiser or just broken. The thing is, she doesn't seem unhappy. She says she's happy, and a lot of the times I believe her.

—And what have you done for her?

—Not sure what you mean.

—Have you altered your expectations in any way?

—Expectations about what?

—Life, love. What it means to be a couple, a family? It may not be any of my business, but I get the impression that she has seriously altered her expectations about a great many things in order to meet yours. Perhaps you could meet her halfway. In any case, she seemed in good spirits when I last spoke to her.

— . . .

—Are you giggling?

—I am. She *is* in good spirits. That's just it. I haven't seen her as giddy in a long, *long* time. Of course, we're gonna die tomorrow, but if that's what it takes to make her feel like that. It's not like I ever wanted her to change. I didn't ask for this. The last thing I want is for Kara to be . . . domesticated. I told her that. I told her a hundred times.

—You also talked to her about building a family.

—Yes. I want kids. Someday. That doesn't mean I want the person I love to turn into something she's not.

—I understand your point of view, but, if Ms. Resnik is contemplating motherhood, she might have her own expectations of what it means to be a mother, a *good* mother. Those might not be compatible with her former self.

—Kara's a smart woman. She knows there are many ways to be a good mother.

—Before Ms. Resnik became . . . Ms. Resnik, she was a little girl, with a mother of her own. No relationship is perfect, and I imagine that this little girl knew exactly what kind of person she wished her mother to be. Do not underestimate how powerful the wishes of that little girl are, to this day.

—I seem to remember your telling me you were in no position to give relationship advice to anyone.

—True. Relationships are not my forte, but without divulging too much information of a personal nature, I can tell you that I did have a mother and father.

—You know, I like that you're taking an interest and you make a really good point. Well, good enough to make me feel like an ass anyway. That would have been a *great* conversation to have, like, five years ago. We have a briefing in a few minutes. I also have a boat to stop. If you can get me instructions tonight, I can try it while everyone's asleep.

—I will endeavor to do so. I can access the blueprints they used for the construction of your vessel. I also know an engineer who can help us disguise your act of sabotage as a normal mechanical failure. If I am not mistaken—

—Yes?

—. . .

—Hello?

—Forget everything I just said. Please tell the captain to increase speed. You must assemble in London as fast as you can.

—What's going on?

—Are you in your room?

—Yes.

—Turn on the television.

—What channel?

—Any channel.

FILE NO. 1440

NEWS REPORT—JACOB LAWSON, BBC LONDON

Location: Regent's Park, London, England

There are tanks on our streets. Over one hundred Scimitar combat vehicles from the Household Cavalry Regiment and the Light Dragoons were called in from Swanton Morley. Fifty-four Challenger 2 tanks from the King's Royal Hussars also arrived during the night from Tidworth. They are joined by countless transport vehicles, and eighteen thousand soldiers, half of whom are reservists, tasked with the evacuation of an estimated four hundred thousand Londoners.

This is the first time such a massive military force has been deployed for civilian protection. In recent years, acts of terrorism have left us accustomed to troops walking the streets of Western cities, but no one can truly be prepared for what Londoners woke up to this morning. In a country that has historically feared militarization, today's scene is more reminiscent of German troops rolling into Paris than of any crowd control or security effort we have seen before.

The three armoured regiments and ground troops gathered in the Park Royal industrial area around four o'clock and headed east along the Westway before fanning out, engulfing Central London in minutes. Soldiers then began knocking on doors, escorting local residents into military transport vehicles. It is not a coincidence that this operation is happening at the weekend, while government and office buildings are empty. Nonetheless, the operation is a colossal one and soldiers will no doubt have to persuade several residents to abandon their homes. Civil liberties have not been suspended, so how much power of persuasion the Army has been given remains to be seen.

The Canning government was under tremendous pressure to act, having lost support from Liberal Democrats, who saw this crisis as an opportunity to silence those who accuse them of being too soft on topics such as terrorism and defence. A Conservative motion to force the evacuation of London was due for a second reading on Monday, and the government no longer had the votes to stop it. Unable to adopt any legislation without support from one of the opposition parties, the current government decided not to delay the inevitable and perhaps put an end to the rumours surrounding an impending vote of no confidence. The British people, on the other hand, appear to be divided on the issue, with 46 percent of the population calling for military action, 42 percent against it, and 12 percent undecided, according to recent polls.

The Prime Minister issued a brief recorded statement early this morning but was not available for questions. Amanda Webb, Leader of the Opposition, saluted the Prime Minister for his courage and called today a proud moment in the history of the United Kingdom. No word yet from the Lib Dems, but we expect to hear from them at some point during the day. It would be surprising if they did not take some of the credit, rightfully so, for putting an end to the government's inaction.

Reactions have been far less positive across the Atlantic. General Eugene Govender, Commander of the EDC, has called today's deployment "a reckless move, motivated by all the wrong reasons." He added, and I quote: "I hope we don't all pay the price for what amounts to a weak kid being bullied into doing something stupid." Dr. Rose Franklin, head of the scientific division, refused to comment. Unilateral action by the British Government could signal the beginning of the end for the EDC—

We'll come back to the EDC's reaction, and comments from other world leaders, in a moment. There appears to be some development on the ground.

Armoured vehicles are now converging on Regent's Park. From our helicopter, we can see what is clearly a carefully orchestrated manoeuvre, as Scimitar vehicles and tanks are slowly closing in on the park from the east, west, and south. The absence of troops or armoured vehicles north of the park can only be deliberate. I would surmise that the Army is leaving an obvious escape route for the alien robot. The military might also wish to avoid making the intruder feel boxed in and provoke an aggressive response. One thing is clear. This operation is meant to send a message: "You have overstayed your welcome in London."

Two armed convoys are approaching the park from the south. One is headed east towards the park on A5205, and a fourth has just turned on Robert Street to enter the park from the east. Armoured vehicles are seconds away from entering the park grounds. I have just been told we will remain on the air for a while longer. We will maintain our position above the south end of the park and give you minute-by-minute updates on the situation.

The closest vehicles, a long line of Scimitars, are on Park Square, now crossing the Outer Circle and entering the south end of the park. Another group of vehicles is entering the south end on York Bridge . . . Our colleagues on the ground inform me that the Secretary of State for Defence has just issued a statement . . . We should have images in a moment, but he thanked the people of London for their cooperation during the evacuation. He also wanted to publicly renew his support for the EDC and assured UN leaders that the military would not engage unprovoked. To that effect, I am told that General Fitzsimmons, who leads this operation, is under strict orders to give the alien a wide berth and avoid any action that could be misconstrued as hostile.

There is a lot of information coming in, and we will hear a lot more from Dana and Mike in the studio in a few minutes. But for now, we will keep our cameras rolling as we witness these historic events unfold. The first convoy now seems to be stopping and entering formation just short of Chester Road, about five hundred metres from the robotic figure. The other group of combat vehicles has also stopped and Scimitars are now lining up inside the Inner Circle. There has been no reaction thus far on the part of the alien robot. It has not moved.

It is now the King's Royal Hussars' turn to enter Regent's Park from the east. The fifty-some tanks have very little manoeuvring room if they wish to keep their distance from the visitor. As expected, the Challenger 2s are stopping only a few metres from the Outer Circle, just shy of the Boardwalk. The last group of Scimitar vehicles is entering park grounds at the west end. They are moving a lot faster than the other groups, heading southeast towards the Inner Circle and away from the Hub and the . . .

The robot has turned its head.

This is the first time we have seen it move since it appeared in London a week ago. It is shifting its feet, slowly turning to the right. Its attention seems to be focused on the combat vehicles sprinting through the park from the west. There is some light coming out of the robot's right hand. White light. It's getting brighter and brighter. It is raising its arm. There is, what seems like, a disc of light inside the robot's right hand, which is aimed at the west end of Regent's Park, where the military vehicles have now stopped their advance.

Our helicopter is moving farther away, but we still have a clear view of the entire—Wha—? There is—what I can only describe as a thin wall of light extending from the robot's hand for . . . it must be at least one or two kilometres long. The light wall is paper-thin, roughly the same height as the robot, sixty or seventy metres high.

It is crossing one of the Scimitar vehicles at the Park's edge! I do not know if it is inflicting any damage. We are too far to the east to make out any details. Our cameraman is attempting to zoom in.

There are electrical wires on the ground, on both sides of the beam of light. There are . . . The robot is moving its arm to the left. It is sweeping Central London very rapidly, turning to its left. It has now stopped after completing a near-perfect half circle . . .

. . .

Dear God.

. . .

Mike, can you call my wife?

. . .

Mike! MIKE!

[*It's all*—]

I know. I need you to call Charlotte. Make sure she's home. I need to know my family's safe.

. . .

I—I need a moment to process what I'm seeing. There . . . There is nothing left in the path of that wall of light, which has now disappeared. There is only a crescent-shaped dirt field where . . . where half this city was. I can see Buckingham Palace at the edge of it. There is nothing but dirt between it and the London Zoo. Half a dozen neighbourhoods have been removed from the London map. Lisson Grove, Maida Vale, Paddington are no more. There is no Marylebone, no Mayfair, no Soho. Bloomsbury, Euston, part of Camden Town . . . All gone.

There is no debris, no fire. Just a perfect half circle of dirt. We cannot—

[*Jacob.*]

We cannot begin to—

[*Jacob! We're off the air. You're talking to yourself.*]

What?

[*The studio. It was right in the middle of it. There is no BBC anymore.*]

. . .

Have you gotten through to my wife?

FILE NO. 1443

MISSION LOG—CAPTAIN KARA RESNIK AND VINCENT COUTURE, EARTH DEFENSE CORPS
Location: London Gateway Port, England

—Vincent Couture. Would you stop fiddling with your flight suit and get on!

—Call me by my last name one more time, Kara. I dare you. I double dare you!

—What are you? Five? Would you just get on this thing, please?

—I'm coming! Why are you in such a hurry? We're not coming back. You know that, right?

—No I don't. And neither do you. You don't want to get on the crane, is that it?

—Of course I don't want to get on that crane. I hate that thing. It's flimsy. It moves in the wind.

—So you're not scared of the alien robot that just destroyed an entire city. It's your fear of heights that's getting in the way?

—Oh, I'm scared of him too. I'm scared of just about everything right now. And it's not so much my fear of heights that bothers me when we're in that stupid cage, it's the claustrophobia. Though it wouldn't hurt to put a piece of plywood on the floor so we can't see through.

—Vincent, we're going up fifty feet, and you get all shaky before we even leave the ground. What would you do if they assembled her standing up, instead of flat on her face?

—I'd teach college.

—All right, EDC. Can you hear us?

[*We hear you loud and clear, Kara.*]

Great. We're in the nacelle—

—That's not a nacelle.

—Shut up, Vincent. We're in the nacelle with . . . What's your name?

[*Lieutenant Martin Crosby, ma'am.*]

We're in the nacelle with Lieutenant Crosby, from . . . You're Army, right?

[*Yes, ma'am.*]

. . . From the British Army. All right, Lieutenant, we're almost there. When we get off on the robot's back, I'll open the outer hatch, and I'll clip this rope ladder to that steel bar here. We're entering the control room through the ceiling. When we're both inside and I tell you to, you're gonna pull the ladder up, and close the outer hatch behind us. Did you get all that?

[*Yes, ma'am. I just want to say, I hope you kill those sons of bitches.*]

I appreciate the vote of confidence, Lieutenant, but we're not here to start a fight.

[*They started it. Kill them all, ma'am.*]

. . .

We're here. Open the gate.

—Kara. Ladies first.

—Oh no. Age before beauty. [. . .] Are you down? Vincent! Are you down?

—Yes! Yes!

—Well, can you step aside so I can . . . Thank you! ALL RIGHT! LIEUTENANT, PULL THE LADDER, CLOSE THE DOOR, AND GET OUT OF HERE AS FAST AS YOU CAN!

—Charming fellow.

—What did you expect? His city was destroyed. You'd be pissed too if they turned Montréal into a sandbox. Can you help me with my harness before you strap yourself in?

—Have I ever not helped you before? I get that he's angry, but he should know we don't stand a chance against that thing.

—Why would he? We've been telling them Themis is invincible for ten years.

—Well, we can't wipe out a city in ten seconds like it did. Here. Snug, not tight.

—Thank you. Now why aren't you strapped in already?

—Ha. Ha.

—EDC Command. We're almost ready to go. Vincent, you're ready? He nods in approval, so I'm . . . pushing . . . up with my arms, knees forward Vincent. And . . . we're up! They told us to follow the highway—what's it called?

—A13, for a while.

—That one—right up until we hit the dirt field the alien made. We might have to step on that highway in a few places. Our apologies to British road workers. EDC, can you tell us how far we are from target?

[*About thirty miles.*]

Is this Rose?

[*Yes, Kara. You should be there in a half hour.*]

Hi, Rose! I just hope Vincent can keep up the pace.

—We'll be there in twenty minutes.

—Nothing more predictable than a man's ego. We're moving. Rose, do we have a death toll yet?

[*We don't know. A lot.*]

Probably better we don't know, anyway . . . So, does anyone still think there's a chance that robot'll calm down when he sees us? No one here is raising their hands.

[*I won't lie to you and say anyone here is overly confident. But perhaps seeing something familiar . . .*]

Rose! You thought sending us was stupid before the Army stepped in. I don't think our odds have gotten any better now that it destroyed half of London.

[*Sending tanks was a bad idea. No one denies that.*]

I don't really care if they deny it or not. What I'd like is for those suits to come up here and take our place. But there's no point talking about it now. We'll be walking for a while. I don't think we have anything to say that'll last thirty minutes, so we should have some music for you in a sec. Vincent, what do we have for our road trip?

—Kim Mitchell.

—Who the hell is Kim Mitchell?

—You don't know "Patio Lanterns"? My mom really liked Kim Mitchell. Used to be my date music when I had someone over for dinner. A long, long time ago.

—Oh God. You mean girls. So Rose, we leave you with some bad eighties music, courtesy of a pubescent Quebecois. Ewww. I can just picture you at fifteen. You had a mustache, didn't you?

—Thank you, Kara . . .

FILE NO. 1443 (CONTINUED)

MISSION LOG—CAPTAIN KARA RESNIK AND VINCENT COUTURE, EARTH DEFENSE CORPS
Location: London, England

—SHIT! I can't see anything. Vincent, are you all right?

—I'm OK. Just . . . disoriented. What about you?

—I think I dislocated my shoulder. What the hell was that?

—I don't know, he must have seen us through the buildings.

[*Vincent, what happened?*]

He shot at us, Rose. That's what happened. And I can tell you that wasn't a push. Whatever he shot us with knocked us on our ass about a hundred feet from where it hit us. In case there was any doubt left, he is *not* happy to see us. I don't think we're gonna shake hands.

[*Where are you?*]

I don't know. We're on our back. Lots of tall buildings. I see one that looks like a pickle. We're not that far from where the damage stops. Must be two or three miles from where he's at.

[*GPS has you in the financial district. That building must be the Gherkin. Did you see what he hit you with?*]

I didn't see anything. Not the robot, especially not the shot. All I saw was a sea of dirt ahead of us. I'm telling you, that robot is pissed. It's still shooting at us! I can see flashes of light above our head every three seconds or so.

—Vincent, what do you say we get out of here?

—And go where? I'm happy where we are now.

—We're lying down in the middle of Downtown London.

—Exactly. How often do we get to do that?

—Vincent!

—All right! I'll turn on the shield if you can move your arm.

—I can hold it up. Getting *us* up will be harder. Ready?

—Say the word.

—AAAARRRRGGGHHH! I'm pushing! We're up! Turn! Turn! Turn! Gimme the shield, now!

—Shield to maximum.

—SON OF A BITCH! AARGH!

[*Kara, what's happening? The helicopters turned away when the robot started shooting. We lost visual. You'll have to talk us through while we switch to satellite.*]

We're getting pounded here! I see him, about a mile away. He must have gotten closer while we were down.

[*Have you tried firing at it?*]

Not yet. We've been busy getting our ass kicked. Vincent, give me the sword, midsize . . . DAMN! Ready . . . FIRE! . . . Did we hit him?

—Yeah. You got him right in the—

—Where?

—You got him right in the legs. He didn't even budge. Rose, we can't fight this guy.

[*Can you—*]

Kara, what are you doing?

[*What's going on?*]

Kara's . . . engaging in diplomacy.

[*She's what?*]

She's giving him the finger. Very mature, Kara.

[*This is—*]

—Run, Vincent! My shoulder can't take much more of this.

—One at a time, please. What did you say, Kara?

—I said run!

—I'm not turning my back to this guy. He'll have us down in one shot.

—I mean run *at* him.

—Why would I do that?

[*I don't think that's a good idea.*]

—AARGH! Damn, that hurts! Because fuck him, that's why!

—Kara, the sword won't go through his shield.

—I don't care about the sword!

—Kara—

—Trust me, Vincent. Run!

—*Tabarnak* . . . EDC Control, we're about to do something really stupid. It was nice knowing you all.

—Faster Vincent! Come on! Faster! Run his ass down!

—I'm trying!

—Almost there! Turn our shield off. UUUGH! You felt that one, didn't you?

—All right, so we tackle him. Now what?

—Now he's not shooting at us, that's what. Get ready to discharge Themis.

—It's not working.

—What do you mean it's not working?

—How the hell should I know? I'm pressing the button and it's not working! Might be his energy shield. How long can you hold him? Kara?

—Not long.

—We're feeding off that shield of his. Themis will discharge all on her own if you hold on long enough.

—He's too strong! I can't hold on! Gimme the sword, midsize.

—There!

—Fire!

—Kara, you're pointing at the ground!

—Shut up and fire the damn thing!

—There! You just made a big hole under our feet! We're knee deep into a giant crater now!

—Make the sword a little longer. Fire! Vincent! I said fire!

—I am! But what are you doing? You're just making the hole deeper. This is bedrock. We won't be able to move!

—Again!

—Ok, that's it! We're in up to our neck! We're stuck! I can't even move my legs!

—Well, he's stuck in that hole with us. Betcha he can't move either.

—That's . . . kinda cool.

—Better than being shot at, isn't it? Now let's see if I can just . . . twist . . . my left arm. Damn, this is tight. There we go. Gimme the shield! Now!

—Wha—

—Shield!

—What size?

—Doesn't matter! Maximum size!

—All right, it's on . . . I don't think it's working. There's no room!

—It's doing *something*. I can see the energy field around him.

—You're right. It's getting brighter . . . It's flickering! Ohhh, I love you, Kara Resnik.

—You love me because I thought of a way to save your ass.

—Hey! It might not work. I'll love you even if it doesn't. That's like 50 percent selfless.

—You're so romantic.

—Kara! Listen!

—What?

—Hear that sound? That's metal grinding on metal. His energy field is down. Is our shield still on?

—It's on all right. I can feel it pushing against my arm.

—Do you think it'll cut through the metal?

—Look!

—YEAHHHHH!

—Booyah! You messed with the wrong girl, asshole. Oh, you like me now Vincent, don't you?

[*What's happening? Are you OK? We can't see anything on satellite.*]

—Hi, Rose! Yeah, we're good. We're just looking at the sky above us. Kara's crazy, we're stuck in a giant hole, but we're OK. A little banged up, but you should see the other guy.

[*We can't see anything. Are you sure he's disabled?*]

I think so. We cut him in half. Don't wanna sound overly optimistic, but I'm pretty sure we won this one.

[*How?*]

He couldn't move anymore. Neither could we. We just let Themis's shield grind against his energy field until it gave out. Then the shield just kept on going.

[*Congratulations! Military folks here are really impressed. No one here would have thought of that.*]

Didn't think of it either. You can thank the psychopath who told me to run at the robot and tackle him.

[*You said yes.*]

Have you tried saying no to Kara? I'd rather face the bad guy.

—Can you stop talking about me like I'm not here? Vincent, what do you say we get out of this hole?

—Sure. Wanna tell me how?

—We could let Themis discharge, like we did in Denver.

[*No Kara! Don't!*]

Why?

—They want the other robot.

—You said we couldn't vaporize it.

—Probably not, but we sliced it open, and the pilots might get wiped out.

[*Vincent's right. It wouldn't hurt if we could talk to them.*]

—OK, fine. So how do we get out?

—Can you move your right arm? We can shoot around with the sword, make a bigger hole.

—Nope. That arm's stuck pointing down. Any other bright ideas?

—I . . .

—Yes?

—I—

—He has no clue. Rose, can you send someone to dig us out?

[*There's a team on the way. It might take them awhile to dig deep enough.*]

I figured as much.

—Kara—

—Don't talk to me! I'm pissed. I wanna get out of here, but you don't wanna hurt the guys that were shooting at us a minute ago. Now I'm stuck in a hole for God knows how long.

—You're smiling.

—Maybe. But I'm pissed.

—You're happy.

—I . . . I guess I am.

—Kara?

—What? Why are *you* grinning?

—Kara Resnik, you have made me—

—Oh no! You're gonna propose *now*?

—I—

—Stop. Stop. We don't want the same things. I'm not ready for the whole family thing.

—I know.

—No kids.

—I *know*.

—Do you really wanna grow old with just grumpy old me?

—No offense, Kara, but I don't think either of us will get to grow old, especially if we're together. The only question is: Do I wanna die young with anyone else?

PART TWO

ALL IN THE FAMILY

FILE NO. 1521

INTERVIEW WITH BRIGADIER GENERAL EUGENE GOVENDER, COMMANDER, EARTH DEFENSE CORPS

Location: New Dynasty Chinese Restaurant, Dupont Circle, Washington, DC

—Sit down, Eugene.

—What's good here?

—You should try the kung pao chicken. The Indonesian rice is also very good.

—I'll have what you're having. How was the wedding?

—It was a surprisingly large affair. I did not think Ms. Resnik—excuse me, *Mrs.* Resnik—

—She'll kill you if you call her that.

—That either of them would want a traditional ceremony, let alone that they would indulge in such a lavish celebration afterwards.

—Oh, weddings aren't about the bride and groom. You propose, or you say yes, because you love the other person. You start imagining your perfect wedding, a small thing outdoors, intimate, with just the people you're closest to. It takes about a week after you announce it before you realize that the proposal was really the only part of getting married that was about you. The wedding itself? That's all about your mother, your aunt who's dying, how it'll look like you're taking sides if this second cousin you never met isn't invited. Still . . . Where was it held?

—**At a hotel in Detroit. You were greatly missed.**

—I doubt they even noticed.

—**They watched you on television after the ceremony. That would suggest they were aware of your absence.**

—Well, I get that they wanted to get married on the anniversary of their victory, but there was another ceremony in London. Someone had to be there. Who has their wedding in December anyway?

—**I thought the London memorial would be on the anniversary of the attack.**

—I guess they wanted to focus on the positive. I don't blame them. One hundred and thirty-six thousand dead.

—**At the risk of sounding insensitive, that number is lower than what I anticipated.**

—A hundred and thirty-six thousand is a lot of dead husbands and wives, sons and daughters. I would call you an asshole, but I thought the same thing. It could easily have been a million.

—**We were lucky.**

—This time.

—**Do you believe they will come back?**

—Don't you? We don't even know what they came for. I don't think it was to pick a fight with the British Army. Do you?

—**I do not. They could have attacked at any time. It is a reasonable assumption that the British Government precipitated this conflict.**

—Well, they're dead now. Their robot's destroyed. Their two pilots were dead when we got there. We don't know if they died when their robot was sliced in half or if they committed suicide to avoid being captured, but the end result's the same. They're dead. At some point, whoever sent them will know something's up. I don't think they're just gonna forget about it. Yeah, I think they'll come back. So young, too. Such a shame.

—Who?

—The pilots. You saw them. Those boys looked like they were what? Eighteen . . . twenty tops. Amazing how much they look like us. Sure, they had their legs backwards, but I've seen Vincent flip his so many times, it sorta looks normal to me now.

—Have we learned anything new from the autopsy?

—Nothing a dinosaur like me can understand. You'll have to talk to Rose. I do know these two were just kids doing their jobs, whatever that was. There'll be some grieving people where they came from. And grieving people make rash decisions. I think they'll come back. I think there'll be a whole lot more of them. And this time, I bet you they won't stare at the scenery for a week before they start blowing shit up.

—That is a very pessimistic view of things. How about the robot? Has it revealed any of its secrets?

—That, I can answer. We've learned so very little about that robot that I actually understand all of it. They pretty much build them like they used to. The basic design's the same. Same number of parts—it fell to pieces a few minutes after it was disabled. The control room is almost identical to ours. The console has a couple more buttons, but that's it.

—Can we put it back together?

—You'd like to have another one. Wouldn't you?

—Well . . .

—Don't get your hopes up. That thing's busted. Nothing works anymore. Themis's shield cut through the control room. The sphere is broken, all bent up, lost the white stuff it was floating in. Whatever it was, it evaporated almost instantly. The torso's cut in half. We can't weld any of it. Duct tape won't work either. The rest of the robot, well, we don't understand how it works any more than we understand how Themis can move. You look at the cross section and, aside from the big hole where the control room was, it's just a big hunk of solid metal. The only good thing I can think of is that the controls are so similar, we might be able to use theirs for spare parts if we break anything. Judging by the way our pilots handle things, I'd say that's likely. The science team will be happy come Monday.

—Why Monday?

—I'm sending the engineers home. The real nerds can play with it now.

—They could not before?

—They could look at it, but I wouldn't let them do anything that could damage it any more than it is.

—Why not?

—What do you think? I wanted another one too. But . . . it's officially scrap now. They can do with it as they please. Spare parts and happy scientists. That's what we get for 136,000 dead.

—That is hardly the only positive that came out of the London events. I thought you of all people would find some comfort in the outcome.

—Me of all people?

—I doubt anyone will question the relevance of EDC anymore. Not in our lifetime anyway. Themis has done exactly what we said, and hoped, she could do. The EDC has saved London, perhaps the human race. There is not a government on this planet that will refuse you funding. You will have all the resources you need, for as long as you need. On a more personal level, no one will question your leadership, ever. In the eyes of most, the tragedy that sent all these people to their deaths could have been avoided had the British Government done as you asked. You are perhaps the only person to ever live to enjoy this much credibility on a planetary level. What you say goes, for everyone, everywhere.

—Give it another year. Today, we're entertaining. People identify. Makes them feel better about their lives. The press is saying nice things about us because that's what people wanna hear. But you eat the same ice-cream flavor every day, after a while . . . At some point, saying nice things about the EDC won't sell as many papers.

—People hardly buy newspapers anymore.

—We're old. Aren't we? Well, a few weeks, six months, a year from now, singing our praises won't sell whatever the hell they sell these days. Then, trust me, they'll try saying bad things. They'll question our research, whether we could do anything against a large enemy force. Funny thing is, they'll be right. It's not that we aren't trying, but we haven't squeezed any new technology out of that thing in ten years. You think we'd have at least a faster toaster, better car brakes, softer toilet paper, but nope. Not a goddamn thing. And don't get me started on how we'd fare against more than one of those robots.

—I hate having to point out the obvious, but we won. We prevailed. Themis fought the alien robot in hand-to-hand combat and she was victorious.

—You call that combat? They dug a hole!

—They immobilized the enemy.

—They dug a hole! What were the odds that their shield could knock out that energy field? They were just lucky. Our guys were in *way* over their heads. Not their fault, we should never have sent them. That was like a schoolyard fight. They were getting pounded by a bigger kid and they panicked. I'm happy it worked, but it doesn't make me feel any better about our chances. The Resnik girl is just insane, if you ask me.

—Some would say she has instinct.

—That's one way to put it.

—It is not the first time her impulsive nature has paid dividends. There are very few people whose careful planning I trust more than her improvisation.

—Maybe. But it doesn't matter. She can't bury more than one of these robots. If they send more . . .

—What do you think we can do to prepare?

—I've asked myself that question so many times. If the stakes weren't so high, I'd find this funny. On paper, I run a military organization, but the one thing we all agree on is that there is no military response to a large alien force. You saw what it did to three armored regiments. Hell, it even took out the city that was around the three armored regiments. Buildings, cars, people, cats, dogs. Didn't even spare the cockroaches.

—Themis can also do that.

—Well, maybe we can give them a hand and wipe out a few cities ourselves. What she *can't* do is hurt these things if they don't stand still. She hit that robot dead on with her weapon. Might as well have thrown insults at it.

—She did give him the finger.

—Too bad the helicopters were gone. That would have made a great picture.

—Or a statue.

—Ha! You made a joke! They could have used that for the memorial. Did you see the monument they made? The alien robot kneeling before Themis? Looks like she's knighting him. Better than Hercules and Diomedes, I guess . . . Oh, you don't know that one. Look it up.

—You have not answered my question.

—My point is this: There's nothing we can do. Not with what we have. Our only hope, if they ever come back, is that my kids will have found something useful by then. I hate to say it, 'cause she's completely crazy, but it's all about Rose now.

—It *is* all about Rose, is it not?

—Yes. That's why I said it.

—She fell on the hand when she was a child. She somehow ended up in charge of studying it. Now we are waiting for a war that we cannot win, and our best hope for survival lies with her.

—Like you said, you're really good at stating the obvious, but is there a point to all this?

—Of course. Did you ever wonder why they chose to bring her back?

FILE NO. 1526

SESSION NOTES—PATIENT EVA REYES

Dr. Benicio Muñoz Rivera, psychiatrist,
San Juan, Puerto Rico

—Tell me about the nightmares, Eva.

—I don't wanna talk about that. You said we could play some games.

—We just did, Eva, and now we need to talk.

—Those weren't fun. I wanna play *real* games.

—Your mother is worried about you, Eva.

—I'm fine! She doesn't need to worry.

—Can you tell me what happened yesterday?

—Nothing happened. I was taking a bath!

—Your mother was very scared. Tell me what happened.

—I . . . I saw something. I wanted to know what it felt like . . . not being able to breathe. I didn't know my mother was in the room. I was just curious. I wasn't trying to—

—She says you spend all your time alone, that you don't talk to your friends anymore.

—I don't have any friends. They think I'm crazy.

—No one thinks that, Eva.

—YES THEY DO!

—Eva—

—You don't know what you're talking about! I'm not imagining it, they say it all the time! They *all* think I'm crazy. My mother thinks that too. That's why I'm here.

—It's perfectly normal for a girl your age to have some bad thoughts, Eva. I don't think they're magically going to go away either. But there are tools you can use to take control of those thoughts. That's why *I'm* here, to give you those tools. I want you to stop being afraid of what's in your head.

—How could I not be afraid? I saw them die, all of them.

—Who died, Eva?

—Those people in London. I saw them dead.

—What did you see?

—They were all dead!

—I meant precisely. Can you describe the images?

—There were thousands of them, everywhere. They were just lying there, on the sidewalk, inside their cars.

—Like they fell asleep?

—All at the same time.

—You saw the bodies?

—Yes!

—But there weren't any bodies in London after last year's attack, Eva. You saw that! It was on television. There was nothing left.

—Yeah, but they're dead, aren't they?

—You just had a nightmare, about a bad thing that happened. It's natural for you to put the two together, but you just said yourself, what you saw isn't what happened.

—They're not nightmares! I'm not . . . Whatever. I know you don't believe me. Can I go now?

—Not yet.

—Then can we talk about something else?

—What else did you see?

—I don't wanna do this anymore.

—Eva, tell me. What else did you see?

—I saw a metal . . . I saw a robot falling into the clouds.

—You mentioned that vision before. How can anything fall into the sky? Was it falling upwards? From an airplane?

—I don't know. Not from a plane, no.

—Then from where, Eva?

—I don't *know*! I'm just telling you what I saw. Can I go?

—That's OK. I just want you to . . . consider the possibility that what you're seeing isn't real? Will you do that for me?

—Sure.

—You have a very vivid imagination, Eva, and that's a good thing, a very good thing. You should find ways to take advantage of it. Do you like to draw?

—Yes.

—Maybe you can draw the things you see. Put them on your wall. I think it might help.

—Help with what?

—It might help you realize it's all in your head, give you some control over your thoughts. Then you might not be so afraid of them anymore.

—I'm not always afraid of them.

—That's good! Can you think of what's different when you're not?

—What do you mean?

—I'd like to know why you're not afraid of some of the things you see.

—They're not all bad things. Sometimes I see good things happening.

—Like what?

—I saw my dad buying a new car. He was happy.

—Did your dad buy a new car?

—No. He's saving for it.

—So not everything you see happens, does it?

—I don't know! But it feels real when I see it.

—Of course it does. Dreams can seem very real.

—They're not dreams! I see these things when I'm awake. I see them all the time! I know what dreams are. I also know when I'm imagining things. This isn't the same! I know you don't think I'm telling the truth, but I am. It's different.

—Eva, I never said you weren't telling the truth. I never thought that for a moment. I know you think what you're seeing is real. I just want you to make room for the possibility that it's not.

—It's four o'clock. My mom'll be waiting downstairs.

—Yes. You can go, Eva. Think about what I said. Next time it happens, try telling yourself it's not real. Say it out loud if you need to. And start drawing what you see. You can bring your drawings with you next time. I'd like to see them. If that doesn't work, we'll try something else. There is a special kind of medication that might make the bad thoughts go away.

—I don't want medication.

—It's just a thought, Eva. Your parents and I, we . . . we just want you to be happy.

FILE NO. 1528

INTERVIEW WITH DR. ROSE FRANKLIN, HEAD OF SCIENCE DIVISION, EARTH DEFENSE CORPS

Location: EDC Headquarters, New York, NY

—Put the gun down, Dr. Franklin.

—Get out!

—Dr. Franklin . . .

—Please! I just wanna be alone! I'm not hurting anyone.

—You are pointing a 9mm handgun at your right temple. I do not wish to draw unfounded conclusions, but I do fear for your safety at the moment. I also know the reason you are distraught and realize I might have been a contributing factor to your current state of mind.

—It wasn't pointed at my head until your guard walked in. And you didn't do anything. Now go! Both of you!

—Dr. Franklin, put the gun down so this gentleman here can leave us alone. I would very much like to talk to you.

[*Put the gun down, ma'am!*]

Young man, there is no immediate danger here. You can holster your weapon.

[*I can't do that, sir.*]

Your name and rank, please.

[*Petty Officer Franklin, sir.*]

Franklin? Are you two related?

[*No, sir.*]

If you are not related to her, Petty Officer Franklin, she will not mind when I have you locked up for the remainder of your short life. You probably know very little about me, but you can trust that, if I apply myself, I can make your existence so excruciatingly painful that you will beg for it to end. And I give you my word: If any harm comes to Dr. Franklin, self-inflicted or not, while you are pointing your weapon at her, I will apply myself thoroughly . . . Good. Now leave us.

[*Sir . . .*]

Close the door behind you . . . Dr. Franklin, please accept my apology for the lack of sensibility demonstrated by your name-sake. The elite unfortunately do not get assigned to night-shift se-curity. More than anything, please forgive me if our previous discussion prompted this moment of despair.

—It's not despair. I just want to put an end to this charade. I shouldn't be here. Rose Franklin is dead!

—That is not what I said. Please give me the gun. We both know you will not end your life today. It is almost 5:00 A.M., so I assume you have been staring at the weapon for hours. I do not doubt your conviction, but your resolve will not magically increase after breakfast.

—It's harder than I thought.

—The will to live is very hard to suppress. It shames me to say it is a subject I am well versed in. Besides, we really need your help.

—You don't need me. You really don't. I haven't done anything use-ful since I . . . since I came back.

—That is not true. No one understands Themis better than you do.

—She's not supposed to be here either, you know that? I was wrong. We weren't meant to find her. She's supposed to be buried, hidden. I'm supposed to be dead. You should dismantle Themis, throw her back to the bottom of the ocean. Forget about her and forget about me.

—It is a little late for that.

—I just want it to stop. You don't know what it's like to be . . . It doesn't matter. Can you please leave?

—It matters to me. If you will not give me the gun, at least put it down . . . There . . . What I told you yesterday was meant to reassure you. It is fairly obvious now that what I said did not have the intended result.

—You just told me the truth. I'm not me! I'm a copy!

—I said nothing of the sort.

—You said they remade me out of thin air!

—They re-created you based on data they had obtained before your death.

—I'm a copy!

—I tried to relay to you information that was given to me by one of the people involved. I can see now that my rendition was less than perfect. It sounded much better in my head. The central point, which seems to have been lost in translation, was that who you are, your essence, was fully preserved in the process. I—

—It doesn't matter! I'm not—

—I was not finished. I have made a terrible mistake in thinking I could convincingly explain things that I barely understand myself. I have done so out of distrust, in a gratuitous attempt to control information that you were clearly entitled to. I was wrong and I am sorry. The person who gave me that information—

—Is he one of the people that . . . made me?

—I believe he is. He offered to meet you and tell you exactly what was done to you. I refused. Before you do anything that cannot be undone, let me contact him and arrange that meeting. Your scientific knowledge is infinitely greater than mine and you should be able to understand a great deal more than I did. I suspect he had to vulgarize things a lot for my benefit.

— . . .

—Will you listen to what he has to say?

— . . .

—Good. I am relieved to see that your curiosity is still greater than your despair. Now, will you give me the gun?

—What if it doesn't work? What if I don't like what he has to say?

—Then I will try something else.

—You can't babysit me forever.

—Probably not. But I can order other people to do so. If you want me to say I will give you back your gun and close the door behind me on the way out, I will not. I will do everything I can to stop you from ending your life, in part because I care about you, but mostly for purely selfish and practical reasons. That being said, you are a very intelligent and resourceful woman, and if you are fully motivated, I will probably fail. Then I will try something else.

—What do you mean?

—You were brought back from the dead once. There is no reason to believe it cannot be done again, and again.

—I . . . You'd do that to me?

—I would do anything I feel is necessary to protect us. I would very much like to avoid having to tell you about "the needs of the many," but this is one of those moments. Most experts, including yourself if I am not mistaken, believe in the impending return of our alien visitors. Even you should concede that your current despondency is inconsequential in comparison. If Ms. Resnik were contemplating jumping into the abyss, I trust you would do everything in your power to stop her.

—Probably. But her role in all this is obvious. I just don't think I can be useful to you anymore.

—Time will tell. May I change the subject for a moment?

—What do you wanna talk about?

—I would like you to tell me what you have learned about the beings that were inside the alien robot.

—Why? There's nothing new to tell.

—Humor me.

—You know all this. You read the reports. We talked about this!

—Are they similar to us?

—Where are you going with this? You know what they look like. You've seen them! They're humanoid. Type V, dark olive skin, knees reversed like the robot. And it's really their knees, they're not digitigrade like we suspected. They have an extra joint in their legs. No eyebrows. Everything else looks human, inside and out.

—How close are they to us from a genetic standpoint? I know that we share 98 percent of our DNA with chimpanzees. Can you tell me how much of it we share with the aliens?

—You've read the report. What more do you need!

—I want _you_ to tell me.

—You should have stuck with Alyssa. She's the expert in all this.

—I wish I could talk to Alyssa about a great many things. But as she is unavailable at the moment, I would like you to tell me what you understand.

—Well, the first part of what you said isn't exactly true. How similar our DNA is to a chimp depends a lot on what you compare. It's really not that close if you look at everything. The short answer for the aliens we found is 0 percent since they don't have DNA.

—I find it difficult to believe that they could be so different from us.

—They're not. They're made pretty much the same way. It's just not . . . Do you know what DNA is?

—Deoxyribonucleic acid. My understanding is that it contains genetic instructions for life as we know it. I realize this is a simplistic answer.

—That's the gist of it. It's information storage. It's a complex molecule that can store an incredible amount of information. And it's stable. The really cool part is that it can replicate itself. That's basically all you need to create life. The ability to hold information for a certain amount of time and to pass it on. And you got the name right. I was asking whether you knew what it's made of.

—Tell me.

—DNA's a nucleic acid, like the name says. It's made up of smaller things called nucleotides. To make a nucleotide, you need three things. A phosphate, a base, and a sugar.

—Sugar?

—Yep. There's sugar in life. If the sugar is the one we call deoxyribose, you get deoxyribonucleic acid, or DNA. If the sugar is ribose, a simpler sugar, you get RNA, which can also store information, but isn't as stable as DNA. The aliens have a very similar genetic makeup, but their nucleotides use a different sugar, a form of what we call arabinose.

—ANA.

—Exactly.

—And that is the only difference?

—Not quite. Each nucleotide also has a base. In DNA . . . Are you sure you want to hear this?

—Please.

—In DNA, there are four possible bases: cytosine, guanine, adenine, and thymine, which we just call C, G, A, and T. That's the genetic alphabet. The alien genetic code doesn't use A but something called diaminopurine. It makes their genetic code a little more stable than ours.

—Is it compatible with our DNA?

—Maybe. It's close enough the two might be able to talk to each other.

—So there is nothing really interesting about the differences.

—Are you kidding? This is probably one of the greatest discoveries we've ever made. People thought DNA was pretty much the only way you could get life. We've been wondering whether life could evolve from an RNA base. It's just recently that people have been able to play with the makeup of nucleic acids. We can make ANA in a lab, we've done it with a bunch of different sugars. We can make di-aminopurine. We can make all this! But to see it occur naturally in the universe in complex life-forms so similar to us . . . Now we know there's nothing really special about DNA. We can change the ingredients and still have a recipe for life. Do you understand what I'm saying? We're this close to understanding how life came about. How you go from a thing to a living thing. It's—

—Fascinating?

—It's not just fascinating. It's awe-inspiring. It's . . . Genesis.

—It touches you.

—Yes. It's—

—That seems like a completely human reaction to me.

— . . . I guess they made a good copy. I know what you're trying to do, but I don't think I'm a robot. Having feelings doesn't make me less of a fraud.

—Does it not? I was not drawing attention to the fact that you can experience emotions, but to what triggered this emotional response. It may be my limited knowledge, but it seems to me you were moved by the fact that the building blocks for life can take many forms. Was it not the point you were making? That there is nothing fundamentally unique about DNA, no magic involved? You were saying that no matter the ingredients, life can shape itself from any molecular structure stable enough to hold information and replicate itself. You were moved because you were able to decompose something you thought was impenetrable into elements you can understand.

—Yes.

—Then should you not feel the same awe over what happened to you? Why would the realization that something as unique as you can be reduced to a stable configuration of atoms not bring you the same satisfaction? I know nothing of genetics, so I am not moved as you are by the discoveries you describe, but I find you extraordinary, and I am absolutely humbled by the thought of something so complex and nuanced being remade from the very fabric of the universe. If your faith is what is torturing you, you should find the miracle in there.

—. . .

—Think about it.

—Your phone is vibrating.

—It does not matter.

—You should answer. It might be important.

—I am here for *you*.

—Pick up. I promise I won't do anything stupid.

—Very well . . . Yes? . . . When? . . . I am on my way.

—What is it?

—Something that unfortunately requires my immediate attention.

—You can go.

—I will not leave you alone. I can ask Ms. Resnik to come and keep you company but I would rather you came with me. Your assistance may be needed.

—What's going on?

—Themis has disappeared.

—What?

—Will you come with me?

—Yes. Let's go!

—Dr. Franklin. The gun? Please?

FILE NO. 1529

INTERVIEW WITH CAPTAIN KARA RESNIK, EARTH DEFENSE CORPS

Location: EDC Headquarters, New York, NY

[*Were the hangar doors closed?*]

{*Do you rememb—*}

—Everyone, stop! One at a time. Euge . . . General, you go.

[*When did you notice that Themis was missing?*]

—Really? Like, five minutes ago, when I called you. You think I went for a manicure first?

[*Watch your tone, Captain Resnik . . .*]

I'm trying, but we're wasting time. Yes, Rose?

{*Were the hangar doors closed the whole time?*}

Yeah they were. I'm telling you, he didn't go for a stroll. He can't walk Themis without me, she falls.

—Ms. Resnik, are you certain Themis was inside the hangar this morning?

—Yes! She was here like ten minutes ago. I saw her. I talked to Vincent!

—**Please tell us everything that you remember.**

—What I remember? It just happened! Is anyone listening?

—**We are now.**

—Vincent got up real early this morning, said he wanted to try a few things by himself so he let me sleep in. I couldn't go back to sleep, so I read a little, then I headed here. I radioed him. He was in the sphere. I asked if he'd had breakfast, he said no. I told him I'd bring bagels up. I went into the kitchen, and when I came back, they were gone.

—**Are you certain you are not forgetting anything? The smallest detail could be important.**

—Yes! I mean . . . He said he wasn't hungry. I told him it'd be a shame to let the bagels go bad—he brings them back from Montréal when he visits. We don't have a freezer here . . . He said OK. I made bagels! Do you wanna know what I put on them? Cream cheese and raspberry jam. Then Themis was gone, with my husband inside. Happy?

—**I am now. Details about the condiments were unnecessary.**

—I think that was the first time I've called him my husband, not as a joke . . . We have to find him!

—**We will. Dr. Franklin, can you tell us where Themis is located at this moment?**

{*There's nothing on the GPS.*}

Could it be malfunctioning?

{*We're picking up everything else. Just not Themis.*}

Perhaps the receiver is broken.

—All three of them? Are you sure you can't see her?

{*According to this, she's not here anymore.*}

That makes no sense. She couldn't have just vanished.

—**Maybe someone tampered with the GPS receiver so we could not locate her.**

—Not a chance.

—I am simply trying to lay down some possible explanations.

—That's not one of them.

—Why is that?

—The receivers are inside the sphere. It takes about ten minutes just to get up there. You'd have to find them, disable them, all before Vincent can pick up a radio. Then what? Even with Vincent, you can't pilot her out of here. That's a two-hundred-foot-tall, seven-thousand-metric-ton piece of metal to move without making any noise, all in the time it takes me to make a bagel.

—Your logic is sound. Can you offer a more plausible explanation?

—Not right now I can't.

—Could the aliens have somehow transported her?

—You mean like the alien robot just "beamed" itself in London? I don't know. Rose?

{*We don't know if it "beamed" itself or if something else "beamed" it. Either way, I don't think so.*}

—It would seem premature to reject this explanation without any evidence to the contrary.

—She's right. If they could just yank Themis away whenever they felt like it, they would have done it when we fought, wouldn't they?

—It is possible they lacked the ability at the time but possess it now. Doing so might require a ship, or equipment that was not present in London.

—But it'd be here now? Without our detecting anything?

—It does sound a bit far-fetched, but we are talking about giant robots from outer space.

—It's not an option anyway.

—I would not blindly discard the possibility.

—I would! If aliens just beamed Themis to their home world, or into space, or whatever, then there's nothing we can do about it. Can we talk about scenarios where we get Themis and Vincent back? And in one piece?

—Certainly. If we ignore, for the moment, the possibility that Themis is no longer on Earth, there would seem to be only two options. Either the GPS is malfunctioning or has been tampered with, or she is somewhere the GPS signal cannot reach. Could she be inside a structure that blocks the signal?

—You mean like here?

—Yes. I know GPS receivers do not function properly inside some buildings.

{*Themis is different, somehow. It takes a lot of interference to block a signal from her. We shouldn't get a radio signal inside this much metal, but it works. GPS won't work on my cellphone inside this building, but it works inside the sphere, and we always see Themis onscreen when she's here.*}

—Thank you, Dr. Franklin. But she could be in a more . . . opaque building. We cannot reject every improbable explanation as there clearly are no probable ones available.

—OK. So either Vincent is being zipped through space on his way to God knows where, or he's here on Earth and we just can't reach him. Can we start making a list of places that can hold a two-hundred-foot giant?

—We certainly can. But without sounding overly pessimistic, you have made a very solid argument that Themis could not simply have been moved in the traditional sense. If aliens did not "beam" her out of this hangar, it would appear someone, or something, did.

{*Vincent and I had talked about the possibility that Themis might be able to transport herself, assuming that's what the robot in London did. We haven't tried anything yet, but it's not impossible Vincent found something on his own.*}

Where could he have gone?

{*I have no idea.*}

[*I hate to interrupt, but the press is coming this afternoon. There's a Q&A with the pilots and some high-school kids.*]

I fear you will have to reschedule, General. Ms. Resnik is unfortunately coming down with a very nasty case of the same flu that kept her husband in bed this morning.

—*Cough.* What can I do while I recover?

—You can help the General make a list of potential domestic sites.

—Where are *you* going?

—Chantilly, Virginia. We should have satellite surveillance of any facility large enough to house a missile silo, or a small army. Who is that at the door?

—That's Amy . . . something . . . She's a civilian employee.

—Is she supposed to be here?

[*She's cleared. She works in Comms.*]

Let her in . . . What can we do for you, Ms. . . . Amy?

<*I'm terribly sorry to bother you, but your cellphone won't work with the room secured. I had a gentleman on the phone who said an . . . Interpol Infra-Terra Red Notice—wow, that's a mouthful— popped up on facial recognition in Helsinki. I have no idea what that means, but he said you'd like to know.* >

Thank you very much, Amy. You can go now.

—What is it?

—A very busy day, Ms. Resnik.

FILE NO. 1532

TRANSCRIPT—FINNISH CUSTOMS INTERROGATION
Location: Helsinki Airport

—I t . . . t . . . told you a hundred times already. My name is Mar . . . Marina Antoniou.

—*And what are you doing in Helsinki?*

—I don't be . . . believe this. I'm not doing anything in . . . Helsinki! I have a c . . . connecting flight. What time is it?

—*Almost 19:00.*

—Gamoto! I've already missed my plane. I've been in this room for sss . . . six hours. Can I go now?

—*Soon. You can take the next flight. Where are you flying to?*

—There is no next flight. The next one is tomorrow. And you have my ticket in ff . . . in front of you. I know you're asking the same questions over and . . . over again to see if I ch . . . change my story, but this must be the tenth time you've asked, and it's written down right here: New York City, so is my name. It's a plane ticket. I can . . . can't go anywhere else with it. If you plan on qu . . . questioning me forever, you should at least find something I could p . . . poss . . . ibly get wrong.

—*These are just routine questions. Airport security has been in-creased and your boarding pass was selected at random.*

—Why don't you tell me what's . . . really going on? You don't select people at random to spend a day being inter—

—*I only have a few more questions . . . for security reasons.*

—No! You don't. You ran out of que . . . questions four hours ago. Can I get some coffee?

—*Soon.*

—You keep looking at your watch. Are you waiting for someone?

—He is waiting for me . . . He did not offer you anything to drink because you would not be allowed to leave this room and he did not want you to soil yourself.

Thank you, young man. You can leave us. I know I need not remind you that you may not discuss your encounter with this woman with anyone. You can, however, discuss your promotion with your superior when you exit this room.

Alyssa Papantoniou. You do not seem surprised to see me.

—I had a feeling you might be coming.

—New passport? Antoniou. I am impressed.

—They told me to make the lie as cl . . . as close to the truth as possible.

—Why Marina?

—My . . . my mother's name.

—Hard to forget. The Russians taught you well.

—They also told me you're t . . . trying to frame me for the Sre . . . Srebrenica massacre. Don't you think that's overreaching?

—Is it?

—You think I would kill people for some . . . outdated notion of eth-nicity?

—To be frank, Ms. Papantoniou, I have absolutely no idea what you believe is worthy of torture or death.

—Torture? I would never purposely inflict p . . . pain on anyone. You really don't know me at all.

—I am the first to admit it. I do not. But you had no compulsions about submitting Ms. Resnik to, shall we say, very unpleasant procedures.

—I never wanted her to suffer! I'm not some psychopath who burned ki . . . kittens as a child. I never took . . . pleasure in hurting anyone.

—You are telling me you had absolutely no part in the events at Srebrenica?

—How can you . . . ? Do you *know* what happened during the Bosnian wars? Or did you just watch the new . . . newspeople get all the names wrong?

—I have no firsthand knowledge of the Bosnian war. I was present during the Kosovo war.

—So you know the difference between a Serbian and a Serb, a Bosnian and a Bosniak—

—Croatians and Croats. I am aware of the difference between nationality and ethnicity. What does this have to do with your involvement in ethnic cleansing?

—My parents, they were s . . . scholars. They met at a conference. My father came from Orthodox Serbs. My mother was Romanian, Catholic. Somehow, that made her a Cr . . . Croat in the eyes of everyone in our town, except for the Croats, who called her a Gypsy. My sister had a Mu . . . Muslim boyfriend. I was an atheist. We were all Bosnians.

—Your point?

—I wouldn't have known which side I was on.

—You were unemployed for over a year at the time of the massacre, yet your lifestyle never suffered.

—Is that wh . . . what bothers you? I was supposed to be a geneticist. There was no research anymore. People weren't getting paid. I was tired of seeing m-m-mutilated people die in front of me, so I quit the hospital. My parents had ju . . . just died. They left me some money.

—Then I suppose I will have to be content watching you be tried in the United States. It says here you had a layover in New York, on your way to Puerto Rico. Why were you going back there?

—Nothing that concerns you.

—I realize we do not know each other very well, but you must understand that you will eventually tell me all that I want to know. Why not save yourself the added discomfort?

—Now who's talking about torture? What are you so ang . . . angry for?

—We both know what you did. If you do not remember, I am certain you will be reminded many times during your trial.

—I only did what needed to be done. Someone had to, even if you didn't have the sss . . . stomach for it.

—Removing ova from Ms. Resnik against her will is something that had to be done?

—It would have been better if she had volunteered, but she didn't.

— . . .

—Yes . . . It had to be done!

—It did not have to be done there and then. You could have waited until she volunteered, or until the circumstances called for more extreme measures.

—No! I couldn't have! You can't wait. You can't worry about other people's feelings. You can't com . . . compromise, hope for the best. Or people die.

—You seem agitated all of a sudden.

—Have you ever seen a village being raided?

—I have not.

—Me neither. Bu . . . but my father told me. I was still in Sarajevo when the siege began. The whole country went c . . . crazy. Everybody fought everybody. The Serbs fought the Croats. Everyone f . . . fought the Muslims. Villages were being raided all the time. Then one day, they came into *our* village.

—Who did? Serbs?

—It doesn't matter. Bosniaks and Croats killed plenty of people too, but yes, they were VRS. Do you know how many men it takes to terrorize a town of ten thousand people?

—Fewer than one would think.

—You can probably do it with fifty men. There were a lot more that day. Two hundred VRS soldiers raided my town while I was away. We had *all* heard of the atrocities. People knew what the VRS did. The villagers weren't defenseless. They had weapons, p . . . plenty of them. People could have fought back. Ten thousand against two hundred. They would have been overwhelmed in minutes. But they didn't. The town leaders called for everyone to remain calm, stay in their home. Don't p . . . provoke them! Don't make things worse! They thought offering no resistance would make things easier.

—Did it?

—Maybe it did. They only killed twenty-seven people that day.

Two hundred men . . . Fffewer than that, because a dozen of them were taking turns raping my . . . raping my sister to death. They made my parents watch, then they killed my mother, let my father live . . . because he was a Serb. They raped and killed a whole lot of people that day. There couldn't have been more than a hundred men left on the street, in the whole town. No one did anything. No one tried. Everyone just . . . hoped for the best. My father killed himself a week later.

That's what happens if you don't do what needs to be done. Vincent and Kara were in their midtwenties. That meant they could be eff . . . efficient for another t . . . twenty years at best. They could have died. They could have got . . . gotten sick. I thought there was a good chance their children could operate the robot, but it would take years to find out . . .

—You do realize there are . . . other ways for people to have children? Did you ever wonder why I would encourage two people in a military unit to pursue a relationship?

—I don't think that's why you did it. I think you liked them. Maybe you thought it would make them work better together.

—If I have, in any way, willingly or not, led you to believe I was remotely interested in your opinion of me, it was my mistake. It will not happen again.

—It doesn't matter why you did it. I was also hoping their children, in the tr . . . traditional sense, could pilot the robot. It would be the best-case scenario. Make a dozen babies, each of them could operate either station. But their ch . . . children would only have half of each parent's ge . . . genes, maybe not the good half. It might not work. I couldn't wait and see. I had to try cloning them too. I had to see if I could splice animal genes into theirs so their legs could bend the right way.

—You are mad.

—Am I? What would *you* have done if they had children? Cut open one of their kids and remove all of his leg bones so his knees would bend backwards? Now *that* would be cruel. I don't think they would have volunteered for that. You just didn't think . . . think this through. At least my plan didn't involve mmm . . . mutilating anyone.

—Were you successful?

—Of course not! You drove me out of my lab before I could even begin. The aliens came sooner than I had hoped, but surely you can see now that I was right?

—Three minutes ago, I told you that I would take great pleasure in seeing you tried for your crimes. To most, that would suggest that . . . No, I do not think that you were right.

—Imagine that the aliens had come a f . . . few years later, and that Kara had been injured. How many more people would have died in London? Would they have st . . . stopped after London? If I had offered you a new pilot to replace her, would you have said no?

—I can imagine a world in which you saved us all and became a hero. In that world, I would ask for your forgiveness and solemnly watch as the president pins a medal to your chest. Fortunately for me, I do not live in that world. Based on my experience, your sentence will probably also be based on facts and not on what could have been.

—I don't think so.

—You do not think it will be based on facts?

—I don't think there'll be a trial.

—Surprising as it may seem, most governments will not summarily execute people if there is no reason to forgo a trial. They view such things as . . . unbecoming.

—I don't think you'll t . . . turn me over to the Americans, not before you get me a f . . . full pardon.

—Are we still in living in this make-believe world of yours?

—You don't seem to like hypotheticals, so let's see how far your con . . . conviction goes in real life. I didn't have time to clone anyone at the lab. I barely had time to grab a few specimens before the Marines st . . . stormed in. I had a fake passport the Russians had given me, but you can't . . . you can't t . . . travel with biological samples without anyone's asking questions. So I stopped by a fertility clinic before I left the island and arranged for them to use the . . . specimens I gave them. There were four eggs. Three didn't take. One did.

—What are you saying?

—I'm saying there is a ten-year-old girl in Puerto Rico with b . . . beautiful green eyes who might just be able to pilot that gi . . . giant robot of yours. Of course, you'll never find out if you don't g . . . give me what I want.

—And what is that?

—A full pardon. And I want to be back on the research team.

—You are insane. Puerto Rico is about one hundred miles across. How long do you think it will take me to find a ten-year-old girl?

—I don't know. P . . . probably a few weeks without records to help. She'll be gone by the time you find her. I was on my way to retrieve her, bring her to Russia so they can s . . . start training her. They'll know I didn't make my flight. They'll go after her.

—What makes you think I will not simply have you killed after you help us find her?

—Oh, I tr . . . trust you. You would find it . . . unbecoming.

FILE NO. 1534

RESEARCH LOG—VINCENT COUTURE,
CONSULTANT, EARTH DEFENSE CORPS
Location: Unknown

This is Vincent Couture recording aboard Themis. I'm . . . I have no idea where I am. I can't see outside. It's pitch-black all around. I don't think I'm in space. There aren't any stars. I can shift the weight between Themis's feet, so we're definitely standing on solid ground. I can hear . . . something. It's a . . . a very low hum. Like a lightsaber that's not moving, if that means anything. My best guess at this point is that I'm in the ocean somewhere and that's the sound of water moving against the hull.

I don't know exactly how I got here, but I have a pretty good idea. I was trying to figure out if Themis could . . . teleport herself when it happened. Rose and I had been talking about it since London. We thought it would make sense for her to move that way. Well, more sense than having little rockets under her feet, or wings that spring out her back. She weighs seventy-two hundred tons, after all.

It was all wishful thinking really, because we were hoping for something quite different from what we saw in London. It came from outer space, so no matter what it used to get here, it must have worked in a three-dimensional space. That would be almost impossible for us to use here on Earth. The planet's surface is curved, there is terrain to consider. Traveling farther than what you can see would be really complicated. You could end up inside a mountain, miles deep into the Earth's crust, or a few kilometers up in the air. What Rose and I wanted was . . . something user-friendly. Something Apple would make: a gizmo that lets you treat the planet as a flat surface and does all the work for you. Just push a button and end up where you want to go, with both feet on the ground, not inside or above it. Anyway, I went to the lab early to try a few things on the console before Kara got there—she gets angry when she can't help. At some point, I hit a key. Everything went white, silent. Then I was here. So, the good news is: Themis can travel anywhere!

The bad news is I think I'm gonna die here before I can tell anyone.

By my watch, I've been here a little more than two days. I don't have any supplies. I only had a bottle of water with me, which is now empty, and I could *really* go for a cheeseburger right about now. Extra cheese, with bacon . . . A large poutine . . . At least air's not a problem, I think. The sphere is about fourteen thousand cubic feet, so I'll die of thirst long before the CO_2 kills me.

If I'm right and I'm in the ocean—I'd most likely be in the Atlantic—there's just no way anyone will find me here. I can probably last a few more days, but I'm having a hard time concentrating already, so if I'm gonna try anything, I think today's the day. I wish I could just walk in any direction, but I can't keep the balance on a flat surface without Kara. Plus I can't see anything, so I'll just end up throwing Themis flat on her face if I try moving.

I listened to the log I made that morning and I took some notes. I'll walk you through them in case this doesn't work. There's a button on the top right of the console, looks like an "M" with a bar across. That's what I started with—we hadn't found any use for it and it looked . . . move-y—and all the sequences I tried were a combination of that, some numbers and "go."

Rose thought we might try something like longitude and latitude, but Themis wasn't made here, but it's hard to imagine a two-coordinate system that would work like that on different planets. Even if you assume all planets rotate on a relatively stable axis, that'll only give you a natural starting point for one of the coordinates, either a pole or the equator, but there's no natural starting point perpendicular to that. Longitude is based on a completely random spot on the east–west axis. I don't think the aliens we're dealing with ever heard of Greenwich Mean Time.

If they were to use a two-coordinate system, it would make much more sense to use Themis herself as a reference point. Coordinates zero, zero would be where she is, and you could go from there. The problem then, if you used something like longitude and latitude, is that the numbers would mean different things depending on what planet you're on. Longitude and latitude measure an angle from the center of the planet, so the distance on the surface for, say, one degree would be greater on a larger planet, a lot smaller on a tiny one. The bigger the planet, the less precise the navigation system would be.

There are other ways to imagine this. What I was really hoping for was a much simpler system. Just point Themis in the direction you want to go, punch in a distance, and that's it. One number, not two. Wouldn't be superprecise over long distances. You couldn't jump from New York to—I don't know—Paris in one shot. You couldn't get the direction precisely right at such a distance, but you could jump the Atlantic, then just . . . hop from place to place and adjust the direction along the way. It had very little chance of working, but I thought it was more fun to search for something I knew I could use.

I started small and tried to make Themis move by a distance of one. I didn't know one what, exactly, but I figured I'd probably end up somewhere on the empty lot in front of the hangar. So . . . I tried what I thought was the MOVE button, then 1, then GO. Nothing happened, of course. I tried in reverse, nope. Hold the MOVE button, one, then release. There aren't that many ways to do this, and I think I tried them all. It occurred to me that it might just not work because teleporting yourself one unit might be stupid, like taking one step. I went crazy and tried with two. No good. I gave up on the simple solution after that and decided to try with two numbers instead of one.

I tried the numbers separated by GO, by a pause. At some point, I tried this: hold the MOVE button, press two, pause, two again, release. Nothing great happened but the console made a sound, like it does when we do something right. I did it again a few times. All I got was the sound. Then I got frustrated and my log is more or less useless after that. I hear myself screaming "two" a few times, then I'm here. In short, I don't know what I did, but it starts with that sequence. I know I punched in at least four numbers, so either we're dealing with a two-coordinate system and I'm an idiot for inserting pauses, or this is a crazy four-dimensional thing and I'm gonna die inside a rock, in space, four thousand years ago.

Anyway, I'm about to try to replicate what I did. I managed to wiggle Themis around so I'm facing in the opposite direction. With any luck, I'll get frustrated the same way and end up right where I started.

Before I inadvertently blow myself up, I have a message for my wife . . . Kara, I love you. I've had two days to just sit and think about how crazy my life has been since they asked me to sign an NDA and go look at some panels in Chicago. I found myself feeling . . . grateful. Grateful Rose trusted me. Grateful we found this big-ass alien thing. But the thing I'm most thankful for is meeting this crazy, stubborn pilot with a chip on her shoulder. Kara, none of this would have been as much fun without you taking jabs at me every step of the way. I got to have my legs crushed, got turned into a T-800 . . . We blew up an airport! I wish we hadn't killed Rose, but it turned out OK, sorta. Hell, we got to wrestle with aliens! Who gets to do *that*? Anyway, if I don't make it, please don't feel like I was robbed of anything. I lived plenty. I had a blast.

I never got to tell you how sorry I was. I'm sorry I made you feel like you had to be something you weren't. I'm sorry I made you . . . dim your light, when all I ever wanted was for it to burn brighter. That sounded good.

I want you to be happy. Find someone. You have my blessing if he's not a dick . . . and not too good-looking. Don't be too happy with him though, but . . . you know . . . be happy. Of course, if you can be happy without the guy. Just . . . I don't know what I'm saying . . . I . . . I don't want you to be miserable because of me. If I'm dead, I'm dead. You can't hurt me. Do what you need to do. I won't be looking down on you from the heavens. I doubt they take pretentious assholes with an accent, and you know how much I'm afraid of heights.

I guess that's it. Oh! Almost forgot! If you find Themis and I'm dead, you might want to clean the floor right behind your station. Seriously, give it a good scrub.

OK. Here we go! Hold. Two. Two. Release. I love that sound. Two. Go. Nope.

Hold. Two. Two. Release. Two. Two. Go . . . Nope.

Release. Two . . . I just did that. Let's do this again. Ho—

. . .

Ah ben calver! It worked! I moved again! It's still dark, so I must not be too far from where I was. I have no idea what direction I'm moving in, but I'm moving! I can do this!

Kara, forget everything I said about meeting someone. Screw him. I'm gonna make it.

Hold. Two. Two. Release . . .

FILE NO. 1539

INTERVIEW WITH RYAN MITCHELL, SECURITY GUARD

Location: Michigan Science Center, Detroit, MI

—How long have you worked here, Mr. Mitchell?

—About a year, sir. Why?

—Do you enjoy your work?

—I . . . What do you want?

—I sense anger in your tone. Are there unresolved issues we need to discuss?

—Ha! You're kidding, right?

—Do you believe I am being facetious or was that a rhetorical question?

—I spent four years in jail after I rescued Kara and Vincent!

—Why would you expect otherwise? There were four years left on your sentence for crushing Mr. Couture into a wall with your vehicle. You had to serve the entirety of your sentence after violating the terms of your parole by leaving the state to join Alyssa in Puerto Rico.

—You could have gotten me out, sir.

—The US Government wanted to charge you with treason. You could be meeting your lawyer to appeal your death sentence. Instead, you are scolding children for running inside a museum. I fail to see what you have to complain about.

—You could have gotten me out!

—Let us not waste time pondering what each of us could have done differently, shall we? You and I both know this conversation will not end with any great moral victory on your part.

—Do you know what I talked about at Fort Carson, before I went to Puerto Rico?

—I have a feeling I am about to find out.

—Nothing. I talked about nothing. Rose visited me a few times, but she's about the only one I talked to. I stayed in my cell as much as I could. They took me to the yard, twice a day, but I mostly kept to myself. I couldn't stop thinking about what I had done to Vincent. I—

—Is that really what you thought about?

— . . . You're right. I kept thinking about what I had lost, about Kara. I couldn't . . . I imagined the way she must have felt about me and I couldn't stand it. I hated myself. I hated myself for a long, long time. I . . . I wanted her to like me again. I kept thinking of the ways I could make it up to her, what I could do to make her see me as a human being again, not as a monster. I'd come up with completely insane scenarios in my head. You know, she gets captured by terrorists and I save the day, that sort of thing. Took about a year for me to stop torturing myself and actually face what I did. I still hated myself, but at least I wasn't living in a fantasy world. It wasn't about Kara anymore.

—Is there a point to this story?

—Yes sir, there is. One day, out of nowhere, I get called in and they tell me I got an early release. Just like that. You can go. I didn't know what was happening, they almost had to drag me out. A day later, I get a call to go to Puerto Rico. Kara's there. Vincent's there. Then things get really messed up and, by the time I realize how far out of her mind Alyssa's gone, I've hurt both of them . . . again. I . . . It was hell. I couldn't believe what was happening, but I pulled together and I did it. I saved them. You know, for real. I wasn't daydreaming. I saved them! I wasn't expecting everything to be perfect after that, but I thought . . . Then you threw me back in jail. Four years. No one came, not even Rose.

—I do not know where to begin. You attempted to kill Mr. Couture. Given the chance to gain their trust again, you chose to help Alyssa keep them captive and perform medical procedures on Ms. Resnik against her will. Finally, faced with something even you could not stomach, you chose to act like a decent human being, once, for about ten minutes. I am truly sorry if you were expecting a medal. As for Dr. Franklin, she was dead, which, if you ask me, is a reasonably good excuse not to visit.

—She came back.

—Yes. She came back, never having met you. Why would you expect someone you never met to visit you in prison?

—You know, sir, this is a lot of fun, but my break's almost over. What are you really here for?

—As we speak, there is a team from Special Forces Operational Detachment-Delta preparing a rescue mission. I would like you to accompany them.

—I can't join a Delta Force team, sir. I'm not an "operator." You have to be . . . well, you have to be Delta Force.

—You would be joining them as an advisor.

—I'm not a soldier anymore! They took that away too.

—I am aware of your dishonorable discharge.

—I'm sure you are, sir.

—Let me rephrase then. There is a Delta Force team preparing a rescue mission. I would like you to accompany them as a *civilian* advisor.

—Do you think sending me on a mission to watch a bunch of soldiers do what I can't do anymore is gonna make me feel better about what happened?

—Your personal feelings are not my chief concern at this time, though I believe you might indeed find some degree of redemption in the process.

—What are you talking about?

—**Do you remember how your mutiny ended at the Puerto Rico base?**

—Alyssa escaped. Everyone else got arrested.

—**Do you remember what prompted said mutiny?**

—Yes. I remember. She said she removed some of Kara's—

—**Ova—**

—Yeah . . . She said she would implant them into another person. She was trying to make—

—**She was attempting to create children who share whatever features allow Ms. Resnik and Mr. Couture to operate Themis. She was trying to make pilots.**

—She's crazy.

—**Crazy or not, it appears she may have been successful . . . at creating a child. No one knows whether Themis would respond to her.**

—It's a girl?

—**Why are you smiling?**

—Kara's a mom! Does she know?

—**Not at the moment.**

—Wait . . . You didn't tell her?

—**I saw no need to alarm her until—**

—You said you would, sir. You told me! You promised me you would tell her!

—**I promised you I would tell her when the time came.**

—It's been ten years! More than that! What are you waiting for? Grandchildren?

—**I had no knowledge of this child until yesterday. Even now, I cannot confirm or deny her existence, nor can I validate the claim that she is the offspring of Ms. Resnik and Mr. Couture. That is what the mission is for.**

—Why send Delta Force? You could just knock on the door and ask—

—I have reason to believe the Russian Government is sending a team of its own to retrieve the child. I do not know what their intentions are, but considering what length they have been willing to go to thus far, I would not put it past them to . . . remove any evidence if they feel their mission will not succeed.

—They would kill the girl?

—If all else fails. I believe their ultimate goal is to assemble an alternate team of pilots and, once they are reasonably confident they can operate her, take Themis for themselves by any means necessary.

—Why?

—They probably feel that the needs of Mother Russia would be better served if the weapon were available to them without the prior approval of the United Nations, preferably on an exclusive basis.

—They want to use it against us.

—I do not believe it is their intent to do so now, but they would certainly like to have the option available, if only as a deterrent. If the London events have proven anything, it is that whoever possesses Themis shall never fear a conventional army ever again. That is a very powerful motivation.

—Why me? What do you think I can do?

—As you said, it may be as simple as knocking on the door. If possible, I would like her to leave of her own accord.

—What about her parents? She must have parents.

—The United States Government would prefer for the child to come alone.

—This isn't a UN mission?

—It is not. Neither the UN nor the EDC are aware of it.

—Why is the US doing this?

—Perhaps they too feel that their needs would be better served if Themis were available to them without the prior approval of the United Nations.

—And you think the parents will just hand over their daughter to a complete stranger.

—You will have to convince them.

—And what if I can't?

—Step aside. Let Delta handle it.

—Step a . . . How long do I have?

—I cannot tell you precisely. Minutes.

—What will Delta do?

—They will do what they need to do.

—And the parents?

—They are not part of the mission. Retrieving the child safely is the primary objective.

—They'll kidnap a kid?

—What do you see as an alternative? They cannot simply ask the parents for their permission.

—Why not?

—Because it would imply telling them where they intend to take the girl, and the United States Government does not want its involvement known.

—So you want me to lie to them?

—I want you to convince them to let their daughter leave with you in under ten minutes. How you achieve that goal is not particularly relevant. That said, I do not believe any parent would willingly let their ten-year-old daughter be trained to pilot a giant war machine should a conflict with powerful alien beings claim the life of one of her biological parents she does not know exist. I would suggest a more compelling story.

—Even if it works, the parents will know something's wrong when their kid doesn't come back.

—Certainly. They will contact the authorities. At some point, they will come to the conclusion that their daughter has been abducted by a human-trafficking ring or something of the sort. You might wish to alter your appearance slightly. Wear a hat. In any case, your story need only last long enough to avoid traumatizing the child.

—This is wrong, sir.

—Indeed. Yet, it is preferable to a dozen men armed with automatic weapons storming the house and grabbing the child. Right is a luxury we do not have at this time. It is an imperfect solution to a less-than-ideal situation. I suspect there will be a lot of those in the near future.

—I won't do it.

—Yes you will. I suggest you grab your personal effects and head over to the airport. Your flight departs in ninety minutes. You will meet with the Delta team at Fort Bragg.

—I can't leave just now. What do I tell my boss?

—I am certain you will come up with something. Think of it as practice.

—That was Jason Bajada with his hit "Down With the Protest." We're live from our brand-new studio in London. You're listening to the *Night Shift* with Sarah Kent on Absolute Radio. So nice to be back on the air with you night owls. It is . . . just before one thirty. Almost time for some freebies! What do we have for you tonight? Oh, you're gonna *love* these. There is something very exciting happening this Friday. You know what it is! I know you know. I'll give you a hint. It's happening in a galaxy far, far away. Yes! The new *Star Wars* movie is coming out and we have two tickets for the . . . let's make it the eleventh caller. The number is: 020 7946 0946. Here's some music while you frantically dial in. This is Muse, on Absolute Radio.

[. . .]

Hello there, you're on the air.

[*Hello!*]

What's your name?

[*Anthony*]

What do you do, Anthony?

[*I work in a bagel shop on Brick Lane.*]

Do you have good coffee in your bagel shop?

[*Yes we do!*]

All right, folks. You heard the man. If you happen to be near Brick Lane and you need a late-night snack, go see Anthony. I'll let you in on a little secret, Anthony. The thing I like most about our new studio is the coffee. We have *the best* espresso machine in the UK. If you hear me go "Mmmm" between songs, I'm having another latte. Well, congratulations Anthony! You and a friend are going to the *Star Wars* premiere at the BFI Imax cinema.

　　I have some great music for you in just . . . What is going on? You probably can't hear it at home but there is quite the ruckus outside. Cars blowing their horns. It's one thirty in the morning, people!

[*Sarah, you need to get out of here.*]

And now I have a visitor! Did you see the big red ON AIR sign outside the door?

[*Look out the window. You need to get out now.*]

There is something happening outside. Probably bladdered Arsenal fans upset over that *humiliating* defeat. Let's not talk about that. I know you're all curious now, so I will look out the window and . . . Bloody hell!

[. . .]

Fuck!

[Door closing]

FILE NO. 1543

INTERVIEW WITH DR. ROSE FRANKLIN, HEAD OF SCIENCE DIVISION, EARTH DEFENSE CORPS

Location: EDC Headquarters, New York, NY

—They're back.

—Themis has returned?

—No. The aliens are back. Look.

—How long have they been here?

—Twenty minutes.

—Where?

—London.

—London? I wonder why they would choose to land in the same city twice.

—They chose to land in the exact same spot. Unless I'm reading this wrong, it's within ten feet from where they appeared a year ago.

—The robot looks different—

—Yes. They don't mass-produce these things. Each seems to have its own . . . personality. This one glows orange, for one thing. Here's a picture from last year. Look at the chest armor. It's a lot smoother.

There are fewer carvings. The helmet is slightly different, the forehead. Look at its face. The one from a year ago had sharp traits, a really severe look. This one looks younger, a bit androgynous. It's almost grinning. We're calling this one Hyperion.

—Perhaps they sent a less menacing figure after our last encounter ended in violence.

—I don't think so. It's 237 feet tall—a foot taller than the last one— and it's standing in the middle of the dirt field the last one left behind. There's nothing *not* menacing about it.

—Is this a live feed?

—Yes. Why?

—I am wondering what those tiny white lights are.

—All around it, I know. I asked myself that same question. There weren't as many five minutes ago.

—Can you zoom in?

—No, that's not our satellite.

—We should try television. It has been there long enough for the press to arrive.

—It's the middle of the night in London.

—People must be aware of its presence. It stands in the one place in the city that is not full of lights. It must be visible for miles, like a lighthouse.

—There. It's on CNN. It's a lot more impressive from the ground.

—I do not see any lights around it.

—That must have been taken with a cellphone. I'll try other channels. There has to be some real footage somewhere—

—Stop. There.

—Wh . . . They're people! People holding candles. There must be a thousand of them. This is so—

—Inspiring.

—I was gonna say stupid.

—The last time the aliens were in London, we sent the army to greet them.

—We didn't send the army to attack them.

—Whatever the reason, the military got involved and we all know how it ended. These people are trying candles and peace signs. Instead of following their most basic instinct and running away, they are trying to make peace with an alien species. I find it extremely courageous.

—I don't doubt their courage, but there's a good reason we have these basic instincts you speak of. This is desperate. It's futile. These people will die.

—I will grant you that this is a desperate act, but it *could* work. Perhaps all it takes is for these beings to see that we are capable of more than what we have shown them during our last encounter.

—Do you really think it'll work?

—I am not overly optimistic about the outcome of this spontaneous endeavor . . . but I could be wrong. Look at them closely. Some of them are still in their pajamas. They rushed out of their homes to show an alien race we do not want a war.

—I'm looking. I hadn't noticed the pajamas. I was more focused on the fact that many of them brought their children with them. Look. There's a baby. He's not courageous, he just has stupid, irresponsible parents. I'm sorry. I don't find that inspiring.

—I must say, I am surprised by your reaction. I thought you of all people would be inclined to join them.

—Because I'm suicidal or because I'm losing my mind? Either way, if that's what you think of me, that should tell you this is a horrible idea.

—Unfortunately, I do not see a better course of action at the moment.

—We can send Themis. It worked once before.

—We do not have Themis. We do not know whether she has been destroyed, or if she even is on this planet, so I should not have to work hard to convince you that sending her is not an option at the moment. Knowing that, would it not be wiser to try to avoid a conflict altogether?

—I'm not sure that's possible after what happened the last time.

—Maybe not, but we have got to try. Whom would you rather send to make peace if not these irresponsible people? I do not think the army is an option.

—It's not.

—Then who? At this moment, a group of ill-advised people with candles is probably our best hope for a peaceful resolution. I believe it is our only hope until Themis is found. I am also worried about the young ones, but one could argue that having children present helps make our message . . . unambiguous.

—I see your point.

—Thank you.

—Don't thank me! I still disagree with you. I think this is a bad way to die. It's pointless. I just don't have anything better to offer. In any case, what I think doesn't matter much right now, since these people *are* there, *with* their children. I don't think candles will help, but it's not like we can send the army to evacuate them. For what it's worth, I sincerely hope it works.

—I do too, but I urge you to help us prepare for what comes next if the robot obliterates these families.

—You don't think I'm trying?

—I—

—Seriously. I don't think I should be alive, but don't you think I wanna find a way to make things better? Don't you think I wanna save these people? Kara, Vincent, you, everybody? I'm trying. I'm trying *really* hard.

—I know you a—

—I don't know how! I just . . . I don't know how to fix this. I'm not smart enough.

—If you allow me to complete a sentence, I will tell you that I never doubted your willingness to help. Moreover, I am absolutely convinced you can, even if you do not share that conviction.

—Why? What makes you think I can do anything?

—Without you, we would not have discovered a giant hand in the Black Hills. We would not have thought to create an argon compound to locate the rest of the pieces. For that matter, we might never have looked for other pieces had you not been so utterly convinced there was an entire body to be found. Without you, we would not have had Themis a year ago. She probably saved millions of people when she defeated that robot.

—That wasn't me. That was all—

—I was not finished. You are, as far as I know, the only person who has ever cheated death. Some people went to great lengths to make sure you are with us today. I admittedly do not know very much about them, but what little I do know tells me that they are not the kind of people to waste time or energy bringing a complete stranger back from the dead without a good reason.

—You make it sound like I'm some kind of messiah. Believe me, I'm not.

—I do not believe you are part of a prophecy. I do not believe you have mythical powers that have yet to reveal themselves. I do not think the people who brought you back even give credence to that sort of thing. While I am reasonably confident you are not "the chosen one," you are without doubt one who has been chosen. I believe they chose you for very practical reasons, for what you are. And as far as I can tell, that is a brilliant scientist who happens to be in the best position to help humanity when it needs it the most.

—What if they were wrong?

—Then we are no worse for it, and I will have had the pleasure of your company for a while longer.

—You said I could meet them, the people that did this to me.

—I said you could meet one of them. I only know of one. I will arrange for that meeting as promised, but I have to take care of a few things first. Are we any closer to finding Themis?

—No. We know for a fact that no one could have physically moved her without our knowing. That leaves two options: Either someone else transported her using technology we don't have, or she transported herself.

—Where could she be?

—If it's on Earth, it has to be underground, maybe submerged. We'd know if she were anywhere above the surface. If Vincent's stuck and he can't make his way back, I'm not sure what we can do but hope he figures it out on his own. If they make it back, I might have found a weakness in the alien robot's defense.

—What sort of weakness?

—Let me show you . . . This is footage from last year in Regent's Park. We can't see the shield unless it rains or something flies into it, but look . . . here . . . when I zoom in on the feet. That's as close as I can get.

—I do not see anything.

—That's my point. That robot's shield extends outwards about one foot. On the ground, you'd expect a hole around and under its feet. There isn't any. The grass is still up right on the edge of its foot.

—Achilles' heel.

—Yes. Wherever that shield ends, it doesn't go all the way to the ground. I'm not sure how that helps us, but it's all I have for now.

—Keep working, Dr. Franklin. We may not have much time.

—I'm trying, but I don't even know what I'm looking for.

—If Mr. Couture were here, he would find an appropriate quote from a fictional character. As I do not share his enthusiasm for science fiction, I will simply tell you that "trying" suggests you lack confidence in your ability to succeed. Find Themis.

—What? I don't get it. What would Vincent say?

—Find Themis and ask him.

—Where are you going?

—Goodbye, Dr. Franklin.

FILE NO. 1544

INTERVIEW WITH LIEUTENANT GENERAL ALAN A. SIMMS, COMMANDER, JOINT SPECIAL OPERATIONS COMMAND (JSOC)

Location: Fort Bragg, NC

—I believe the president was very clear when he said this mission was of the utmost importance. I know, because I was standing next to him at the time.

—He was. He was very clear about it eight hours ago. I'm sure he would have said the same thing three hours ago. But two hours and fifty-five, no, fifty-six minutes ago, a giant alien robot appeared in London, again. The last time one of these things was here, it killed over a hundred thousand people, so you'll understand when I tell you that things that were "of the utmost importance" not so long ago are a little farther down the list right now.

Now, I'm a Lieutenant General in the United States Army, which means I'm a pretty big shot in *my* world, but you probably don't give a crap about what I have to say, so go ahead. I know you have the Office of the President on speed dial. I'll wait.

—I do not need to call the president. If you are unwilling to proceed, I know other people who will.

—Not right now, you don't. The CIA nut jobs at the Special Activities Division might be crazy enough to say yes, but they'll find out very quickly there isn't a single tier one unit available. No SEALs, no

Marines, no Special Forces, no ISA, no STS. Everyone's grounded. The only Delta you're gonna get is Delta Airlines if you want to fly down there, but you'll have to do it alone.

—Where is the Delta team right now?

—Here. They never left. Your assault troop was still prepping when that happened. I gave the abort order in person. We're shutting down every live op we have until this clears.

—What about the civilian I sent you?

—We flew him back where he came from. He was pissed, said to tell you he would handle things himself if you didn't. Now if you'll excuse me, I have to get some very unhappy people out of Syria.

—I must insist. It is imperative that they leave now and complete their mission. You can have them back in twenty-four hours.

—Insist all you want. Their mission, as I understand it, was to retrieve a child who may or may not be able to pilot the EDC robot when she grows up. Am I missing anything?

—That is a reasonably accurate, though somewhat simplistic, summary of the objective.

—Then no. The president agreed to this because having a team of American pilots would provide a strategic advantage to this country. That was then. If we're on the brink of a global conflict with an alien species, there's no point in even thinking about getting the robot for ourselves ten years from now. We follow the plan and put all our resources with the EDC. I'm not gonna waste a Delta team we might desperately need here and risk pissing off everyone else at the UN when we might be begging for Themis a few hours from now. Your Boogeyman op is NO GO.

—This mission is also important for the EDC.

—Is it? Then why haven't you made the request through them? You'd have your team if the EDC requested it. Hell, you could have a platoon!

—Did you agree with the mission?

—You didn't answer my question.

—Perhaps another time.

—Cute. And yes. I did agree, twelve hours ago. I agreed because it made strategic sense at the time. At *peace*time. We cheat and we lie at peacetime because we know the other side does it too. This might be war, and in war, you don't try to scam your allies. Except for you.

—What do you mean?

—Unless I'm mistaken, you're the one who started the EDC.

—That would be an overstatement, but I did play a role in its creation.

—Then why are you trying to screw them out of a pilot now?

—I am trying to help this country.

—Nice try. Having one pilot would give us leverage with the EDC, but not enough to take control of it. I don't know what you're hiding from them, but at some point your secret will come out and we'll get caught with our pants down. The more I think about this, the more I think we're being played.

—You have a vivid imagination.

—That must be it. Look, you have your answer. We're not going. If the Russians are stupid enough to go get her now, let them. They couldn't do anything with just one pilot. We'll sort this out . . . Excuse me one sec.

. . .

—What is it?

—Another giant robot just appeared on Scatarie Island.

—I am not familiar with the name.

—It's a wilderness reserve near Cape Breton Island, Nova Scotia.

—Is it attacking?

—There's nothing to attack there. Besides, it's ours . . . well, yours. Would you care to tell me what Themis is doing in Canada?

—I have to go.

—I guess not. It was a pleasure talking to you. Come back anytime . . .

INTERVIEW WITH BRIGADIER GENERAL EUGENE GOVENDER, COMMANDER, EARTH DEFENSE CORPS

Location: EDC Headquarters, New York, NY

—Damn robots are everywhere!

—I thought the second one was ours.

—Yeah, Themis is back. She's on her way here, actually. Vincent insisted on . . . "beaming" her back, whatever that means. He's OK. He said he should be here in an hour or so.

—Did he tell you where he was?

—In the ocean.

—Where?

—That's what he said. I wish I could tell you more. I didn't exactly have a lot of time to chat. There are robots showing up every ten minutes.

—There are more?

—Yeah. Eleven of them! Haven't you heard? This is a goddamn invasion! We ran out of Titan names on the last one.

—Where are they?

—You already know about the one in London. The next one appeared on the tracks at Shinjuku Station in Tokyo around 4:00 A.M. About five minutes later, one popped up in Jakarta. There are two in India, one in Delhi, one in Calcutta.

—**All at the same time?**

—All of them showed up in the last hour. These guys are well coordinated. There is one in Cairo, taking a footbath in the middle of the Nile. It's a hundred feet from the 6th October Bridge. You know what the bridge is named after?

—**The start of the Yom Kippur War.**

—Yeah. I think they'll soon have a good reason to rename that one. There's also one in Moscow.

—**London and Moscow. Things will not go well at the Security Council.**

—No they won't. The French have theirs too. You should see the pictures of that one. It's on Place Charles de Gaulle, perfectly centered in front of the Arc de Triomphe. Whoever is piloting that one has a good sense of aesthetics and a huge flair for the dramatic.

—**Have any appeared near us?**

—Not yet. The closest one is in Mexico City. There's another one in São Paulo. The one in Mexico didn't even bother to find an open space. It just crushed a small art museum, appeared right on top of it. Maybe the pilots just aren't any good. There's a pretty large city park across the street.

—**Finding good pilots is very difficult. You mentioned London, Tokyo, Jakarta, Delhi, Cairo, Moscow—**

—You forgot Calcutta.

—**Thank you. Paris, Mexico City, São Paulo. That makes ten. You said there were eleven.**

—Johannesburg.

—. . .

—I know . . .

—Is your family in danger?

—They live a few miles from where it showed up. They are trying to leave the city. I just spoke to my sister. She says the roads are still open. I don't know how long that'll last. Some of my former men are with them. Things are gonna get ugly. Delhi and Calcutta are the worst right now. The roads were useless about five minutes in. People have to leave on foot. I wouldn't wanna be in Tokyo either.

—We could—

—We could what? Save Johannesburg? Since when is Africa on anyone's list of priorities? I appreciate the sentiment but you know that won't happen.

—Probably not. I am sorry.

—Did you notice anything about where they chose to land?

—They appeared in some of the most populous cities on the planet.

—Yes they did. And what does that tell you?

—That they understand resource optimization very well. The cost of an eradication effort is, generally speaking, inversely proportional to the population density.

—That's a nice way to put it. It's cheaper to kill the rats if they're all in one place . . .

—It is certainly less time-consuming than to kill us one at a time. If that is their intention, they can possibly exterminate one-quarter of all humans with a handful of robots in a very short amount of time. Once all major cities have been destroyed, there would be no government to speak of, no supply chains. A significant portion of the surviving population would die of disease or starvation within months. Whoever is left would offer little or no resistance. You have to admire what they can do with twenty-two people.

[*I'm sorry to bother you, General, but you'll want to read this.*]

—Thank you Jamie . . . Make that twenty-four.

—Another one? Where?

—Beijing.

—There might still be another explanation. They have not attacked us.

—Not yet.

—It is entirely possible that they are using this tactic to scare us into submission.

—Then it's working.

—Would you surrender if given the option?

—Wouldn't you? I'll put up a fight because I don't think they give a crap whether we surrender or not. But you know Themis can't fight them all. Hell, she can't fight any of them right now.

—I was under the impression that Themis was recovered intact.

—Oh, Themis is fine, but she can't fight a dozen of these.

—She can try.

—She's not going anywhere, not with a pilot missing.

—You told me Mr. Couture was on his way here less than five minutes ago.

—Oh, Vincent's fine. It's Kara we're missing.

—Ms. Resnik? She was here yesterday.

—She was. And now she's not. Can you tell me where she is?

—I was completely unaware of her absence until a second ago. What makes you think I would know where she is?

—She left a note for you on my desk. It said: "Don't know when I'll be back. Please give this to him." I'm assuming she meant you.

—Can I see it?

—I can tell you what it says. I memorized it.

—You opened it?

—Of course I goddamn opened it! The world is coming to an end. I'm missing a pilot. I don't give a rat's ass about your privacy! Wanna know what it said or not?

—Please.

—Fuck you!

—...

—That's what it said!

—Anything else?

—Nope. Just fuck you. One exclamation point. Are you gonna tell me or do I need to ask?

—Ask what?

—What did you do, you conniving son of a bitch?

FILE NO. 1550

EMAIL FROM RYAN MITCHELL TO CAPTAIN KARA RESNIK, EARTH DEFENSE CORPS

Dear Kara,

I know I'm probably the last person you wanna hear from right now, and I know a drunken email is probably not the best way to mend a relationship. I would have sent a real letter but there isn't enough time. They'll send you and Vincent to fight again and I think there are things you should know before you go. As for the drinking, well, I was already drunk. I would have liked to sober up some first, but like I said, there isn't enough time.

You have a child in Puerto Rico, a daughter. I think she's about ten or eleven. She lives in San Juan, at 559 Concepción. Alyssa took out some of your ova (I think that's what they're called) while you were unconscious and put them inside some woman in Puerto Rico when she escaped. She used Vincent's stuff, so he's a father too.

I feel terrible because I'm the one who helped Alyssa put you out so she could do this, but I swear on my brother's grave I had no idea what she planned to do. I thought she just wanted to do some tests. When I found out she was trying to make babies, I got you and Vincent out of there as fast as I could. I didn't know she was going to put your child inside another woman. She said she wanted to try, but I thought I could stop her. I thought I did. I didn't know she had actually done it until today.

That's what I wanted to tell you. I was supposed to go to San Juan today with Delta Force to bring her back here, but we're not going anymore. There might have been some Russians on their way to get her too. I don't know if they're still going after what happened tonight. Your daughter might be in danger if they are. My job was to knock on her door and try to convince her to come back with me so Delta wouldn't have to take her by force. I think if anyone knocks on that little girl's door, it should be you, not me or some Russian guy she doesn't know. Of course, she doesn't know you either, she has parents, but you're her mother so she should meet you, not me.

I had it all planned in my head. I had a great story. She would have left with me and we would have gotten to know each other on the plane. Then I could have introduced her to you, you know. I think it would have been better for her if she already knew someone when she met you. I would have liked to see the smile on your face when you found out she was your child. I don't know. Maybe you wouldn't have smiled right away, it's a lot to process, but I would have liked to be there.

I think you'd be a great mother. Well, you're already a mother, but I think you'd be great with the kid. You can be a little rough sometimes, and you don't always react well to change, so it might take a little while before you're comfortable with her, but it's OK. She'll need time too because she'll have lost the only parents she's ever known if she comes here. Still, once you've both gotten used to your new life, I think you'll be great.

I know what you're going to say: I should have said something, but I didn't know about the child. I only knew about the ova. When Alyssa escaped, our friend with no name said he wanted to wait until Alyssa got caught before he told you. I said you deserved to know, but he insisted, so it's not my fault. I would have told you. In hindsight, it's probably a good thing I didn't. You would have been worried for nothing all this time. Ten years is a long time to wonder if someone is making your babies in a lab, somewhere.

I want you to know I'm not a bad person, even if you think I am. I made a mistake. Several mistakes, really. What I did to Vincent was awful. But after that, all I tried to do is help. I saved him after that. That should count for something. I saved you too. I'm not saying we should be best friends, but maybe we could.

When we were training together, all I could think about was you. I wanted you to open up to me. When you didn't, I felt like I was the one with a problem, like I didn't deserve you. Now I know it had nothing to do with me, that you just weren't ready. I wish I had figured that out at the time. I would never have hurt Vincent if I had. I wouldn't have sent you running into his arms by being so pushy. I realize that now. I know it's too late for us to be together, especially now that you and Vincent have a child, but I think we'd be good together, even as friends.

Being a parent is a lot of work, and with everything that's going on, you're going to be really busy. You could probably use all the help you can get. I want you to know I'm here for you if you need anything. Your daughter isn't a baby anymore, so I'm not offering to be your nanny, but I could be like a big brother to her. I can give you a shoulder to cry on when you need it. You know, I just want to be there for you.

Anyway, that's what I wanted to tell you. I think I said that already. I wanted you to know before they sent you to fight again because, well, you could die there. I know you're ready for that, but I thought you might wanna see your daughter before you do.

That's it. I wish you all the best and I hope you will let me know how things turn out.

Your friend,
Ryan

PART THREE

FLESH AND BLOOD

FILE NO. 1554

INTERVIEW WITH VINCENT COUTURE, CONSULTANT, EARTH DEFENSE CORPS
Location: EDC Headquarters, New York, NY

—Where's Kara?

—**We will discuss her whereabouts in a moment. There is a lot we need to cover today, Mr. Couture. First, I would like you to tell me how you and Themis ended up in Canada.**

—Well, it's hard to move around when you can't see anything. I thought I had turned Themis completely around, but I was about thirty degrees off. That's how I ended up in Canada. All things considered, I think I did OK.

—**The question was not meant as a reprimand, I was simply curious as to whether or not you chose that destination.**

—I had no idea where I was, or where I was going. I kept moving forward until there was enough of Themis above water for me to see outside. I didn't know where that island was either until I turned on my cell and Google-mapped it. From there, I stuck to shallow waters all the way to New York. That gave me some time to figure out how that thing really works.

—**Dr. Franklin told me you had talked about the possibility that Themis could transport herself. She seemed to suggest the odds of**

discovering anything we could use were not in our favor. Should I take your ability to return to base in one piece as a sign that we have beaten those odds?

—Oh yeah. It's even better than I thought. When I managed to get Themis moving again at the bottom of the ocean, I was convinced we were dealing with a multiple-coordinate system. That could have been a nightmare for us. Turns out it's a lot more user-friendly than I thought. It's . . . point-and-shoot, more or less. You orient Themis in the direction you want to go, then you punch in how many units you wanna move forward. What confused me is that you get to define those units beforehand. The shortest distance she can move is about fifty, sixty feet. That's a very short step for Themis. So for short distances, you can use that as a unit, then enter how many times that you want to move forward. The console will take three digits tops, so the biggest number you can enter is 777. That's in base-8. In base-10, that means 511.

—If I understand correctly, the farthest Themis can transport herself is 511 times 50 feet, which is roughly 25,000 feet.

—It's 25,550. That's about 7.8 kilometers. If you want to go farther than that in one jump, you can increase the unit size. You can use three digits for that too.

—So the maximum distance we can travel is . . . 511 times 50 feet . . .

—Times 511. In the neighborhood of 4,000 kilometers. I wouldn't recommend jumping that far unless you end up in the ocean again or in the middle of the desert. It's easy to use when you see where you wanna go. We'll need a map or something for longer jumps. I'm supposed to talk to the guys downstairs. It shouldn't take them long to program something we can use.

—Can it be used safely?

—For us, yes. It really does all the work for you. It'll put you on the ground at the distance you told it to go. It's not so safe for anyone at the destination. People, cars, buildings, well, whatever can't support the weight will be crushed. We'll have to be careful, but it'll be a hell of a lot faster than taking her apart and loading her on a boat. I can't say I'll miss spending a week at sea either. I know Kara'll be happy. Where is she?

—We will discuss your wife shortly. Has General Govender made you aware of the current situation?

—He said that the aliens are back in London. That can't be good.

—I wish that were all. Since then, several more robots have appeared in largely populated areas on four continents. The last one materialized in Rio de Janeiro nine minutes ago. There are now thirteen robots on Earth, all nearly the size and shape of the one you battled a year ago.

—He said the one in London hadn't made a move yet.

—That is still true. None of them have. However, given our previous encounter, we cannot ignore the possibility of an attack. The density of the population in the areas where they have landed would make a simultaneous strike incredibly lethal.

—Just so you know, if they start vaporizing everyone, I'll go. Kara will too, but you have to realize we can't beat all of them.

—You may be our only hope.

—That's not hope. I'm not selling us short, it's just simple math. We might get lucky again one time, maybe twice, but not thirteen times in a row. I don't think our odds are even close to fifty-fifty, but say they were. You can't flip a coin and get heads that many times. We'll go. We'll go because it's better than just sitting here watching, but we won't win. You need a better plan.

—NATO is planning a nuclear strike in case you are defeated. However, even if that strategy proved to be successful against the alien robots, the fallout from thirteen large-scale nuclear explosions all over the world would be devastating and would be felt for decades. That cannot be our first option. I feel obligated to tell you that, if the aliens turn hostile, the order to send Themis *will* be given if she is operational.

—What do you mean operational? I brought her back in one piece.

—I suppose now would be a good time to discuss your wife. Themis is not damaged, but she is not operational because she is missing a pilot. Ms. Resnik has left the base unauthorized.

—Kara's gone AWOL? Is she in trouble?

—Given the current state of affairs, military discipline is not the issue. What concerns me is not that her absence is against military rules but that she is absent. Without her, this organization, and perhaps the entire world, is absolutely powerless against what could be the prelude to a full-scale alien invasion.

—Where did she go?

—I believe she intends to visit the Commonwealth of Puerto Rico.

—Puer . . . Why?

—Read this.

—What is it?

—It is a letter—an electronic letter—from Ryan Mitchell to Ms. Resnik. That letter is what sent your wife on what I can only assume is a rescue mission, the purpose of which will become amply apparent as you continue reading. I should also remind you that the content of this letter, while shocking and inflammatory, only represents one side of a much more complex story. You should—

—I'm done. Is he lying?

—Already?

—I'm a fast reader. Is that sack of shit lying?

—He is not. Mr. Mitchell does not possess all the facts; he is being irresponsible, shows a complete disregard for the consequences of his actions, and appears to be on the verge of a complete breakdown, but he is being truthful.

—So it's true? I have a child?

—That, I honestly do not know. It is true that Ms. Papantoniou removed biological samples from both of you while you were being held, and that evidence left at the laboratory suggests that she intended to attempt in-vitro fertilization. What Mr. Mitchell failed to mention in his missive—which would have been very helpful for Ms. Resnik to know—is that all of the information he is so eager to divulge, from the existence of a child to her parentage, not to mention the threat of a Russian kidnapping, also comes directly from the mouth of Ms. Papantoniou. I need not explain why I do not take everything she says as gospel.

—You found Alyssa?

—I did not personally locate her, but she is indeed in custody.

—Do you think she's lying?

—She faces charges that could normally carry a death sentence or several lifetimes of imprisonment. The circumstances under which she committed her crimes make a public trial unlikely, but she is well aware that the United States Government would like nothing better than to see her . . . retired. She knows that without a bargaining chip of some sort, she will in all likelihood disappear without explanation, or fall victim to something more mundane, get lost at sea, or succumb to a mysterious disease. She therefore has ample reason to lie. That said, I am tempted to believe her. She could only buy a few days by sending us on a wild-goose chase.

—Where is she now?

—In a safe house under twenty-four-hour surveillance.

— . . .

—What are you thinking?

—A child?

—A daughter, yes.

—Now?

—She would have been born a decade ago. We are only finding out about her now.

— . . .

—Mr. Couture?

— . . . What?

—You do not appear angry?

—You mean at you?

—Yes. I did hide what I knew about what Ms. Papantoniou intended to do a decade ago. If I had to do it again, I would still conceal that information, but that makes you no less entitled to some form of anger.

—Oh, I'm angry all right. I'm just . . . I can't imagine what Kara's going through.

—I am fairly certain Ms. Resnik did not react so calmly to the revelations contained in the letter you are holding.

—I'm sure she didn't. She must have gone mad when she read this. But that's not what I'm thinking about. She didn't want . . . I tried real hard to make her change her mind, but she didn't want children. But I did, and I pushed, and I pushed.

—And now?

—Now? Now the world is ending. Would you bring a child into this world? Today?

—As I previously stated, she would have been born several years ago.

—How do we find Kara?

—You stated that she was against becoming a mother. Do you believe she will attempt to contact the child?

—She'll go. She won't come back until she finds her. She won't stop looking. There's a reason she didn't want a child. I think she was afraid it would consume her. Now that she has one, it—

—She very well may not—

—Doesn't matter. Now that she *thinks* she does, there'll be no stopping her.

—Are you worried?

—Yeah, I am. I'm afraid she'll do something stupid.

—I am truly sorry if I—

—I really don't care. I'll deal with you when this is over. What did you plan to do with the information Alyssa gave you. Oh, and how the fuck does Ryan know?

—I did not want to share the information with anyone at the EDC until I could at least confirm that some of it was accurate. I requested help from the United States Government.

—What did you promise them? A pilot?

—Not in so many words, but I did leave open the possibility. They agreed to send a Delta Force unit to retrieve the child. In the event that a child did reside at the address Ms. Papantoniou provided, I asked Mr. Mitchell to accompany the Delta team and to make the experience less traumatic. There was also a strong possibility that there would indeed be a child living there, but that she would later prove not to be the offspring of Ms. Resnik and yourself. My request was later denied when the robot appeared in England.

—Let's say they had gone and found a little girl. Say it was our daughter like Alyssa said. Would you have told us?

—Of course I would have.

—How do I know that?

—I understand that your trust in me may have been irreparably damaged. Trust, however, is not a prerequisite in this case. Simple logic will suffice. The sole reason I would have—that anyone would have—to hide your daughter from you is to use her as a pilot in the future. I, or anyone else, would first need to determine if she can activate one or both helmets inside Themis. This could perhaps be accomplished without your knowing. That said, she would eventually need to be trained. Themis requires not one but two pilots, hence the child's training would demand that you or Ms. Resnik be present. It would most likely have to be you, since you are the only one whose anatomy is compatible with the lower body controls. I would surmise that her ability to activate the controls, coupled with a likely physical resemblance to one or both of her parents, would make it near impossible for me or anyone else to hide her lineage from someone of your intelligence.

—Really? Flattery? And what do you suggest we do now?

—We wait. Now that the information I was trying to conceal is out in the open, I will renew my request for a Delta Force extraction, this time through the EDC, and *sans* Mr. Mitchell.

FILE NO. 1556

NEWS REPORT—JACOB LAWSON, BBC LONDON
Location: London, England

[*Thirty seconds, Jacob.*]

—No! No! Don't put me on the air. We're walking away.

[*What do you mean, away?*]

I mean that my cameraman and I are leaving. We're five minutes away from the van.

[*Why? They're ready for you in . . . twenty seconds. What's going on Jacob?*]

Stall them. The bloody thing moved. I'm getting the hell away from it.

[*What do you mean it moved? I'm looking at it on channel two. It's not doing anything.*]

I'm telling you, Jack, the robot moved. It . . . shifted its weight. It moved its hands.

[*Shifted . . . You can't do this to me Jacob. What am I supposed to air for three minutes?*]

Weather report. Show some footage from this morning. I don't give a shit. The last time one of these things moved, a hundred thousand people died. It happened—oh, wait—right here.

[*You're being paranoid. We're all looking at it now and I'm telling you: It's not moving.*]

Paranoid, Jack? We're walking on dirt, Jack! Do you understand what I'm saying? We're walking on dirt because the last of those bloody robots vaporized every bloody thing that was here. We're too close anyway. I can get a better view from farther away.

[*Where are you going to go?*]

Where there's no dirt! We'll take the van and get to one of the downtown buildings on the edge of the levelled area. I can get you some footage from there.

[*How long will that take?*]

I don't know. Give us . . . twenty minutes to set up.

[*Jacob. The edge of the dirt field is two kilometres away. It should take you two minutes to get there.*]

There are fifty thousand people here, Jack. Children everywhere, more tents than you can count. There's a food station ahead of us with—I don't know—fifty barbecue grills. Hundreds of people waiting in line for hamburgers. These people have built a community here. It's difficult to *walk* through the crowd. We'll need to clear a path for the van.

[*And these fifty thousand people, are they leaving as well?*]

No, Jack, they're not leaving. There are people coming and going but I don't think anyone is fleeing.

[*And neither should you. You're a journalist, for goodness sake. Even the children are not as skittish as you are.*]

Go to hell, Jack. We're leaving.

[*What does your cameraman have to say?*]

Janet, do you want to stay?

{*Go to hell, Jack!*}

[*OK! OK! I'll kill your segment.*]

What will they air?

[*I'll have them improvise for three minutes. They won't be happy. You could lose your job for this, Jacob. Both of you.*]

You know me, Jack. I went to a dozen wars for you. I took a bullet for you.

[*Your bag took a bullet for me, Jacob. You were never injured.*]

Another six inches and we wouldn't be talking. My point is I don't scare easily. I'm telling you: I have a bad feeling about this.

[*I hope you're right, or there'll be hell to pay.*]

I sincerely hope I'm wrong. We're at the van. I'll call you when we get there, Jack.

[*No, you won't. Don't hang up. I'll put you on the air just before the weather, but I need you in front of the camera five minutes from now.*]

Janet, Jack says we have five minutes.

[*What's she saying?*]

She's smiling.

[*That's more like it.*]

Janet, look in the mirror behind us. Can you see that?

{*Yes, what is it?*}

[*What is what, Jacob?*]

The air . . . It's hard to explain, the air around the robot is becoming . . . thicker, like . . .

[*Like fog?*]

Not quite. It's like a mist slowly forming all around it. Whatever it is, it doesn't look like a natural phenomenon. I see people running away.

[*Is the robot making it?*]

I think so. I can't see where it's coming from. The air is whiter now, opaque. I can't see the robot's feet anymore. It's not fog. It looks like . . . like smoke from dry ice, a *lot* of dry ice. Janet, can you drive faster? I think it's gaining on us.

[*Is it dangerous?*]

How the hell should I know? It's moving a lot faster than anyone can run. We're about three hundred feet from the road but it's right behind us.

Floor it, Janet! There! That way! We're in the city. Take Golden Lane. Bloody thing's all over us now. We can't see ten feet ahead of us.

Bloody hell! It's coming through the back door of the van. Through the floor. Janet STOP!

[*Jacob?*]

. . .

[*Jacob!*]

I'm here. Fuck! We . . . we hit a parked car. My head, it's bleeding. Janet! Janet! Janet's unconscious. I have to get her out. Come on, girl. Let's get you out of here.

[*I'll send help. Tell me where you are.*]

I'm taking her inside Cromwell Tower. Jack, you better hurry. She's . . . Her veins are dark, almost black. Her skin is all pale.

[*Is she dead?*]

I don't fucking know! I have her in my arms. I can't check her pulse. The smoke, it's coming inside the building, even with the doors closed. I have to get her away from it. I'll try the lift.

[*Jacob, is she dead?*]

I'm getting on the lift. I'll take her to the top floor. Hopefully whatever is hurting her won't reach us there.

[*The police won't answer.*]

. . .

[*Did you hear what I just said?*]

. . .

[*Jacob!*]

She's dead. Janet's dead. Bloody aliens killed her. She's . . . hard. Her skin . . . It's like someone sucked all the blood out of her— . . .

[*Jesus.*]

They're doing it again, Jack. They're killing us all.

[*I'll find some help. I'll come get you myself if I can't.*]

You worry about yourself, Jack! The fog will have crossed the river by now. It will reach you soon.

[*You think it will make it this far?*]

I'm looking through the window now. It's everywhere, as far as I can see. Anything smaller than twenty-five or thirty storeys is completely covered by the cloud. It looks like a white sea, with a few tall buildings rising out of it. Get everyone out of the office and to the top floor. You should be safe there.

[*What about you?*]

I breathed as much of this smoke as Janet did. I don't know why I'm not dead and she is. I feel fine. I'll stay here until it dissipates.

[*Be safe, Jacob.*]

Goodbye, Jack.

INTERVIEW WITH DR. ROSE FRANKLIN, HEAD OF SCIENCE DIVISION, EARTH DEFENSE CORPS

Location: EDC Headquarters, New York, NY

—Dr. Franklin.

— . . .

—Dr. Franklin. What are you doing?

—I'm . . . I'm not doing anything.

—You are sitting on the floor with your eyes closed, surrounded by a thousand body bags. You are doing *something*.

—There are 861. It seems random. Why not eight hundred, or a thousand?

—I assume it is the number of cadavers they could fit inside the cargo plane that brought them here.

—I guess so.

—You have not answered my question.

—What was it?

—What are you doing?

—I was trying to imagine what four million body bags would look like. Could I see them all? Or would it look like an endless sea of dead people in every direction?

—I do not know the answer. It should be relatively easy to calculate if it is important to you.

—It's not. It's just hard to get a sense of what four million really means. Did you know it would take about three months with no sleep just to read their names out loud?

—I see you have been giving this number a fair amount of thought. You should know that four million is only an approximation of the death toll based on other very rough figures. We do not know how many people were able to leave London before the attack, how many people lived in the area affected, how many were gathered near the alien robot, and so on. The final count, if there is ever one, may be significantly different.

—It doesn't matter. It's still sad.

—Four million dead is indeed terribly sad.

—I don't mean that. I mean it's sad that their deaths aren't as important just because there are so many.

—I do not see how the magnitude of the event makes their passing any less tragic?

—It just does. Kara told me how devastated I was . . . how the other Rose was when eight people died in Flagstaff while we were looking for giant body parts. I can only imagine. I sure felt the weight of the 136,000 who died during the first London attack, but I'm certain it wasn't 136,000 times what I would have felt for one. I'm not four million times sorrier now.

—That seems perfectly normal.

—Is it? Don't you think I owe it to every person I killed to feel their death equally?

—You did not kill anyone, Dr. Franklin. It is only human to feel a certain part of responsibility—I certainly wish I had been able to prevent this tragedy—but you did not kill anyone. Aliens did, without having so much as a conversation with us first.

—I started this, they didn't. I fell in a hole and I started all this. I had a chance to put it all behind me, but I managed to not only find the hand again, but to put Themis together entirely. How many people get a second chance? I got one. Look what I did with it. I should have stopped looking.

—**Technically, you are not the one who kept on looking. The . . . other Dr. Franklin did—**

—I should have stopped looking! I should have left Themis alone. She knew. She killed me for it.

—**Mr. Couture and Ms. Resnik killed you, however unwillingly.**

—You don't think it means anything that I was killed by the robot I put together? By the robot whose discovery put everyone's lives at risk? I see poetic justice, but please tell me you at least find it a bit ironic.

—**You discovered parts of a very powerful weapon. There is risk in dealing with dangerous things. People die every day because of their proximity to handguns, or power tools, or chemical drain cleaner. You found a two-hundred-foot-tall alien weapon that weighs thousands of metric tons and is capable of destroying armies. You worked with it all day, every day. Had your insurance company been aware of what you were doing, your premiums would have increased a thousandfold. Your death was devastating, but it was also highly probable. Furthermore, I do not believe you had a choice. I suspect you were steered towards the hand by forces well beyond your control.**

You did, however, get a second chance. You are here now. You are here so that you can help us save people. You will not be able to save them all. I could have told you that long before the attack. But I am convinced that you can save some. That may not sound wonderful, but there is a strong possibility that saving some of us is the best that we can hope for at this juncture. With that in mind, and with all due respect to your disproportionate feeling of guilt, I would like to know what you have managed to learn since these bodies arrived from London.

—They died a horrible death. There are a dozen medical examiners doing autopsies around the clock, but the twelve they've looked at all died the same way: extremely severe sepsis. Inflammation quickly spread throughout their entire body. They would have had a very high fever. Blood clotting would occur very quickly, restricting blood flow to the entire body. Without oxygen, all the major organs would start failing. The kidneys, liver, and lungs would go first, then death. They died burning up from the inside, gasping for air.

Do you still think it was a good idea to bring children for a picnic around the alien robot?

—I never thought of it as good. I merely stated that it might have been our best chance of showing them our peaceful nature. I still believe it was our best chance.

—It didn't work too well for these people.

—It did not. Therefore, we must proceed knowing that peace is no longer an option. How long did it take for the victims to die?

—It happened quickly. I'd say under a minute. We're getting video surveillance from all over London. The gas reached a uniform height of 230 feet. It spread in a perfect circle, approximately twelve kilometers in every direction—that's about 450 square kilometers—in just under eighteen minutes. Everyone was dead after twenty. The alien robot vanished shortly after. Has there been any sign of it?

—It reappeared in Madrid almost immediately.

—Are they evacuating?

—General Govender is coordinating with local government in the thirteen cities under immediate threat.

—The other robots, are they . . . ?

—No. Fortunately for us, none of the others have sent out any gas, up to this point. We can assume it is only a matter of time before they do. If the survival rate is as low as it was in London, and only half of the population remains in these cities, we could have one hundred million dead within thirty minutes.

—How many have survived? I was told only a few hundred.

—We are finding more as rescue teams sweep the city. The latest figure I received had the number of survivors near fourteen hundred.

—That's still horribly low.

—It is. Most of them were found within five kilometers of the point of origin. The density of the population affected decreases as we move away from it, as more people were able to get away. I would not expect the number of people who came into contact with the gas and survived to increase significantly from this point on.

I have requested that some of the survivors be sent here for examination.

—They're here. They arrived an hour ago.

—**Have they been examined?**

—No, but they've all given blood samples on the plane. We should have those results in an hour. I talked to four of them already. I'll interview the rest when they come back. I sent them all to get something to eat.

—**How did they manage to stay clear of the deadly gas?**

—They didn't. From what they told me, there was no way to escape it. They tried to seal themselves inside a room, block every orifice with whatever was at hand, but the fog—that's what they called it— found its way in as if nothing was there to stop it. They say it came in through the walls. I know many of them didn't even make it inside. Some were part of the group gathered around the alien robot. They were exposed to the gas, breathing it, for over an hour before it dissipated.

—**How did they survive? Were their symptoms any less severe?**

—What symptoms? They had none. They're all perfectly healthy. That's not true; one of them has a pretty nasty case of the flu, but I doubt it has anything to do with it. He says he's been sick for days. Whatever this "fog" does, they're completely immune to it.

—**Do you have any idea why?**

—No. They're all physically very different. They come from different parts of the world. I'll try to get as much information about them as I can, see if they share eating habits, some activity. It could be something they're in contact with at work, or at home, the kind of soap they use, their shampoo. The ones I talked to aren't on any medication. I'll keep asking. It's possible something will come up when I talk to the others but, in all honesty, I doubt I'll find anything. There's a six-year-old girl in that group and an eighty-year-old man. How much of their daily lives could they have in common? I'm not the one who should be doing this.

—You should stop doubting yourself, Dr. Franklin. I have every confidence in your ability to solve this puzzle.

—You keep talking about me like I'm some sort of *savant*. I'm not. I'm good at what I do, but this isn't it. There is one thing, though. The person you want me to meet, the one who helped bring me forward in time, could he be a descendant of the aliens who left Themis here on Earth?

—What if he were?

—It's just a thought, but if these people, the survivors, were descendants of the people who built Themis—they're obviously not full-blown aliens but say they were only part human—it would make sense for the attackers to spare them.

—I was thinking the very same thing. I find it extremely difficult to view the survival of the people that were brought here as coincidental. If, as my contact suggested, people of alien descent have been walking among us throughout history, they might have some form of immunity to the gaseous agent used in the attack. Can you think of a way to confirm this hypothesis?

—Like I said, this isn't my thing. I don't have the knowledge or training to deal with any of this. What you need now is a geneticist.

—I may know someone who can help.

FILE NO. 1570

INTERVIEW WITH DR. ALYSSA PAPANTONIOU
Location: EDC Headquarters, New York, NY

—Are the handcuffs really necessary?

—**They are not. This is a secure facility, and the odds of a successful escape are infinitesimal. However, given your history with the members of this team, I believe the restraints will help keep everyone at ease.**

—It's really hard to work with my hands t . . . tied together.

—**The chain is fourteen inches long. I have requested it to allow you some freedom of movement. If any of the tasks you must perform require that your hands be farther apart, I have provided you with an assistant whose freedom of movement is unimpeded.**

—We're on the sssame side. You realize that, don't you?

—**You have made a habit of changing sides whenever it suited you.**

—Four million dead. What I meant was that there *are* no sides anymore. It's us and them. I don't think they would t . . . take me on their team even if I wan . . . even if I wanted to.

—Sixty million people died during the Second World War. There are still sides.

—How many dead will it take for you t . . . to trust me?

—Rest assured, Ms. Papantoniou, I personally do not fear you. The restraints are not for me. That said, I believe that Mr. Couture would like you to keep them on even if you were the only two people left alive. That would make the answer to your question approximately 7,125,000,000.

—Why is Vincent still here? Haven't you sent Th . . . Themis?

—What we have and have not done does not concern you. You were brought here for a very specific purpose.

—I was just mmm . . . making conversation.

—Then converse about the people who died in London. The medical examiner said they all died of sepsis.

—Close enough.

—Are you saying they did *not* die of sepsis?

—Not exactly. They died of a systemic inflam . . . matory response, but sepsis implies there is an infection present. There's no harmful pathogen in the gas, no virus, no b . . . no bacteria, at least that's what I think.

—What you think? Did you not analyze the gas samples they sent you?

—There was nothing to analyze. The ca . . . canisters were empty when I received them. But, based on the cell samples I looked at, I believe the gas contains a really, really smart molecule, one that binds to long DNA chains and causes the gene to cr . . . create a different protein, one that the body doesn't recognize. The body thinks every cell is infected and starts attacking itself. The reaction is extremely severe, and almost ins . . . tantaneous.

—Is there anything out of the ordinary about the genetic makeup of the victims?

—I didn't check, but no.

—I brought you here because of your expertise in genetics. I cannot understand why you would not see it fit to perform even the most basic genetic profiling on the victims.

—I didn't count the bodies in London m . . . myself, but the report you gave me says that about four million people were exposed to the gas, and that around two . . . two thousand people survived.

—Exactly 1,988, by the latest count.

—That's about five out of ten thousand, 5 percent of 1 p . . . percent. That means 99.95 percent of the people exposed to the gaseous agent died. I don't need to do a lot of t . . . testing to tell you that there's nothing really unique about 99.95 percent of the population. The living, all 1,988 of them, are a lot more . . . interesting.

—Very well. What can you tell me about the living? I trust you have at least examined the survivors we flew here.

—I've done a full genome sequencing on all t . . . twenty-seven of them. They have really bad ge . . . genetics.

—How so?

—They all share a co . . . cocktail of genetic variations and mutations, most of which are bad for you. These people shouldn't even exist.

—Because of poor genetics?

—Because of rrr . . . because of rare genetics. There shouldn't be more than one person with all these anomalies.

—Please explain.

—There are little "errors" in everyone's DNA. Most of them are SNPs—

—Pardon me, I know very little about genetics.

—They're differences in only one base pair of nu . . . nucleotides, one pair of letters. Replace a T and an A with a G and a C, that t . . . type of thing. The vast majority of these differences are in noncoding areas between the ge . . . genes and no one really cares, or knows anything about them. Those that occur inside genes are usually more interesting, and we're beginning to understand how . . . some of them work. Differences that are more common are called p . . . polymorphisms, those that occur in less than 1 percent of the population are called mutations. People shouldn't share multiple mmm . . . mutations.

—And the survivors do?

—A lot of them. Enough so that the molecule in the alien agent doesn't re . . . recognize any of the long DNA chains it's looking for. This many people should definitely not share this mmmany mutations. It just doesn't happen.

—It obviously does. How unlikely is it?

—Well, let me give you an example. All the people you s . . . sent me have a mutation in their TREM2 gene. One of the things TREM2 does is help re . . . regulate immune response to disease and injury in the brain. There are all sorts of mutations that can make TREM2 not function p . . . properly. These people all have the same one: variant R47H. That one is rare. It occurs in a little more than half a percent of the po . . . population in certain places like Iceland, and it's even harder to find everywhere else. All of the survivors have the same TREM2 mutation, in both co . . . copies of the gene. That's rare enough, I don't even have frequencies for it.

—Is it debilitating?

—It's been shown to increase the risk of developing Alzheimer's, but most people with the mutation won't get the d . . . the disease, so no. There is also a mutation in the BCR2 gene. It increases your risk of br . . . breast cancer.

—Do all the survivors have it?

—They do. Both copies of the gene.

—How uncommon is that mutation?

—It's ha . . . hard to tell. It's more frequent in certain ethnic groups, but overall, it's found in less than half of one percent of the general population. You see w . . . what I'm getting at. Assuming the two mutations are unrelated, half a percent times half a percent means that out of a mi . . . million people, you should only find about twenty-five with both mutations. Of course, that's not all the survivors have in common.

—Do all the mutations shared by the people you examined increase their risk of contracting a disease?

—No. Most of them will have no effect at all. They do have one g . . . good thing going for them. They have a variation in their PCSK9 gene that leads to lower bad cho . . . cholesterol. That one is found in about 3 percent of the po . . . pulation. If you do the math: There should be no more than three people with just these three mutations in the four million who were exposed to the gas in London.

The people I examined share hundreds of SNPs; fifty-seven rare gene mutations. You should not be able to find two people on Earth with so many rare t . . . traits in common, there aren't nearly enough people. I'll need blood from all the survivors to confirm, but I'm willing to bet they all have the same t . . . traits, even if it's . . . impossible. It's not a coincidence that these people survived.

—Could all the survivors be related? Having common ancestry would increase the likelihood of their genetic similarities if I am not mistaken.

—Some of them are. Of the t . . . twenty-seven people you flew here, six are related to one of the others, two brothers, one brother and sister, one mmm . . . mother and daughter. Beyond that, no. Sixteen are of British descent, one is from Denmark, one from Morocco. There are four people from India, one Ca . . . Canadian, two Frenchmen. The mother and daughter are Russian. These people are related the same way you and I are related. You'd have to g . . . go back a long long time to find a common ancestor.

—Do you believe that these people were spared on purpose?

—Yes. It has to be by design. Well, it doesn't *have* to be, but it makes mmm . . . more sense that way.

—How so?

—In theory, it could be that the aliens just don't know that these p . . . polymorphisms exist and that's just a flaw in their weapon. But the molecule they built targets really long DNA ch . . . chains and, at least from what I understand about genetics, that's a lot more complex to create, and t . . . totally unnecessary. They could have made a much simpler molecule that targets short DNA chains that everyone has. They could have used a poisonous gas. Making bo . . . botulinum toxin would be child's play compared to this. With the same delivery system, there are a m . . . million things they could have used that wouldn't have left *anyone* alive and are much easier to build. They went through a lot of t . . . trouble to make it the way it is.

—Assuming, for a moment, that these people do indeed share a common ancestry, could the molecule you described have been programmed to specifically spare their descendants?

—That's an interesting idea. But no, it wouldn't work. You can't know what part of your genetics your ch . . . children will inherit.

—It cannot be a completely random process. Surely, some of it is predictable?

—Some of it is. There is a sss . . . small portion of your genetics that only comes from your father, and a small portion that only c . . . comes from your mother.

—Could that DNA—is it DNA?

—Yes.

—Could that DNA have been used to program the alien molecule?

—No. It w . . . wouldn't work over long periods of time. How can I explain this? Imagine that you wanted to target the desce . . . all the descendants of a John Doe who lived a thou . . . thousand years ago. The only genetic material you can be certain John Doe passed on is his Y-chromosome DNA, that is the sss . . . sex chromosome. You could use the markers in that DNA but it is only passed on in a direct p . . . paternal line, from father to son, to son, to son. No women. If it were the p . . . progeny of a Jane Doe you wanted to save, you could use mitochondrial DNA. That is only passed on by the m . . . mother. You would get the opposite results, only women in a d . . . direct maternal line. That's an infinitely small portion of one's lineage and these direct lines tend to die out. All it needs is for one father to not have a son, or for a mother to not have a d . . . daughter. You can look at it the other way, you have sixteen great-great-g . . . grandparents, yet you share Y-chromosome DNA or mitochondrial DNA with only four of them.

—Could you not target specific markers from . . . normal DNA, which I believe is passed on from both mother and father?

—It's called autosomal DNA. Like you said, you get more or less half of it from your mother, half from your f . . . father. You have two copies of each gene, but you only pass on half of your genes to your ch . . . children, and you don't get to pick which ones. It's called recombination. Autosomal DNA recombines every generation. That means how much DNA is shared with a specific ancestor gets cut in half every time. The parts that are shared also get shorter and shorter. Over time, there will be almost no . . . nothing left that is shared by all the descendants of a specific person, certainly not as much as what these p . . . people have in common.

Take whatever mutation the survivors had, both of their parents must have had it, but probably not in both c . . . copies of the gene. The parents would have died in London. The little Russian girl saw her father die. The same is true for their children. A lot of the survivors had children and they all died, except for one. Their children didn't have all the same genetic tr . . . traits since they got half of their DNA from the other parent. Genetics gets really mixed up over long p . . . periods of time. If they were trying to save people from a single family, the gas would have wiped out most of their lineage, except for a com . . . pletely random few.

—Then, could you ensure that *only* descendants of these specific individuals survived, even if most of them were killed?

—Maybe. A very small and very random fraction of them.

—Is there anything . . . out of the ordinary about the genetics of the survivor?

—Have you been listening to wh . . . to what I said? Yes, having so many genetic variations in common is d . . . definitely out of the ordinary. I thought I had made that clear.

—You had. I meant taken individually. If you do not consider their shared genetics, or even the number of genetic mutations they possess, is there anything you would not expect to find in an average human being?

—I'm not sure I understand what you mean.

—I want to know if you can confirm with absolute certainty that they are entirely human.

—Human? I . . . I do not . . . Some of their gene mmm . . . mutations are rare, but they are just that: rare. There is nothing really unique about their genetics other than the f . . . fact that they share a lot of it. I have never examined alien DNA so I have nothing to compare it with.

—I will give you access to the remains of the two alien pilots who died a year ago during the first attack. Can you compare their genetic makeup to that of the survivors?

—Do they even have DNA?

—Not exactly. I do not pretend to fully understand the distinction or its implications but, if I remember correctly, the sugar in their nucleic acids is . . . arabinose—

—That can't be right.

—Dr. Franklin was also excited.

—She sh . . . should be. That is . . . extraordinary. Is there anything else?

—You can read it for yourself, see for yourself. I will provide you with the report from the geneticist who first examined them. How soon can you tell me whether their genetic structure matches that of the survivors in any way?

—I'm not sure that I can. You're really talking about apples and oranges, but I will cer . . . certainly try. Thank you!

—Do not thank me as if I have in some way done you a favor. You are probably the one person on this Earth I am the least inclined to please, and if anyone had told me a year ago that I would grant you access to everything you dreamed of, I would have told them. . . . Well, I suppose this is as close as we will ever get to hell freezing over.

FILE NO. 1571

TRANSCRIPT—ONLINE GAMING CHAT ROOM SURVEILLANCE—REYNARD PROGRAM
World of Warcraft—Aegwynn Realm

[Eva002]:   Essie! I can go!

[SkyJumper]:   Hi Eva! Go where?

[Eva002]:   To your place. I can go! I can sleep over.

[SkyJumper]:   Ur mom?

[Eva002]:   She said yes.

[SkyJumper]:   ??

[Eva002]:   I can do what I want.

[SkyJumper]:   How come?

[Eva002]:   Mom believes me now. It happened just like I told her.

[SkyJumper]:   What happened?

[Eva002]:   Those people in London. I saw it.

[SkyJumper]:   That's messed up.

[Eva002]:   She thinks I'm talking to God.

[SkyJumper]:   RU?

[Eva002]:   NO! Can I come?

[SkyJumper]:   Dunno. Everyone's scared. M&D stopped going to work. Can't go out when it's dark.

[Eva002]:   Same here. Soldiers everywhere. But PLEASE! I'll bring you those rocks I found.

[SkyJumper]:   I'll ask. Eva, those people are dead. U not afraid?

[Eva002]:   I am. I was scared before everyone was. But I wanna see you.

[SkyJumper]:   When?

[Eva002]:   I don't care. We can make jewelry. I have new charms. Lots.

[SkyJumper]:   I'll ask.

[Eva002]:   I need to get out of here. Please say yes!

[SkyJumper]:   OK. Stop! I said I'll ask! Wanna play this or not?

[Eva002]:   OK, but we should switch servers. Paladins everywhere.

[SkyJumper]:   Pallies suck. Later though. Told Miguel we'd duel here.

[Eva002]:   Be back in a sec.

[SkyJumper]:   WHAT? NO! Raid is starting!

[Eva002]:   Lots of noise downstairs. I hear Mom screaming.

[SkyJumper]:   ??

[SkyJumper]:   ??

[SkyJumper]:   ??

[SkyJumper]:   ??

[SkyJumper]:   ??

—End intercept—

FILE NO. 1574

INTERVIEW WITH LIEUTENANT GENERAL ALAN A. SIMMS, COMMANDER, JOINT SPECIAL OPERATIONS COMMAND (JSOC)

Location: Fort Bragg, NC

—Is the Delta team in position?

—They arrived in San Juan a few hours ago. They're set and ready to go. We were waiting for you.

—Thank you. And thank you for your help in this matter.

—Anything for our friends at the EDC. All right, let's get this show on the road, shall we? Can we get GSSAP-2 on the big screen, please? Thank you. The target should be in this house right here. The red dots are Delta-3. We have four men in the van across the street. These four will hide behind the pool shed once they get over the fence.

—How long will surveillance last before they breach?

—We're going in now. We've had satellite over since last night. The van's been there for two hours. There's been no movement in or out. No lights on. I would give it more time but, given the circumstances, we'll have to make do with what we have. Plus, we're going in in broad daylight. Armed men jumping fences in a cozy neighborhood, it won't be long before someone dials 911.

Boogeyman, this is Mother Goose, what's your status?

[*In position. Status is go.*]

—What are their orders?

—Locate and extract a young female, approximately ten years old. Grown-ups are potentially hostile. Use of force is authorized.

—They should also be on the lookout for an American woman in her midthirties.

—Stand by, Boogeyman . . . Who is she?

—She is an Army chief warrant and a Captain in the EDC. She would not be in uniform. She cannot be harmed.

—Anything else you wanna tell me? Now is not exactly a good time for surprises.

—That is all.

—She better not be holding a gun.

—If she is present, and alive, she would most likely be armed.

[*Mother Goose, what's the holdup?*]

—This is bullshit. Stand by, Boogeyman! . . . Does she know we're coming?

—She does not.

—I'm sorry for your Captain, sir, but if she points a gun at them, they'll put her down.

—They cannot. They have to be clear on that.

—And what's she gonna do when she sees a bunch of guys with M-16s wearing face masks?

—I cannot say.

—You cannot say. Like I said, I'm sorry, but that's not the mission. If you can't warn her, you better pray she doesn't get in the way. My men come first.

—Let me be abundantly clear. Our planet is under attack by alien forces. Our only viable weapon is a two-hundred-foot-tall alien robot in New York City. That woman is one of two people required to operate said robot. I sincerely apologize for the late warning. I

was hoping she would make contact. That said, the lives of your men most definitely come second to hers.

—We're looking for Kara Resnik?

—We are indeed.

—Boogeyman, this is Mother Goose. New intel.

[*Oh, great.*]

Watch for a female friendly, midthirties in civilian clothing. She is armed and may treat you as hostile. Do not fire, even if fired upon.

[*Mother Goose, can you repeat that?*]

You heard me.

[*Mother Goose, I'm gonna have to—*]

It's Kara Resnik—

[. . . *Roger that, Mother Goose. Relaying orders.*]

—What is that on the next street?

—Looks like a man walking his dog. GSSAP control, tag him. Can we shoot this man if need be? Or are you about to tell me Vincent Couture is also missing, with his dog?

—Mr. Couture does not like dogs. You are free to shoot both the man and his pet if you are so inclined.

—Boogeyman, there is a man walking his dog about to turn the corner, coming at you from the west.

[*Roger that. We'll keep an eye on him. Approaching target.*]

If anyone is having second thoughts, now would be a good time to say so.

[*Mother Goose, this is Boogeyman. Requesting go for breach.*]

Breach is authorized, Boogeyman. I repeat: You are go for breach.

[*Roger, Mother Goose. Gentlemen, on my mark. Three, two—*]

—What was that flash? Are they under fire?

—They're using stun grenades.

[*Clear! . . . Clear! . . .*]

[*Bravo-One, back rooms are clear.*]

[*Clear!*]

[*Garage is clear.*]

[*Roger, Bravo-Two. Front is clear. Checking upstairs.*]

[*We've got your back Bravo-One. Close the doors. Cover the windows.*]

[*Clear! . . . Clear! . . . Clear!*]

[*All clear! Mother Goose, this is Boogeyman. We have two dead civilians in the master bedroom.*]

Roger, Boogeyman. The child?

[*No sir. Two adults.*]

Is one of them . . . ?

[*One Hispanic female, one black male. No sign of Captain Resnik.*]

—It must be the parents. They should check the closets, under the beds. The child may be hiding.

—Boogeyman, give me a full sweep.

[*Bravo-Two, I want a full sweep downstairs. We're looking for a tiny human.*]

[*Roger that.*]

—Lieutenant General. My Spanish is far from perfect but I believe—

—Boogeyman, this is Mother Goose. Local police are on their way. ETA three minutes.

[*Roger, Mother Goose. Bravo-Two, bedrooms are clean. We found a trap for the attic. Going to take a peek. Exit in two minutes.*]

[*Downstairs is clean.*]

[*Holy shit!*]

[*Bravo-One, everything all right?*]

[*All good. Just a big-ass rat. Attic is clean.*]

[*Mother Goose, this is Boogeyman. The house is clean. No sign of target. Requesting instructions on the bodies.*]

—Is that it?

—That's it! She's not there. Thank you, Boogeyman. Leave them be. Return to nest.

[*Roger that, Mother Goose. We'll be home for dinner.*]

Hurry up. It's meatloaf night. Mother Goose out.

FILE NO. 1576

INTERNAL MEMO—DEPARTMENT OF HOMELAND SECURITY

From: Commissioner, Customs and Border
Protection (CBP)

To: Deputy Secretary of Homeland Security

Object: El Paso

An estimated sixty thousand Mexican nationals are now gathered on or near the Paso Del Norte Bridge and more people seeking asylum in the United States are arriving daily in Ciudad Juárez. Isolated acts of violence have already been reported on the bridge and their frequency is increasing rapidly.

BORTAC units were deployed this morning at the request of the Port Director. Attempts at clearing the bridge with 37mm gas guns were unsuccessful.

It is the opinion of this office that CBP personnel, even with increased support from the National Guard and local law enforcement, are no longer able to secure the port of entry within current use-of-force parameters.

It is our recommendation that use of lethal force be authorized on a discretionary basis immediately, at all southern ports of entry.

FILE NO. 1578

INTERVIEW WITH BRIGADIER GENERAL EUGENE GOVENDER, COMMANDER, EARTH DEFENSE CORPS

Location: EDC Headquarters, New York, NY

—Goddammit! They're gonna kill us all!

—**Have all the robots released their gas?**

—Yes they did, simultaneously.

—**All thirteen of them?**

—All but the one in Madrid. He might be waiting for his friends to catch up. We'll know soon enough. If it's anything like London, they'll be done in twenty minutes.

—**How are we responding?**

—Responding? What the hell do you want me to do?

—**I meant the countries under attack. Have any of them retaliated?**

—They sent some ground troops in India.

—**Through the gas?**

—They wore masks. I know, stupid.

—**Did the robot vaporize them?**

—It didn't have to. They died before they even got out of the transport trucks. It's mayhem over there. Mass panic. People trampled to death, thousands, maybe tens of thousands. There are cars, trucks driving through crowds. Elephants . . . Human nature is ugly sometimes. The Russians and the French sent fighter planes after theirs. Nothing happened, except for a big hole half a mile wide. They tried bombing Moscow about ten minutes ago.

—To no avail, I presume.

—It's hard to see through the fog, but we know the robot's still there. There's probably not much left of Moscow around it. Pretty ballsy, bombing their capital.

—What did they have to lose?

—Hmmm. They blew up the Kremlin all on their own.

—There would be no one left alive inside.

—Maybe, but there would have been something to go back to, in two hours, or two weeks, or two years. Now there's probably a decade of construction waiting for them if they ever want to make Moscow habitable again.

—Perhaps they wanted the satisfaction of knowing the aliens will not be able to use their infrastructure when they land in masses.

—You think they're here to colonize?

—Why else would they use a gas to get rid of the population? They have the ability to obliterate everything in an instant. The only reason I can think of is to keep the buildings intact.

—I don't think so.

—Can you think of another reason?

—Nope. But I still don't think so.

—Do you wish to elaborate, or is that the extent of your reasoning?

—You've seen where I live.

—You live in a hotel.

—I meant outside the city.

—I have, but I fail to see the point.

—If you could build these things, these robots—they can make giant structures with a more or less self-sustaining energy source, solid light that can cut through metal, and God knows what else—would you wanna move in that crappy house? I have a white picket fence and a sick crab apple tree. The plumbing is like a hundred years old, the windows are drafty. There's a good view, but that house is shit! Why would they want to live in there? I can't imagine downtown Moscow has a lot more to offer.

—Then—

—I think you're right. I think there's a reason they're using that gas and not vaporizing everything. I don't know what that reason is, but I don't think they're looking for a place to stay. I just can't figure out what they could possibly gain by wiping us off the planet.

—**Whatever their incentive may be, they will undoubtedly succeed if we do not find a way to stop them.**

—I don't think you or I will be the ones to do it. If the science guys don't come up with anything, there isn't much we can do but watch.

—**NATO is preparing for a nuclear strike.**

—What? Are they crazy?

—**I did not suggest it, but as I do not have a viable alternative, I could not find a good reason to argue against it.**

—Goddammit! How about they'll blow up millions of innocent folks? It won't stay there long enough for us to evacuate. They'll nuke a city full of people.

—**People who will undoubtedly die when the aliens attack.**

—Maybe, but at least we're not doing the job for them! Oh, and it won't work. You know it won't work.

—**I do not know that.**

—You should. There'll be fallout for hundreds of miles. They'll contaminate the water, the soil, everything. People'll get sick. People'll die. A lot more people than that gas will kill, I tell you. They'll die a shitty death too. This is a dumb idea. There's no way to explain how dumb an idea this is.

—There could be eighty million people breathing alien gas as we speak. There might be eighty million dead in less than twenty minutes. We have to do . . . something.

—I told you: Rose can do something, the science team can. You and I can't do anything, you made sure of that.

—That is not true.

—You're a real piece of work, I hope you know that. I'm the commander of the EDC. That means I control the one and only thing on this planet that could fight, or at least distract the bad guys. Only that one thing is sitting in a hangar because someone didn't wanna tell my pilots they had a daughter.

—I did not know that they had a daughter.

—You told me they did! That's why I'm missing a pilot.

—I merely relayed the information that was passed on to me by Ms. Papantoniou. I was never able to verify said information.

—Well, you must think she's telling the truth. You have that psychopath working in my lab now.

—Her knowledge of genetics is the sole reason for her presence in this facility. She is unarguably a competent scientist and a very intelligent woman. However, neither of these things is any indication that she is telling the truth.

—Then why not tell everyone? You've known for like a decade.

—What I knew ten years ago and what Ms. Papantoniou is claiming now are very different things. The reason for my silence, then and now, should be self-evident. Ms. Resnik would have scoured the world to find her. She would have done so a decade ago.

—And yet you thought it was a good idea to tell that criminal moron all about it.

—I will admit that sharing vital information with Mr. Mitchell was a miscalculation on my part, one I am trying very hard to remedy, and that the timing of my mistake was unfortunate.

—It's the end of the world.

—*Very* unfortunate.

—That's better.

—**If you allow me to focus this conversation on the problem at hand rather than on my personal shortcomings—**

—By all means.

—**When I said: "That is not true," I was not refusing responsibility for our inability to act, I meant that there was something we could do. You are correct in stating that a permanent solution, if there is one, will come from Dr. Franklin and her team, but you and I should do what we can to give her some extra time.**

—How do you suppose we do that?

—**If we cannot stop the aliens from killing people, we can at the very least try to make the task more time-consuming.**

—How?

—**We could ask everyone living in large urban areas to find a less populated place of refuge.**

—Every city in the world? Are you out of your goddamn mind?

—**We could start with every city of over two million people.**

—Have you looked out the window lately? There are forty-five thousand soldiers patrolling the streets of New York, twenty thousand police officers pulling sixteen-hour shifts. There's looting, people are getting killed. They're barely able to keep things under control, and that's with us lying through our teeth telling them there's nothing to worry about. What do you think's gonna happen if we tell people they should leave? Besides, where would they go?

—**Farmland, perhaps.**

—They're not ready for that. There's no rural area in the world that can handle millions of refugees with no advance warning. There will be violence, sanitary issues, food shortages. Even if it worked, wouldn't the places where people cluster become just as good a target for the aliens? If they can decimate a city in half an hour and move on to the next one instantaneously, I don't think we'll accomplish much by moving people around.

—**I was not suggesting that a mass exodus from urban areas would go smoothly. Not everyone would be able to leave, and many** would no doubt perish or be injured in the process. I also did not imply that the resulting communities would be sustainable. They would exist in a state of complete lawlessness, and those who do not die in the violence that ensues would soon face famine, drought, and disease. That said, they could survive for a few days. Should Dr. Franklin and her team come up with a means of disabling the alien robots during that time, it will mean this many more people left alive. If they are unable to find a solution within a few days, I do not believe we have to worry about anyone facing dehydration or food shortages. My point is simply that it will take longer for them to kill us all if they have to do it one hundred thousand at a time.

—OK, then. Let's move some people around! I'll get the UN to coordinate with governments. If we can get some NGOs involved, it might make things go a little easier.

—Very well. I will leave you to it.

—What are *you* gonna do?

—Dr. Franklin and Ms. Papantoniou are going over the data from the London survivors. I will see if I can be of service.

—What did you do with them? The survivors.

—They have been quarantined.

—Quarantined! I thought the whole point was that they weren't sick.

—I cannot explain why they were unaffected. I felt it was safer to keep them isolated.

—Do you think they had anything to do with the attack?

—I do not believe they were directly involved. I am, however, absolutely convinced that their survival was not coincidental. These people were chosen, somehow, whether they are aware of it or not.

—Why?

—I do not know. I have no hard evidence that they are anything but extremely lucky. However, I cannot help but think that they might not be entirely human.

—Not entirely human . . . Like that friend of yours you won't tell us about?

—No, not quite. I believe my contact, despite never having actually stated that he is of alien descent, to be well aware of his extraterrestrial heritage. I would be surprised if these people were aware of anything. He is also . . . physically unique. I suspect his lineage leads fairly directly to the first aliens to descend upon us. The survivors—the ones I have had a chance to look at—seem perfectly normal. They do not show the same physiological peculiarities. They could be . . . distant cousins at best.

—Ever thought of just asking them?

—Unfortunately, I have.

FILE NO. 1580

INTERVIEW WITH JACOB LAWSON, REPORTER AND SURVIVOR OF THE LONDON ATTACK
Location: FBI Safe House #141, New York, NY

—STOP! Nooooo! AAAAAARRRRGGGHHH! Please stop! Please!

—**Tell me why.**

—My name is Jacob Lawson. I'm a reporter for the BBC. This is illegal. You can't do this.

—**Evidently, I can. Tell me why.**

—I want my government to be notified. I wanna speak to a lawyer.

—**Tell me why.**

—Why what? I don't fucking understand! NO! Stop! AAAAGGGG-GGGHHHH!

—**Tell me why.**

—My name is Jacob Lawson. I'm a British citizen. Under the Vienna Convention, I ask that the British Consulate be notified of my . . . NO! No! No! AAAAGGGGGGGGHHHH! STOP! Stop this! I can't. . . . Why are you doing this? I . . . AAAAGGGGGGGHHHH!

—**Gentlemen, stop. Sir, take a moment to gather yourself. No one will hurt you now.**

—Why are you doing this? I've done nothing wrong!

—Are you calm?

—I don't know what I'm doing here. I want to speak to the person in charge.

—You should by now have little doubt as to who in this room is "in charge." I asked if you were calm.

—Am I . . . Yes. I'm calm.

—Then, tell me why.

—WHY WHAT?

—It would seem really selfish to tell you how much I loathe these debriefings, given our respective situations, but I *will* tell you that I find your lack of cooperation disturbing. If it had not become such a cliché, I would tell you about the definition of insanity, but, in short, you should not expect the outcome to be any different if you keep refusing to answer. Again.

—No! No! Don't! Stop! STOP! NOOOAAAAARRRRGHHH!

—Tell me why.

—AAAAARRRRGHHH!

—Tell me why.

— . . .

—Tell me why.

— . . .

—He is not responding. Wash his face with cold water. Thank you. Now please apply the ointment on his fingertips, generously.

— . . . Oh God. Ahhhh! Thank you! Please make it stop.

—This will numb the nerve endings in your hand. The needles these gentlemen have inserted in your fingertips caused a severe nervous reaction when they hit the bone. The pain should completely subside in a moment.

—Thank you. Please stop hurting me!

—Gentlemen, please remove the needles. Your body is in shock now, and you are slowly losing feeling in your right hand. Take a deep breath. They will not reinsert these needles into your hand.

—Thank you! I can't take any more of this.

—On the contrary. I am taking great pains—if you will pardon the pun—to inflict as little damage to your body as is humanly possible. In some sense, most of the discomfort you have experienced here is your own creation. The needles these men are using are small, yet the nerve endings in your fingertips are very sensitive and the impulses they send to your brain and spinal cord leave you experiencing a suffering that is truly disproportionate to the physical damage that is being done. If you simply answered my question, you would recover very quickly from this unfortunate encounter, with little or no residual symptoms.

—But I don't know anything!

—I was not finished. Should you, however, choose to persist in your refusal, minimal injury also means that these proceedings could go on almost indefinitely. You will not die of pain, but you will never get used to it. Pain is unique in that it does not show habituation or neural adaptation, like smell, or touch.

—I don't know what you want me to say! I haven't done anything!

—That said, you have already sustained some nerve damage in your right hand, and any new discomfort we attempt to produce will be proportionately diminished. I will let you rest for a minute or two, and when the pain is gone, we will start fresh with your left hand.

—NO! Not the other hand! PLEASE! I'm begging you.

—I realize you are in an unfamiliar locale, being questioned by people you do not know, but the events of the last twenty minutes should have made it clear that asking me to stop, however politely, will not be successful.

—I'll tell you anything you want.

—I have been asking one very simple question ever since you arrived, and you have refused to answer every single time.

—I don't know what you want me to say. I don't know anything! Tell me what you want and I'll say it! Just stop. Please!

—This is not my specialty. I am, however, acquainted with people who perform these debriefings on a regular basis, and they tell me that the anticipation of the pain that is to come is often harder to cope with than the pain itself. I do not know what shames me most, that I associate with these people, or that I have come to know that their claim is absolutely untrue. Shall we go again?

—No! No! No!

—Gentlemen, the left little finger, please.

—No, no . . . AAAAAARRRGH!

—Again.

—AAAAAARRRGGH!

—Tell me why.

—*Cough.*

—Deeper.

—No . . . AAAAAAAAARRRGGGHHHH!   AAAAARRGGHHH!— *cough.*

—Let us pause for a moment, so you can reflect on your answer.

—*Cough.* Why what? What do you think I know?

—I do not believe you know anything.

—You . . . You wouldn't be doing this . . . It's safe to say you think I know something, something important.

—Is it? Safe? As we speak, nearly tens of millions of people are dead or dying. What I believe is rather inconsequential at the moment. What I can prove is of the essence. I can no more afford to trust my feelings than I can afford to trust you. Shall we continue?

—Wait! Wait! Please! What do you want to know? Why the aliens came to London? Why they attacked us? Why I'm alive and all those people died?

—The answer to any of these questions would spare you more pain than you can possibly imagine.

—But I don't fucking know! I don't know why those bloody aliens came. I don't know what they want with us. I don't know why they chose London. All I know is that everyone I ever cared about is dead, and I'm not.

—**Tell me why.**

—Don't you think I would tell you if I knew? My son is dead! My wife is dead! My friends, my family. Do you think I wanted them dead? That I wouldn't trade places with any of them if I could? Do you have any idea how much I wish I had died instead of my son?

—. . . I do.

—You believe me?

—**I do.**

—You believe me!

—. . .

—You won't stop, will you? Just tell me!

—**I will not stop.**

—Why?

—**So there can be no doubt. So that I do not have to do this to anyone else.**

— . . .

—**Gentlemen, the left ring finger.**

—MY NAME IS JACOB LAWSON! I'M A BRITISH CITIZEN! UNDER THE VIENNA . . . AAAAGGGGGGGHHHH!

FILE NO. 1585

COCKPIT VOICE RECORDING—US AIR FORCE
B-2 SPIRIT—NATO DEPLOYMENT
Location: Somewhere over Portugal

09:15:31 [HAMAL 11]	Anderson House, this is Chris Parker, approaching Spanish airspace. Speed is 560 mph. Altitude: thirty thousand feet.
09:15:40 [AIRCOM]	Thank you, Chris Parker. Begin final checklist.
09:15:45 [HAMAL 11]	Roger that.
	. . .
09:18:03 [HAMAL 11]	Checklist complete. We are ready for bed.
09:18:10 [AIRCOM]	Roger, Chris Parker. Thirty seconds to bedtime.
09:18:14 [HAMAL 11]	Anderson House, are we really doing this?

09:18:17 [AIRCOM]	Affirmative, Chris Parker. Bedtime is a go. I repeat: Bedtime is a go.
	Twenty seconds.
09:18:24 [HAMAL 11]	Anderson House. This is Chris Parker requesting you reconfirm with Mother.
09:18:28 [AIRCOM]	You have your orders, Chris Parker. Ten seconds till bedtime.
09:18:31 [HAMAL 11]	Anderson House. I'm gonna have to ask again for a reconfirm.
09:18:33 [AIRCOM]	Mother is here, Chris Parker. Bedtime is a go. In five. Four. Three. Two. One. Now. Now. Now.
	Chris Parker, this is Anderson House. You have missed the drop zone.
	. . .
	Chris Parker, this is Anderson House. Please respond.
09:18:57 [HAMAL 11]	Roger Anderson House. We're having some . . . technical problems with the drop hatch.
09:19:09 [AIRCOM]	Chris Parker, I understand. No one here is thrilled either but we have a job to do. Change heading to two seven zero for another pass.
	. . .
	That's an order, Chris Parker, not a suggestion.

. . .

	Chris Parker, respond.
09:19:31 [HAMAL 11]	Roger, Anderson House. Heading two seven zero now.
09:19:35 [AIRCOM]	Roger that. Stay on course.

. . .

	Chris Parker, bedtime is in five. Four. Three. Two. One. Now. Now. Now.
09:20:10 [HAMAL 11]	Anderson House, this is Chris Parker. The kids are asleep.
	Holy sh . . .
09:20:22 [AIRCOM]	Chris Parker, this is Anderson House, say that again.
	Chris Parker, what's your status?
	We lost you on radar, Chris Parker, please respond.
	Chris Parker, please respond.

. . .

FILE NO. 1587

INTERVIEW WITH DR. ROSE FRANKLIN, HEAD OF SCIENCE DIVISION, EARTH DEFENSE CORPS

Location: EDC Headquarters, New York, NY

—The aliens just destroyed Madrid.

—They did not, Dr. Franklin. They did not.

—Look! There's nothing left. Absolutely nothing.

—I am well aware that Madrid has been removed from the face of the Earth. I was merely stating that the aliens are not to blame. We did this to ourselves.

—What do you mean? Did we bomb Madrid?

—We did more than bomb it. Approximately twenty minutes ago, an American B-2 Spirit dropped a B83 thermonuclear gravity bomb with a yield of 1.2 megatons on the capital of Spain. There was no visible explosion, no mushroom cloud. Only an electromagnetic pulse that knocked down nearly every electronic device in Spain, and a bright white light, approximately thirty-two miles across, that covered the entire city for about three seconds. When the light disappeared, there was nothing left. Only a large robotic figure standing at the bottom of the largest hole anyone has ever seen.

—I don't believe it . . . On the news, they said the alien robot attacked, just like in London.

—What did you expect them to say? That the democratically elected government of Spain asked the North Atlantic Treaty Organization to drop a nuclear warhead on a city of six million people?

—How many people were they able to evacuate before they dropped the bomb?

—There was no evacuation, no advance warning. They wanted to be absolutely certain that they would hit their target. They did.

—Did you do this?

—I had nothing to do with it. I tried to stop them, but I have to come to terms with the fact that the scope of this crisis dwarfs any influence I might have had in the past. I have felt my . . . grip on the world loosen these past few years, but it is possible that I have finally outlived my usefulness completely.

—That's not true. These are just . . . unusual circumstances.

—I fear there may not be many *usual* circumstances left in our future.

—Maybe not.

—Dr. Franklin, I feel it is my responsibility to keep everyone around me focused on their task, no matter the outside circumstances, and the last thing I want is to be a burden on anyone, or for my personal feelings to ever get in the way of our moving forward, but at this very moment . . . Why are you laughing?

—You want a pep talk from *me*?

—I would ask Alyssa if she were here—

—You made a joke! Where is she, by the way?

—I sent her to London to examine more of the survivors.

—What happened to the ones that were here?

—On the plane with Alyssa. I saw no need to keep them here any further.

—All of them?

—**All but one. Mr. Lawson, unfortunately, did not make it.**

—The journalist? What happened to him?

—**He had a heart attack.**

—When? How?

—**He had a heart condition I was not aware of. He collapsed during his interrogation and we could not reanimate him.**

—His interro . . . You had him tortured?

—**It is, as most things are, a matter of . . . Yes. I had him tortured.**

—Why?

—**I thought he might know something. He did not.**

—And he died.

—**That he did.**

—I don't know how to respond. Do you want me to say it wasn't your fault?

—**No. I bear complete responsibility for his death. I should have obtained his medical records before debriefing him. I was careless.**

—What bothers you is not that you tortured a man but that you forgot to ask for his medical records?

—**Do not judge me too harshly, Dr. Franklin. Goodwilled, intelligent people just dropped a nuclear bomb on their own people. The United States Government gunned down over six hundred people at the Mexican border less than twelve hours ago. Those were unarmed men, women, and children, families seeking refuge.**

—Is that what we've become?

—**I have asked myself that question many times. The person who offered to meet you—the one who may be of alien descent—mentioned once that if we did not seem responsible enough, the people who built Themis might choose to send us back to the Stone Age and let us mature for a few millennia. I believe those were his**

exact words. I sometimes wonder if that might be exactly what we need.

—A fresh start.

—A fresh start.

—I should be appalled that you tortured a man. I'm not. I think I'm becoming as cynical as you are.

—I am not cynical, but we are indeed very different creatures.

—We're not so different.

—Oh, but we are. No matter how much you believe you have changed, we are still very different animals, you and I.

—I think you're wrong.

—Let me ask you this: Do you believe the American government lied to the people about weapons of mass destruction before invading Iraq?

—What's this got to do with anything?

—Just answer the question.

—Yes. I do.

—Do you believe that was wrong?

—What do you mean? Of course that was wrong!

—Why?

— . . .

—Because lying is bad?

—Something like that.

—You see, I believe that the invasion of Iraq was a mistake but for completely different reasons. At the time, the people in power believed—some of them did—that a strong military presence in the Middle East was crucial to the preservation of our way of life. They believed that the very survival of democracy, freedom of speech, everything we hold dear, hinged on our military presence in the Middle East. Imagine for a second that you also believed that to be true. Let us make this easier, imagine that through some

unexplained magical phenomenon, you actually *knew* it to be true. Would you have lied to the American people if it increased your chances of establishing that vital military presence?

—No. I wouldn't have.

—And therein lies the fundamental difference between us. You would not sacrifice your principles for a greater good. I would not stop to think about it. I am . . . pragmatic, and you, Dr. Franklin, are an idealist.

—Is that such a bad thing?

—Not at all. What would people like me do without ideals to defend?

—I think you're having a crisis of conscience because you've crossed one line too many and you're trying to rationalize everything that brought you here. You did what you did because you thought it was right.

—I did what I did because I thought there was a small chance it might save people. I never thought for a second that it was right.

—So what's next? I take it Mr. Lawson didn't spill the beans about the great alien master plan.

—He did not. However, I still find it likely that his immunity to the alien gaseous agent was due to genetic traits he inherited from ancient alien visitors, but I can now say with a good measure of certainty that, if *Homo sapiens* were not the only species in his ancestry, he was completely unaware of it.

—For what it's worth, I think you're probably right. It would make sense for them to spare people they feel related to. What does Alyssa have to say?

—She has found nothing conclusive as of yet, but she is working around the clock. I must say, I have rarely seen anyone so enthusiastic, about anything. If she fails, it will certainly not be for lack of trying.

—She *is* dedicated. I'll say that about the woman.

— . . .

—What is it?

—An alien robot materialized at the north end of Central Park.

—Here?

—I am afraid so. Can you turn on the television?

—There. It's already releasing gas.

—How long before it reaches us?

—What do we do?

—Dr. Franklin, how long?

—At twenty-five miles per hour, I'd say . . . five minutes, maybe less.

—We need to get Themis to safety. We cannot risk the alien robot destroying her after we evacuate.

—I'll call Vincent. He's probably still in the hangar bay.

—Very well. I will direct everyone here to the helipad.

—Don't! Eugene took the helicopter to Washington this morning. Get them to UN Headquarters. The gas shouldn't reach above the twentieth floor.

Vincent? It's Rose. We have an alien robot in New York, about two miles from here . . . Yes, Vincent. It's already releasing gas so we don't have much time. Grab whatever you can and get Themis away from here . . . I don't know, somewhere safe. Anywhere but here. Yes, I know. I'm sending everyone there . . . Thank you, Vincent. Good luck to you too.

Intercom . . . Where's that button? There. Attention. This is Dr. Rose Franklin. If anyone is in the building, you must evacuate immediately. The city is under attack and a deadly gas will reach this facility within a few minutes. Make your way to the main UN building and get to one of the top floors. This is not a drill. I repeat. You must evacuate this building and find shelter above the twentieth floor in the main building. Again, this is—

—That is enough, Dr. Franklin. We must go, now.

—You're still here! I thought you were seeing everyone out.

—I was. Now they are out. It would be ungentlemanly for me to leave without you, Dr. Franklin.

—You should go, I'll catch up.

—What are you doing?

—I can't leave my notes behind.

—The computer files are saved every night.

—I know. I write everything down in notepads.

—Why would you do that?

—So you don't read everything I put in there.

—I hope I remember to be offended if we live through this. Why are you stopping?

— . . .

—Dr. Franklin, why are you looking at me that way?

—I don't think we have enough time.

—Unless you can present me with an alternate course of action, it would seem preferable to "chance it" than to simply sit here and wait for what you described as a very unpleasant experience.

—The clean room. It's glass-enclosed.

—Are you confident it will isolate us from the gas?

—I don't know. It's rated for biosafety level 3—

—Are you certain we cannot reach the main building in time?

—Pretty sure.

—Then to the clean room we go.

—Follow me . . . In here. Once both doors are sealed, nothing should get in or out. The gas will have to go through the glass walls to get to us.

—Is there not a ventilation system?

—I shut it down. We'll run out of breathable air after a few hours, but that should be long enough for the gas to dissipate.

—Carbon dioxide poisoning seems preferable to what the alien agent will do to us.

—Don't you have anything nice to say?

—You and I have read the same reports, you have talked to the survivors. They tried to do exactly what we are doing now, and they could not escape the gas. Besides, there are at least half a dozen doors between here and the outside world. If the gas reaches this far, I fail to see how one layer of glass will make a difference. What is so special about it?

—It's thick. It's . . . I have no idea, but you can let loose a deadly airborne disease in there and it'll contain it. It has to work.

—I am happy to see you have a newfound will to live.

—Like you said, it's a bad way to go . . . Not like that. I'd also like to talk to that friend of yours.

—I can call him now if you wish.

—Why don't we wait until this is over? I hope my staff made it to UN Headquarters.

—They are young. They can run the whole way. I believe they will make it.

—I hope they made it two minutes ago. Look at the main door.

—It is also coming in through the walls.

—It won't be long before it fills the lab completely.

—I hope this glass will be more efficient than the laboratory walls.

—It's very expensive glass—

—Let us hope our tax dollars have been wisely spent. I would hate for us to perish because someone saved a few pennies on substandard materials.

—We'll know soon enough, there's gas all around us now . . . See! I told you we'd be safe in here.

—Look down, Dr. Franklin.

—No! It's seeping in through the floor!

—And now through the glass.

—No it's not!

—Look closer.

—How does it . . . ? I thought—

—It was a good idea Dr. Franklin. Come sit with me.

—It's coming in slowly.

—Indeed, this glass is slowing down the gas considerably. It was well worth the price you paid.

—I mean it's *really* slow! We might have enough time. It takes—

—Dr. Franklin, it takes hours for the gas to dissipate. Even at this rate, we might have . . . ten, twenty minutes before it fills this room.

—Maybe if I turn on the ventilation—

—Dr. Franklin—

—There's got to be—

—Dr. Franklin!

—I don't wanna die!

—I know. Come sit with me over here.

—It seems I won't get that meeting with your . . . friend after all.

—Perhaps not. Is there anything you want to know that I might be able to answer?

— . . .

—Dr. Franklin?

—What? There are . . . There are so many things I wanna know.

—We may not have time for so many things. If you could only ask one question, what would it be?

—That's easy. Who are you? Who do you work for?

—I said one question.

—I—

—It does not matter. The answer to both questions is really one and the same. I am . . . no one.

I was a college professor. I taught American literature at Montgomery College. I was . . . I was a different person. I married really young. My wife wanted me to become a writer. I never . . . She died of cancer when our son was twelve years old.

—I'm sorry.

—That is kind of you. It was a difficult time. I was not the worst father that ever lived, but I certainly was not good enough to raise a young man on my own. Henry, my son, seemed to forgive my shortcomings easily. We had a good relationship for a while. Parents feel a great deal of responsibility for the way their children turn out, but there is very little a parent can do that will remotely rival the influence a friend or lover can have. My son met a girl when he was fifteen, the daughter of a US senator. Nice girl, a year older than him. I thought she would be a good influence on him. My son turned out to be a bad influence on her. He had tried drugs before, but he could not afford an addiction. I had chosen to keep the house after my wife died—I wanted some stability for my son— and there was little money left after the mortgage. But she had money—her parents did. Two rebellious teenagers in love, with what must have seemed like unlimited means. A few months later, they were but shadows of themselves. I thought cocaine would claim the life of my son, but it was alcohol that did it. They got into a head-on collision with a drunk driver on their way to the video store.

The driver had two prior convictions for driving under the influence. He was charged with vehicular homicide but was found not guilty because of a tainted blood sample.

—You must have been angry.

—I was. I was left with nothing. My wife and I had lots of friends, but they were *her* friends and they forgot all about me soon after she died. I had stopped going to work. I lost the house. All I had to hold on to was the anger. I withdrew whatever money I had left from my bank account—a thousand dollars or so—and I asked a friend of Henry's to buy as much cocaine as he could with it. Then I found out where the driver lived. I put on my best suit, told his landlord I worked for the government, and asked to be let into his apartment. I hid the drugs and left. Later, I made an anonymous call to the police.

—Did it work?

—Of course not. I had made my discontent very clear to the police on several occasions. It did not take long for them to figure out who that mysterious government employee really was. They arrested me four hours after I made the call. I knew I was caught. I did not wear gloves. They would soon find my fingerprints all over the bag of cocaine.

—Then what happened?

—I was let go. Two men, both wearing a better suit than mine, picked me up and drove me home. A week later I received an invitation to the home of the senator.

—The father of the girl your son dated.

—Exactly. I did not know it at the time, but he was also the ranking member of the Senate Committee on Homeland Security and Governmental Affairs. You do not get to that position without knowing the right people. Just one more favor called in and I was a free man. We had a long conversation about parenthood and the world we live in, some very good whisky.

—Did you talk about what happened?

—Not a word. It took nearly a month before I heard from him again. We met in a fancy Italian restaurant in Washington. That time we talked. He said I had shown both courage and stupidity, but that to achieve what I had set out to do—

—To get some justice.

—No. What drove me was not a sense of injustice but pure, unadulterated rage. All I wanted was vengeance. The senator told me that to get it, my commitment would need to be much greater. I remember feeling ashamed when I told him I would not murder the man who took the life of our children. He then asked me what I would be willing to sacrifice. I felt such a relief. I had nothing left, not even the desire to live so I did not hesitate before giving him the answer he was looking for.

After dinner, I was taken to a small apartment outside the city and a nurse came in to draw my blood. I do not know how much blood I gave, but I had to lie in bed for two days afterwards. I got up when a man dropped a large envelope at the door. It contained five hundred dollars, a bank card, and a copy of the newspaper from that morning. On page three, it read: "Man arrested in murder of college professor." The driver of the car that killed my son had been found unconscious in his own bed, covered in blood—my blood—with a knife on the floor. My home had been ransacked, there were signs of struggle, a large pool of blood on the living-room carpet. Witnesses said they saw his vehicle stopped on the side of the road near the Potomac River . . .

—Don't stop!

—Apologies. I was distracted by the gas approaching your shoe.

—Oh my God!

—Perhaps we could continue our conversation on this desk, once we liberate it from all its . . . Dr. Franklin, you are trembling like a leaf.

—We're gonna die, aren't we?

—We were always going to die, Dr. Franklin. Would it be terribly inappropriate if I placed my arm on your shoulder? There. Where was I?

—You were dead.

—Oh yes. My body was never found. I watched my own funeral from a distance. Having so few people attend made giving up my former life that much easier.

—How did you end up working for . . . ? You never told me who you work for.

—I was not entirely sure myself, but it soon became clear I worked for the senator. He had his own private agenda and I was to help him advance it in any way that I could. My bank card gave me access to a CIA slush fund the senator had tapped into. He told me to find a quiet place to stay. I chose the small town in Northern Virginia where my wife was born. It took almost a year before I heard from him again. Several of the rebuilding contracts he had helped secure after the Iraqi Kurdish Civil War were getting some unwanted attention from the Defense Contract Audit Agency. He wanted me to "convince" the DCAA to look the other way. I refused, of course, but it was made abundantly clear to me that I did not have a say in the matter.

—What did you do?

—I bought a better suit. Then I met with the director of the DCAA.

—You just sat down with him.

—I thought I could persuade him.

—And?

—My powers of persuasion were not all that I thought them to be. He had me arrested, by the FBI this time.

—Was the senator able to get you out again?

—Indeed, he was. The director of the FBI came to see me personally. He took me out for a walk and asked if he could be of assistance. I told him I could use his help with the DCAA. The next day, the DCAA director was caught in some prostitution scandal and had to resign. After that, people in law enforcement and the intelligence community seemed to know who I was. I tried to find out what had happened at the FBI several times, to no avail. Years later, I was told that the director of the FBI received a call from the Oval Office saying that I worked for "an organization that has the best interests of the United States at heart." I have heard it worded in various ways, but that is the one I like the most.

—I assume you don't work for that senator anymore.

—Oh no. He died not long after that. Bone cancer.

—So who do you work for now if it's not him?

—Well, he was the only person who really knew anything about me. I had no name, a growing reputation in the intelligence community. I had a bank card. I traveled for a few months, then it occurred to me that, perhaps, I was in a unique position to effect some positive change in the world.

—It can't be just you. Are you telling me there's no secret worldwide organization pulling strings all over the world?

—I can tell you that if such an organization does exist, I have never heard of it. I certainly never worked for one. Over the years, I have made numerous connections all over the world, and the means at my disposal are considerably greater now than they once were, but I do not work *for* anyone, if that is what you are asking. I am what you would call . . . self-employed.

—I'm . . . That's insane! And it works? People believe you?

—Why would they not? I have what they want most.

—What's that?

—I offer tranquility of the mind. People choose to believe I am part of a greater entity because it lets everyone sleep better at night. The world we live in is terrifying. There is war, global warming, disease, poverty, terrorism. People are scared. Everyone is. That is especially true of powerful people. They are scared of the world and the part they play in it. They are petrified, paralyzed by responsibility, unable to choose for fear of making the wrong choice. I offer exoneration, peace of mind. I peddle God in the form of an all-knowing, all-powerful global institution that will right every wrong and keep the world safe.

—Why this project?

—Ah! In 1999, an incident on an archeological site in Turkey was brought to my attention. Evidence found onsite, though inconclusive, led me to believe that technologically advanced beings might have been present in the area several millennia ago.

—You knew? Who else was aware of this?

—I knew nothing. I suspected. When the NSA granted funding to your research project in Chicago, I became aware of your childhood discovery and I immediately took an interest.

More than anything, I saw this project as a potential legacy. What I do, it is . . . It takes a particular mindset. It is not unlike law enforcement in that regard. I started out thinking I could remove the bad from the world one piece at a time until there was none left. The world, unfortunately, does not work that way. Perhaps it needs a certain equilibrium to function properly. Whatever the reason, it soon became obvious that what I had set out to do was very much like digging a hole in the mud. Remove a bad man from power, and a year later the person you put in his place is just as corrupt. If a policeman stops a drunken man from beating on his wife, what are the odds he will never have to go back? Can he really prevent anything, or is he just delaying the inevitable? I came to realize that good and evil were out of my reach, that time was the only thing I had any control over. I could buy time, create intervals. I could not *truly* make the world a better place, but I could make part of it a better place for a short while. I came to peace with that. Some cannot. As I said, it takes a particular mindset.

But as you grow older, you realize there will come a time you cannot keep digging, and the idea that your hole in the mud will fill itself completely, as if you never existed, becomes harder to bear. Permanence is the Holy Grail in my line of work. I saw this as an opportunity to leave a mark.

—If you could go back in time—

—Perhaps I could.

—That's true. Do you wish things had been different?

—Besides the world coming to an end?

—That's not what I meant. Would you rather have lived a . . . normal life?

—I wish my son had never died. I wish my wife were still here. If I could not change that, I would probably choose the same path. It has not always been easy, but overall, I believe I have done more good than harm.

—I guess that's all any of us can ask for.

—I do have one regret.

—What's that?

—I wanted someone to continue what I started. I did not know that I would run out of time. I had hoped to find a successor, to take someone . . . under my wing. I was looking for—

—A son.

— . . . Perhaps. I wanted to leave some form of legacy. For a while, I thought Mr. Couture was a good candidate—

—He could still do it.

—He has a family now, a child. He has too much to lose. I was saying I thought Mr. Couture was a good candidate until I realized you were the ideal one.

—Me?

—**It had to be you. You are intelligent, dedicated. You do not have a family and you have expressed no desire for one. When I first met you, you were too naïve, too . . . fragile, but since your reappearance, you have become more resilient, less—**

—I tried to kill myself.

—**A momentary lapse in judgment. I meant to say you have become less . . . vulnerable to what the world has to throw at you. I can tell you that your former self would not have remained as collected as you were these past few days.**

—I don't give a shit anymore, is that what you're trying to say?

—**I said that you could replace me. That was never meant as a compliment.**

—I couldn't do what you do. I'm not . . . James Bond!

—**I was not looking for someone to blackmail world leaders. I wanted my replacement to safeguard the Themis Files, preserve a record of these world-changing events. That said, I have accumulated a tremendous amount of sensitive information. If you knew what I knew, you could get what you want from just about anyone.**

—Thank you, for thinking of me. I—

—**I am sorry to interrupt, but it appears we have run out of things to climb on. Shall we stand?**

—It's all over my feet. Do you feel anything?

—**Not at the moment.**

—What will happen to them? Your files?

—**I do not know. Everything I collected in my—I hesitate to call it a career—is on a hard drive in a safe-deposit box. The key and access card are in my jacket pocket. I can only hope that whoever recovers our bodies has a curious mind and an adventurous spirit. The most recent files are on a thumb drive, also in my jacket. Figuring out the password should be easy with this recording.**

—What is it?

—The name of my son.

—Tell me something more about you.

—What do you want to know?

—I don't know. Anything. Tell me how you met Eugene. You two seem to be close.

—That is a very interesting story but also a very long one. It was an honor knowing you, Dr. Franklin . . . —*cough*

—Sir?

Sir?—*cough*

. . .

. . .

FILE NO. 1588

MISSION LOG—VINCENT COUTURE, CONSULTANT, EARTH DEFENSE CORPS
Location: EDC Headquarters, New York, NY

—This is Vincent Couture. I'm in the control room next to hangar one. Everyone's gone. I sent them to UN headquarters. They'll be safe on the top floors if they get there in time. I hope Rose makes it. She was in the lab when the robot appeared. That's a lot farther from the main building.

I'm taking the backup drives from the safe. Some comm gear. I'm not sure what else I can grab before I head out. Hopefully, the building won't be destroyed and it doesn't matter.

I wish I could fight that thing. A whole lot of people have died already but it's different when it's home. Our neighbors, the dry-cleaning guy across the street, I wonder if any of them will survive. Probably not. I feel bad that I have a way out and they don't. I can't believe I'm saying this but I even feel sorry for the asshole at the coffee shop who keeps hitting on Kara. I'm heading to hangar one now. I'll take Themis up north in case that robot decides to rip her apart.

Crap! Almost forgot. Gotta make a quick stop by our lockers. Kara left some personal stuff in hers: an old picture of her mom, some trinkets I gave her. I have a signed picture of David Prowse in mine. Oh, and my wedding ring's in there. *That's* why I'm going. If I die out here, tell my wife I went back for my wedding ring. She'll be impressed.

—She'll think you're a complete idiot.

—Kara? Is that you? Oh my God! Come here, you're crazy!

—OK, stop! You're choking me.

—Sorry.

—Vincent, meet Eva. Eva, this is Vincent.

— . . .

—Vincent? You OK?

—Yeah . . .

—Then say something, either of you.

—It's nice to meet you, Eva. Would you like to see Themis?

[*She's here?*]

I'll take that as a yes—

—Vincent, there's a lot I need to tell you.

—I know. Our "friend" filled me in.

—That asshole, I'll—

—Later. We *really* need to go. There's a big robot shooting poisonous gas about a mile away from here. Eva, it's that way.

—How long do we have?

—I don't know. It travels fast. Three minutes maybe? Is she . . . ?

—I can't say for sure. She kinda looks like me, don't you think?

—Not *kinda*. It's a bit eerie.

—Shhh. She's right behind us!

—Does she know?

—No. I haven't told her. She's been through enough already. She's . . . she's a bit dark.

—How dark? "Dark" like her favorite band is The Cure? Or I'm-an-abomination-I-should-be-burned-alive-Rose-dark?

—She's . . . She's not what you'd expect. One minute she's a normal ten-year-old, the next it's like—

—Like what?

—She talks about people dying, how they felt. She's . . . dark. She saw her parents die.

—Poor kid.

—Yeah. The Russians got there before me. Three men broke in in the middle of the night. They killed her parents right in front of her.

—Where did you find her?

—In Haiti.

—Haiti? How the hell did you end up there?

—I knew they couldn't take her back on a commercial flight and there were no private planes there with Russian tags. I figured they'd hop islands and fly out of Cuba. My plan was to go from port to port, hoping someone would remember three big men with a weird accent. I got lucky on the first try, right there in San Juan. They had chartered a boat to the Dominican Republic. I ran into the captain's wife on the docks. I caught up to them at Punta Cana and followed them across the island all the way to Port-au-Prince.

—How'd you get her back? Please tell me you didn't fight three KGB agents.

—I think they were mercs. And no. I paid the Haitian police to arrest them. That reminds me, we don't have any money left.

—Oh great. My wife spent all our savings on crooked cops.

—Not all of it. I had to rent a car.

[*Whoa.*]

—Yep. Here we are! She looks bigger in person, doesn't she? How'd you like to go inside, Eva?

[*Really?*]

Yep. For real. Let's go for a ride.

—Are you sure we can walk Themis away from here? We can't fight with Eva on board.

—Oh, we're not walking . . . There are a few things I need to tell you too. By the way, how could you leave while I was missing?

—I thought she was in danger.

—And not me? I was stuck at the bottom of the ocean!

—Really?

—Yeah, but my point was—

—I didn't know what to do! All I did was watch other people trying to find you. I was in the way, I felt . . . Shit!

—What?

—The elevator doesn't work—

—I was afraid of that. I think the power went out like five minutes ago.

—But the lights are on!

—Yeah. I heard the generator kick in when I walked in the control room. I guess the elevator isn't on it. You know what that means—

—Can you do it?

—We're about to find out. Every time we go up the elevator, I look at that ladder and I think: "Who would be stupid enough to climb up that thing?"

—Eva, the elevator doesn't work, so we'll have to climb up that big ladder. Vincent'll go first. You follow him.

—Why do I need to go first?

—Trust me, Vincent. If you have someone's feet too close to your head, you'll wanna look down, and you don't wanna look down.

[*I'm scared.*]

—That makes two of us, Eva.

—Vincent's afraid of heights. You'll have to keep him calm. Go Vincent! We don't have all day! OK, now it's your turn Eva. Just keep your eyes on Vincent. I'll be right behind you.

—How high is the hatch again?

—Think about something else. You said you were at the bottom of the ocean?

—I'm not sure if talking about the time I thought I was going to die is the best thing to keep me from thinking about how I'm going to die.

—Never mind then. Are your palms sweaty? Those bars can get slippery when they're wet.

—Ha! Ha! Very funny. Eva, how do you say asshole in Spanish?

—Don't answer that, Eva. He just wants some attention. Speaking of assholes, Vincent, you said Mr. Warm and Fuzzy filled you in?

—Yeah he did. I think he felt bad you had to learn of all this from Ryan of all people.

—Fuck him.

—I told him you'd be mad.

—I'm not mad. I just don't wanna see him again. Ever.

—Good. Glad I was wrong. I hate it when you're angry.

—You're not? He lied to you too, you know.

—He didn't exactly . . . You know what? We're being rude. Let's talk about something else. Eva, I don't know the first thing about you. Tell me something, anything.

[*I don't—*]

Come on! It'll keep your mind off that ladder. Never mind that, it'll keep *my* mind off that ladder. I don't know about you but I'm scared shitless, in a . . . really . . . manly way. Tell me something interesting.

[*Hmmm . . . Do you know who I was named after?*]

I'd say Eva Perón.

—Eva's from Puerto Rico, Vincent, not Argentina.

[*I was named after a robot.*]

—That *is* interesting.

—Oh yeah. You have his attention *now*.

[*I was born on the day of the parade when the EDC was created. My parents were the biggest geeks ever, huge science-fiction fans. Themis was the greatest thing they'd ever seen. They wanted to name me after her, but they somehow thought everyone would start naming their kid Themis, so they named me after another big robot.*]

A robot?

[*Yes. Eva's a common name in Spanish, but apparently, it's also the name of a giant robot, from a Japanese anime they really liked. It's old. I never saw it.*]

—Eva is for Evangelion? That is so cool!

—Of course, Vincent knows all about it.

—Yeah! It's awesome! But ours is bigger.

—Eva, I think you have a fan now.

—I . . . *We* have it on DVD, you know.

—Oh, do we?

—Yep.

—OK! OK! If Eva's never seen it, we can watch it together . . . He's smiling, isn't he?

[*Yes. So are you.*]

I guess I am—

—Well, it's not as cool as being named after a giant robot, but I was also named after a TV character.

—Really? Who?

—Ron Perlman, with makeup. My mom told me once how much she liked watching *Beauty and the Beast* while she was pregnant with me. It was in French, of course, and whoever dubbed Linda Hamilton had a really phony accent, but my mom loved it when she called the Beast by name. Oh *Vincent*! That's where she got the name.

—How come you never told me that?

—I kinda forgot, to be honest.

—Your parents named you after the Beast. That's strange.

—Oh, I said that's where my mom got the name. I'm sure she never told my dad. He never would have gone along with that. Though I can't imagine my father spending much time looking for baby names. She was probably on her own for this.

[*Hey, guys? There's white stuff storming into the room below us.*]

Shit!

—That's what I thought. Vincent, can you pick up the pace a little?

—I'm going as fast as I can. How fast is the room filling with gas?

—Well, it's higher than it was a second ago. I'd say fast. Eva, try to go a little—

[*AHHHH!*]

It's OK. I got you.

[*Are you OK?*]

I'm fine. Your shoe almost tore my ear off, but I'll live.

—Is everyone all right? I don't want to look down.

—We're fine, Vincent! Keep climbing! Go Eva! Go! I'll catch you if you fall.

[*Kara?*]

Yes.

[*You should take my place. I'll go behind you.*]

We're almost there, Eva. Vincent, a couple more and that's it.

—I'm at the top. I can't reach the hatch.

—It's a couple feet away. You have to hold on with one hand.

—I can't!

—Sure you can! Hold on with your left hand and stretch your right arm.

—I can't reach it.

—You have to look, Vincent. Hurry! There! Just a bit to the right. You got it. Now climb down one step and grab the ledge.

—I'm scared!

—You got this! Let go of your left hand and push with your legs. Hard! Yes! You got it! Climb in and I'll give you Eva! . . . Eva, I want you to lean against the shaft. Put your legs on that bar here and let me climb between you and the ladder. See, I got you. Vincent, we're running out of time, I'm gonna hold her with my right arm and give her to you. You have to grab her.

—Hurry, the smoke's right below you.

—I know! Are you ready? Ready Eva? Go! Grab her! Grab her! Do you have her?

—Yes! Come on Eva! Get inside.

—There's no time, Vincent. Close the hatch behind her.

—Kara, don't be stupid! Come on Eva, pull yourself in. I have to get past you to get Kara. Hold on, Kara! I'm coming.

—There's no time.

—Yes there is! Just one sec!

—You're a father now. Take care of her.

—No DON'T!

—I love you.

—Don't close the hatch! KARA! NO!

[*Stop.*]

KARAAA! Eva, move out of the way!

[*No. Don't.*]

I said MOVE!

[*We'll die if you open that door.*]

That's your mother out there!

[*I know. But she's gone now.*]

PART FOUR

NEXT OF KIN

FILE NO. 1591

PERSONAL JOURNAL ENTRY—
VINCENT COUTURE, CONSULTANT,
EARTH DEFENSE CORPS

Don't be stupid.

That's the last thing I told Kara, the last thing I said to my wife. I didn't say I love you, I told her she was an idiot. It doesn't make sense . . . That's not how it was supposed to go. She's not supposed to be dead. I . . . All I had to do was to get inside Themis a second sooner, climb a little faster. That's not how it was supposed to happen . . . I swore I would never let anyone down because I wasn't strong enough. But I was afraid, and I wasn't fast enough, and now she's dead. She knew. She knew before we started climbing. That's why she went last.

I shouldn't have been there to begin with. I should have been with her. I was the one who . . . I told her a million times how much I wanted children. She thought I couldn't go, so she went after our child. What did I do? Nothing. I found out and I stayed behind. I didn't go help my wife. I didn't go find my daughter. They said they were sending someone, and I said . . . OK! I'm a coward. I'm a fraud.

Certainly not a dad. What a joke! I'm nothing. Parents are supposed to protect their children. I can't do that. I couldn't protect my wife. I never could. She was the one protecting me. That kid ran out of parents the moment Kara closed that hatch. Crazy thing is, I would have opened it again. I would have opened that hatch without hesitation, and we'd all be dead. I would have killed my wife *and* my daughter on the same day. But Eva stopped me. She's ten and she saved *me*.

I don't know how I convinced myself I could do this. In my mind, it was so . . .

It was about me. I'd hold my baby girl and be filled with pride seeing how safe she felt in my arms. I would show her the things I knew about the world, and she'd listen, wide-eyed and smiling. I'd be there for her when she needed me, and it would feel good to be there for her. And I'd never yell, and I'd listen, and I'd feel great about seeing how happy she was. I'd be a great dad. We'd be a great family, like the Tremblays across the street when I was eight years old. Their kid was my age, and he played baseball, and he was good at it. His parents never fought—or so I thought—and they were always smiling. We weren't friends, but I went over for a few hours one summer. He had a pool. We ate KFC in the middle of the afternoon. I wanted to be him. I wanted his family. Maybe that's what I've been chasing the whole time.

Kara knew what it would be like. She knew what it would take, and she knew I wasn't ready. She'd have been better off with Ryan. I hate that asshole more than anyone in the world, but maybe that's why. He wouldn't have climbed slow and he wouldn't have climbed first. He'd have carried them both if he had to.

Now the world is ending and somehow I've managed to make that about me too. Millions of people are dead, so my grief isn't that special. But I've killed the one person who was needed to save the world. Themis can't fight anymore. She's a paperweight now. I do my best to avoid going outside. I can't stand to look at her. I can't bear the thought of walking into that sphere and seeing Kara's gear hanging from the ceiling. I always had my back to her in there but I could feel her presence behind me. I would follow her voice, her breathing. There's no Themis without Kara.

I'm useless here now. I can't help Rose. I can't help Eva. I don't know what I'm supposed to do.

FILE NO. 1593

DISCOURSE TO THE UNITED NATIONS GENERAL ASSEMBLY—BRIGADIER GENERAL EUGENE GOVENDER, COMMANDER, EARTH DEFENSE CORPS

Location: UN Headquarters, Geneva, Switzerland

Mr. President, Mr. Secretary General, members of the General Assembly, ladies and gentlemen. I am here today . . . I am here today to tell you . . . Ah, to hell with my notes!

I was asked to provide a summary of our current situation, but you already know we're in deep shit. We're up to our eyeballs in it. There are thirteen alien robots on Earth. All of them have the ability to transport themselves anywhere on the planet in a nanosecond. They can also release a gaseous substance that kills, almost instantly, 99.95 percent of the human population in a twenty-mile radius, all in a matter of minutes. I should point out it *only* kills humans; cats, birds, bugs, they're all fine. Each robot has done so twice in the last five days, except for the one in Madrid, which didn't get a chance. As of now, London, Tokyo, Jakarta, Delhi, Cairo, Calcutta, Paris, Mexico City, São Paulo, Johannesburg—I need to catch my breath—Beijing, Seoul, Mumbai, Buenos Aires, Istanbul, Karachi, Bangalore, Shenzhen, Santiago, Kinshasa, Riyadh, Kuala Lumpur, Sydney, and New York are all ghost towns. Moscow is in ruins, with a population of zero. Madrid is now a crater.

You may also have heard rumors that we lost one of our pilots. The rumors are true. Captain Kara Resnik is dead. She died in New

York two days ago. We're working on a contingency plan, but it's a long shot at best. That means, for now, we can't use Themis for anything but transport. We can teleport her, but she can't walk. And she can't fight. Right now, she's lying in the woods, covered with branches and a whole lot of camo netting.

The alien robots are immune to . . . well, to everything we've got. Just ask India how effective their ground assault was. Russia dropped more firepower on Moscow than they did during World War II. It didn't do anything. A nuke didn't work. Let me say that again. *A nuke didn't work.* Half of Europe will glow in the dark for the next decade or so, but the Madrid robot's still standing. I told you people all of that the last time we met, but you didn't listen. You got scared, and you did stupid things like scared people do. You need to stop that now. Stop fighting. You can't win! They are better than us. Stronger. *They* have the upper hand.

I see by your faces you were hoping for something a little more positive. There's nothing rosy about the situation. There are over one hundred million dead—one hundred million. Probably a lot more coming. Civil liberties have been curtailed, everywhere. Most of the governments represented here have imposed some form of martial law. We're losing lives. We're losing our way of life. We're losing, big-time.

I lost someone . . . someone very close to me. He's the reason I'm standing here today. He got me into this mess. I didn't want this job. I didn't want to be a general either, but I understand the army. This? I'm a soldier. The last thing I wanted was to deal with you people. But he thought that was a good thing, and he convinced me. For those of you who know who I'm talking about, you know how convincing he could be. To be honest with you, I was really counting on him to make everything better. He won't. He's dead. Lots of people are. I came *this* close to losing my whole family. I didn't. I was lucky. I know some of you weren't that lucky. You have my deepest sympathy. A lot of people are grieving today. There isn't anything I could say that would make it . . . better.

The only piece of good news I have is that they've stopped killing us for now. It's been thirty-six hours. They stopped shooting out gas, all of them. They're not moving around. They're not doing anything.

Why? I don't have a goddamn clue. Maybe they're waiting to see if we'll nuke ourselves into oblivion. How long will it last? I don't know that either.

So . . . Why am I here? What do I want? Before I can answer that, we have to talk about the giant elephant in the room. Why should you listen to me? What good is the EDC without its only weapon? Well, I don't know if we're good for anything! I don't know that anyone is. What I do know, and what I told you before, is that *if* there's a solution to the goddamn mess we're in, it won't be a military one, it'll come from our science team. We don't have a big robot we can use anymore, but we still have what matters most: smart people. Big brains! They're working right now, in a cave, trying to save this world. Let them do their job.

There might be a way to stop these things. There might be a way to neutralize that gas. Even if we can't, roughly one out of every two thousand people survives it. They do more than survive. They're completely immune to the alien gas. We have no idea why. I'd call them lucky, but most of them have had to watch their loved ones die in front of them. Still, if we can replicate whatever makes them . . . not die . . . Well, I'm sure all of you would like to have that pill.

There's a . . . security guard in the garage at the EDC; not sure what his name is. This morning, just before I left, he said: "You know, sir, they might just leave." Seemed so goddamn naïve. I felt like slapping him on the back of the head. It must have shown because he got all defensive, and he said: "They might!" You know what? He's right! They might leave! Truth is we know nothing about these people. We don't know why they're here. We don't know what they're thinking. We don't know *how* they're thinking and we might not understand it if we did. I'll keep working on the assumption that they won't because it would make no sense for them to pack their bags now. But it doesn't have to make sense. If there's one thing we should have learned by now, it's that we're not the greatest thing in the universe, certainly not the smartest. Seems logical there'd be a great many things in it we can't comprehend.

I do have hope. I believe there is a solution out there, waiting. There's always a solution, at least that's what I think. If we don't survive this, it's because we'll have been too stupid, too selfish, too greedy to find it.

I realize I've been wrong about one thing this whole time. I've let my ego get in the way. I thought . . . I still think our best hope for survival is with the EDC. I thought you people were just getting in the way. I forgot that the EDC is supposed to be an extension of this room, that you're all a part of it, in a way. It was stupid of me to ask you to stand aside and do nothing. God knows I couldn't. I know you're all as vested in this as we are. I know you wanna help.

This morning, I've asked my people to share all the data we had on the alien gas with each and every one of your governments. You should have it by now. I know many of you were working on a cure already, but if you weren't, get your best people on it. Hell, get your *worst* people on it. You never know. We will also share everything we have on the alien robots, all of it. We'll make that data available to everyone. Our data should be on the EDC website this evening. Tell the world. The key to our survival might be in the hands of a really smart kid, somewhere. Make sure he knows. That is what I want from you. Help us. Do not send your armies to die in vain. Do not launch more missiles. Help us.

I *have* hope.

That's all I have to say. Now go home. Go home and tell your family you love them. Tell them ten times, a hundred times. Do it while you can. And if we somehow survive this, keep doing it. In the end, it's all that really matters.

INTERVIEW WITH VINCENT COUTURE, CONSULTANT, EARTH DEFENSE CORPS
Location: Shadow Government Bunker, Lenexa, KS

—You can sit down Vincent.

—Thank you Rose. Can I still call you Rose?

—Why wouldn't you?

—I don't know. You're in his chair. You're taping this. Feels weird to have you sitting in front of me and not him.

—Believe me, it feels a lot stranger being on this side of the table.

—Are you sure he's dead?

—I was there, Vincent.

—I know. I just thought . . . I thought he'd be able to weasel his way out of this, twist God's arm, tell him he had nude pictures of him or something.

—He was very human in the end. He really liked you, you know?

—Yeah . . . I thought so. He . . . When I woke up in the hospital after Ryan crushed my legs into a wall, he was there sitting by my bed. He must have been sitting there for hours. He could have asked the hospital staff to call him, but he chose to stay. For years, I tried to figure out what he had to gain. Over time, I . . . I guess I got used to the idea that he might have just cared. Then again, maybe he thought gaining my trust was important for the project. Who knows?

—Probably a bit of both. But he did care. Strange as it may seem, you were the closest thing he had to family.

—He called me Mr. Couture.

—That was a sign of respect.

—Strange man. I wish I knew something about him, who he was.

— . . . Me too.

—Rose, I—

—What is it?

—I don't want you to take this the wrong way. I'm so happy, relieved, that you're here, that you're safe, but how—

—How did I survive the gas? I'm not sure. Alyssa's back from London. She's analyzing my blood now. I assume I have the same genetic anomalies that every other survivor has.

—Does that mean you're . . . ?

—An alien? Part alien? I don't know. I guess so. I was having a hard time figuring out who I was before. This is just—

—Could they have altered your DNA when they . . . brought you back?

—Ten years ago, they said my genetic profile was an exact match to . . . well, to mine, to hers. They said I was me. It's possible they missed something back then. I won't know until Alyssa runs more tests. To be honest, it would be a relief, somehow. If I weren't really Rose Franklin . . . I know how this sounds, but—

—You'd have a reason to feel the way you do. You'd know you're not . . . crazy. I'm sorry. That's not what I meant.

—No, no! That's exactly what *I* meant. Thank you. On the other hand, if I was one of them, if I had some alien blood to begin with, it would explain why they chose to bring me back from the dead.

—Seems like a lot of trouble to go through to save a distant cousin. I think you guys may be wrong on this whole alien thing.

—Maybe. I wish I had a better explanation. We keep talking about me, but how are you holding up?

—I'm . . . I don't know how I feel. I'm still . . . numb.

—If anyone could cheat death, I thought it would be Kara.

—I know, right? Spit in its face. Kick it in the teeth. It's my fault she's dead, you know?

—Vincent, there's—

—No, no. It's true. If I'd climbed the ladder a tiny bit faster, if I hadn't been scared of heights, if I'd reached the hatch on the first try . . . There are so many things I could have done. I just had to get up there—what?—two, three seconds faster. Kara would still be alive. I'd have a wife. Eva would have . . . someone to call Mom. But I didn't, and she fell. She's dead. She doesn't exist anymore. She was a person. Now she's not.

I'm smart enough to know I haven't quite come to terms with what happened yet. I can say it, I can explain it, you know. Kara's dead. My wife's dead. But it's not *real* yet. I can't believe I'm telling you this—I feel like an asshole for thinking it—but what bothers me most, now, is not knowing what she was thinking when she fell. Did she blame me? I don't want her last thoughts to have been how her husband killed her. Awful, isn't it? How selfish is that? *Moi, moi, moi!*

When I killed you ten years ago—

—Vincent, don't.

—Please, let me finish. I've killed you, so some of this feels familiar, but with you, it hit me right away. I felt it. The pain, the guilt. The realization that you'll never feel any of what you felt with that person ever again. Might be because it's the end of the world, but it all feels like a movie now. It's . . . muffled.

I see her fall over and over again in my head, so I'm sure it'll sink in at some point. The hatch was closed, but I can *see* her. I don't think the image would be any clearer if I'd been watching. She's falling backwards into the void, her arms spread. She fades into a sea of white smoke. Then she's gone. Repeat. She's falling backwards into the void, her arms spread. She fades into a sea of white smoke. Repeat.

—Did you cry?

—Did I cry? I cried when it happened, inside Themis. I cried for a long time. But no, I haven't cried since. Why do you ask?

—I haven't cried either. Kara's really the closest thing I had to a best friend. I could try and explain how much she meant to me, but it doesn't matter. *I* know. But I haven't cried. I watched a man die, right in front of me, thought I was next. How many people died in New York? Two, three million? Kara died. Today I'm here setting up the lab. All in a day's work. Don't torture yourself, Vincent. Nothing feels real anymore. Nothing.

What are you smiling about?

—I was thinking about Kara. It's just . . . never mind. Stupid memories.

—No, I wanna know.

—Did I ever tell you about our wedding night?

—Tell me. Well, not everything.

—Oh, I can tell you the whole thing. I spent the night with a traveling salesman. Bob. No really, that was his name. There was a reception at the hotel after the ceremony, but as soon as people started leaving, Kara dragged me and some of her childhood friends to this bar where they used to hang out. Shitty place, but we had a good time. I danced with her friends.

—Kara doesn't dance.

—No she doesn't. But she beat everyone at the pool table. Kara can . . . Kara could play. She loved playing pool. Her friends were buying her drinks, lots of drinks. Never the same one. That's what happens when you take a bunch of grown-up people with jobs and families and you let them pretend they're twenty years younger for a few hours. They get stupid real fast. Kara threw up on the pool table after a shot of . . . I don't remember what it was. Something nasty. We got kicked out, of course. I had to use the conspiracy puker to talk the staff into letting us back in.

—I'm sorry. The "conspiracy puker"?

—Oh, you don't know that one.

—I've never been kicked out of a bar.

—I told them we were having a good time, minding our own business, when this kid with a White Sox baseball cap bumped into us and threw up on my feet. Right on my shoes. I went to the bathroom to clean it up, but Kara was so grossed out she threw up herself. You know. What kind of establishment are you guys running? People throwing up on other people's shoes! This is my wedding night!

—Did they let you back in?

—Of course. Twenty minutes later, Kara got into a fight with two guys who were harassing a girl. She didn't even know the girl, they just pissed her off. They took it outside, so we didn't get thrown out again.

—Did Kara win?

—What do you think? Kara can't handle her liquor, but she can take two assholes anytime. Could. But she fell on a piece of broken glass, cut her hand pretty bad.

We took a cab to the hotel. We were both done for. Kara could barely walk. She was bleeding. We must have been pretty loud because we woke up Bob in the next room trying to get our door to open with that stupid plastic card. He was pissed at first but then he saw Kara's hand. It was a pretty nasty cut. He said we had to disinfect that thing and put a proper bandage on it—she'd Scotch-taped a few napkins on her hand at the bar before we left. We sat in the corridor while Bob went to the lobby to get a first-aid kit. They didn't have anything, so we put Kara on the couch in Bob's room and he drove me around town looking for a CVS or anything else that was open. By the time we got back, Kara was sound asleep. I tried to wake her up, but she was just gone. We cleaned her hand and put a nice white bandage on it—well, Bob did—and we let her sleep. I stayed up with Bob. He didn't know who we were, so we emptied the minibar talking about what it's like to sell plumbing supplies across the Midwest. Fun night.

—I'm sorry your wedding night didn't go as planned.

—No, I meant it! It was a fun night.

—I miss her. So much.

—She loved you like a sister.

— . . . What about Eva? That's her name, right? How is she?

—Eva is . . . Eva's OK . . . I guess. She knew. Somehow she knew Kara was her mother.

—How did she know?

—I have no idea. I haven't talked to her about it. I figured that meant she also knew about me, that I'm her father, and I can't be *that* right now.

—You're gonna have to be *something* to her, Vincent. You're all she's got.

—That's . . . what I wanted to talk to you about. I—

—What is it?

—I'd like you to take care of her.

—Vincent, this is—

—Just for a while. I need to get away from all this.

—She needs you.

—I'm no good to her right now.

—Vincent, the parents she's known all her life were killed right in front of her. Then she somehow figures out Kara's her biological mother, and she has to watch her die the very next day. Now the world's coming to an end and she's all alone in an underground military base. She needs her father, not some strange woman she's never met. She needs you, and I don't think she can wait until you get over your grief. You don't know how to be a father right now? Fine! I'm sure she has no idea how to be your daughter either. You're just gonna have to figure this out together.

—I'm not saying I'll give her the silent treatment for the rest of her life. I'm not ready to be her father now, today.

—Vincent, I don't think you're listening. No one cares whether you're ready or not. It's not up to you. You're her father, you can't change that.

— . . .

—What would Kara say?

—That's not fair. I don't know how! I can't! I think the kid is doing better than I am anyway.

—Like I said, I haven't met her yet.

—You haven't asked her to try Kara's station?

—She's a minor, Vincent. I would need her parents to sign off on it. That's you.

—You haven't asked me either.

—I was afraid you'd say yes.

—You don't want her to try?

—Oh, I want her to try. I'm curious, like everyone else. Part of me also wants us to put up a fight. But if it were my daughter, I wouldn't let her go anywhere *near* that robot.

—I wanna fight them too. I don't want us to go quietly. I . . . I want to avenge Kara more than anything. But I don't want Eva's life to be just that. Violence.

—What will you do?

—I have no idea.

—You said you needed to get away. Take her with you.

—And go where?

—Anywhere you want.

—I could—

—What?

—I could, maybe, take her back to Canada, find a quiet place, as far away from the city as possible. You know, try to give her something that feels like a normal life, even if it's only for a short while.

—That's a beautiful idea.

—No it's not. It's a stupid idea. It's a movie scene: small wooden shack, by a creek. Young girl playing in the grass. I'm not a farmer. Even if I were, I won't buy a farm! We'll end up sleeping in my car, begging for food.

—You don't have a car.

—I don't have papers to cross the border with a ten-year-old either.

—I'm not sure people care about these things anymore.

—Oh, they care. I'm not the only one who thought Canada might be safer. There are tens of thousands of people massing at the border. So far, they've used tear gas, rubber bullets. About a dozen people were killed. I don't think they're letting anyone through, even with the right papers.

—You can stay here. It doesn't have a creek, or grass, but it's safe, at least for the moment.

—Not sure how safe it is for Eva. I don't think they'll just let her leave.

—Who is "they"? Eugene is in Geneva trying to stop everyone from bombing their own people. It's just me running this place right now.

—There's a guard on Eva's door.

—Why?

—You know why. We're guests here, Rose. You may be running what's left of the EDC, but this is an American base, full of American soldiers, and they don't take orders from us.

FILE NO. 1597

INTERVIEW WITH MR. BURNS, OCCUPATION UNKNOWN

Location: New Dynasty Chinese Restaurant, Dupont Circle, Washington, DC

—Good morning, Ms. Franklin. Can I call you Rose? I've heard so much about you!

—Of course. What do you want me to call you?

—Mr. Burns will do just fine. I'd like to keep *some* anonymity. Half of it anyway.

—You have something in common with . . . with our mutual friend.

—We have a lot more in common than you think. He will be missed. I don't know by *whom*, but he will be missed. I'll certainly miss his sense of humor. He was a funny guy!

—I'm not sure "funny guy" is how I would describe him.

—Maybe you just need a better sense of humor. I was surprised to get a call from you. I was even more surprised you knew about this place.

—He had it in his notes.

—You read his notes? I'm so jealous! What did it say?

—New Dynasty, Dupont Circle. Mr. Burns. Kung pao chicken.

—What else did it say? Do you know who killed Kennedy?

—There was nothing under "K."

—Too bad. You should look at the menu. Our waitress will be here soon.

—I assume I should have the kung pao chicken.

—It might not be ready. I've never been here this early. I'm surprised they're even open, given all that's going on.

—I'm sorry. I really needed to talk to you.

—Sure! Talk! What can I do for you, Rose Franklin?

—Am I? Rose Franklin?

—I certainly hope so! Otherwise I'm at the wrong table, and the lady over there looks mean. Look at her! She looks like she's about to stab someone with her fork.

—She could be a really nice person. There are a lot of friendly-looking people who aren't at all.

—You might be right. We do discriminate a lot based on first impressions. Except for that woman. I know she's just mean. Look at those eyes! Ah! Finally!

[*Are you ready to order?*]

Yes! My friend here would like the kung pao chicken. I'll have . . . Oh, what the hell, make that two. Two cooling teas.

[*It'll be right up!*]

Thank you!

—You haven't answered my question.

—Really? "Am I Rose Franklin?" You came all the way to Washington to ask me *that*?

—He said you would—

—I said I would talk to you and explain what happened as best I could. That was before people started dying by the million! But now? Boohoo! I'm not meeee! Seriously, who cares?

—I care.

—You know, our "friend" was a lot more fun! You had a car accident and you woke up a bit later than you thought you would. That's what happened to you. Can we move on?

—He said I was a copy.

—Oh, crap. I thought you, at least, could understand. If it makes you feel any better, I used the same device that brought you back to transport myself a dozen times. You don't hear me whining about it. I'm a copy of a copy!

—It's important to me. I need to know.

—All right . . . You think you have a soul. You think you're special. The idea that you could just be a big pile of matter makes you feel unimportant. Well, you're not special, no more special than every other magnificent thing in the universe.

—That's not—

—Don't interrupt. Just give me a sec. I have something to show you . . . Here! Do you know what this is?

—That's a picture of the Pillars of Creation. It's a giant mass of gas and dust in the Eagle Nebula. That picture was taken by Hubble some years ago.

—So you know it!

—I love that picture. I was always fascinated by it.

—What do you love about it?

—It's a stellar nursery. The gas clouds in that region collapse on themselves to form new stars.

—It's big, isn't it?

—Oh yes.

—How big?

—The nebula? I don't know exactly. Probably *trillions* of miles.

—OK, so it's a very big pile of dust. What do you find so fascinating about it?

—Well, that's it! It's a huge cloud, larger than anything we can imagine. Yet it's just a tiny speck in the universe. And it spits out stars! Stars that will have planets.

—And some of these planets will have life! And some of that life will be sentient.

—Yes! It's awe-inspiring. It's—

—God?

—Maybe.

—It's also gone, you know. The Pillars of Creation. They were probably long gone by the time the light from it made it all the way here for that picture.

—Probably.

—Well, you, Rose Franklin, are made of the exact same stuff as the Pillars of Creation. No more. No less. That's how special and insignificant you are.

— . . .

—That's all I'm gonna say about it. I hope that's enough for you to learn to live with your soulless self. I, and some associates of mine, took a high-resolution scan of you when you got into that car crash—

—You were there?

—I held your head, so you wouldn't bang it on the door. After you died, we used that scan to reconstruct you. Whether or not you existed before makes absolutely no difference. I swear to you, you are as much who you are as you ever were.

—I—

—Yes?

—Do you always carry a picture of the Eagle Nebula in your wallet?

—I do!

—Why?

—I like the colors. Can we talk about something fun, now? I really miss the other guy, you know.

—Why save me? Why bring me back?

—Hmm, let me think. So that you'd be less dead. I think that was the idea.

—But why me?

—I'm beginning to wonder myself. Because you're important.

—He told me the same thing before he died. I'm not! I'm not a messiah. You just told me I'm not special at all. *Insignificant*, you said.

—I didn't say you were the second coming. Maybe *important* wasn't the right word. *Useful?* How's that? Are you OK with being useful?

—Useful how? I know this has something to do with the aliens coming, but . . . I'm not . . . I'm not smart enough to do this on my own.

—Well, you're not *that* smart, but you are smart enough. *Just* enough. This isn't an intelligence contest, you know. If we wanted a genius, we would have picked your colleague, Alyssa what's her name?

—You picked me?

—Geez! Louise! You're really not that smart! No wonder we had to help you.

—Help me?

—It never struck you as . . . *convenient* that you fell on a giant hand as a child, then ended up studying that same hand, as part of your very first job?

—What are you saying?

—I'm saying that A-minus students from one of the most unrecognized schools in the country aren't often admitted to major research universities.

—You mean you got me in at the U. of C.?

—Getting you into the right school was the easy part. Getting you to study physics—

—I don't believe you. I always liked science, ever since I can remember.

—You were good at it. We just made sure you had the opportunity to figure that out.

—...

—You can talk now. I was done with that sentence.

—You just told me I don't have a soul, that it doesn't matter if I'm a copy or not, that my entire life has been orchestrated for me, and that I didn't really deserve any of the things I'm most proud of. I . . . I'm not certain how I'm supposed to react.

—Meh, deserve, schmeserve. You're allowed to be proud. You did all the things you did on your own. I didn't do your homework for you. I didn't find that robot. You just needed a little nudge from time to time, to point you in the right direction.

—But why me? Why am I . . . useful?

—Oh, I wasn't gonna tell you more, but now that you've asked me twice!

—...

—Now, do you have anything interesting to ask me? You know, something that might not be entirely about you?

—Why did the alien robots stop moving around? Why did they stop shooting gas?

—That *is* an interesting question.

—Then why?

—I have no idea. You'd have to ask them. Maybe they're on a break. Maybe they're unionized. Maybe they're giving you a chance to respond.

—I don't understand. To respond to what?

—How should *I* know? But they're killing a whole lot of people. They must have a reason.

—They might be angry that we used Themis in North Korea. He thought they didn't want us to kill one another with their weapon. They might be angry just because we have her. Maybe we weren't supposed to find Themis.

—Like I told our friend, they couldn't care less whether you kill one another, with or without their weapon. Besides, it would be pretty stupid to kill millions of people because you might kill some people. They really don't like to interfere in the affairs of others.

—They don't like to interfere? They're wiping us out! I'd call that interference.

—Then maybe they're looking for an excuse to stop.

—Why do I get the feeling you want to help us but you also don't want to help us?

—That sentence makes absolutely no sense. Do you know the story of the fisherman and the seagull?

—Please. I would love to hear it.

—Oh! Now I'm beginning to like you! Here it goes. There was a king crab fisherman in Alaska. Every morning during the fall, he took his little fishing boat to sea to catch some king crab. He and his crew would visit every spot where they had dropped a trap—they call them pots—lift it up, grab the crabs that were the right size, throw in some bait, and send the pot back to the bottom. One day, the fisherman was sorting through the crabs in a pot when he noticed one of the little crabs—the ones that get thrown back in—wasn't a crab at all. It was an oyster. The fisherman opened it and, lo and behold, found the most beautiful pearl inside.

He thought of how the pearl would change his life, of everything he would buy for his wife and kids, then he put the pearl in a small box next to the boat's wheel and went on with his day. While he was sorting through another pot of crabs, a seagull landed on the ship's wheel, grabbed the pearl from the box with its beak, and flew away before the fisherman could do anything about it. He was . . . destroyed. His dreams crushed. Soon his despair turned to anger. He became convinced that the seagull had stolen the pearl only to hurt him, that all seagulls were creatures of evil, feathered demons out to steal the dreams of man.

Of course, the seagull just thought it was a piece of food it could feed its newborns with. Back at the nest, none of the baby seagulls were able to chew the pearl, so it just lay there—something shiny for the baby birds to look at while waiting for mom and dad to return.

The fisherman tried shooting at the birds. But the first shot—he missed—scared them away. They still circled the boat but kept their distance from whatever made that loud noise. He tried setting traps, but he wasn't really good at it, and the seagulls always managed to leave with the bait, unscathed. The fisherman tried a slingshot, ended up hurting his hand. He tried aiming fireworks at them. Yep, that was a stupid idea.

Finally, after he took care of the burns on his hands, the fisherman brought poison with him on the boat, lots of it. Heck, he had enough poison to kill every feathered thing in all of Alaska. He stuffed poison inside small fish, bread, the muffins he had brought for breakfast— that was a shame, they were really good muffins. He put poison into whatever he could find, and threw it into the sea for the seagulls to eat. Some did, and died, but most of the deadly bait sank to the ocean floor. You should have seen how happy the crabs were. Look, Mom: free food falling from the sky! Muffins, even! The crabs gathered all of it and organized the biggest crab party anyone had ever seen. They had crab music, and a really long and narrow dance floor. They danced sideways until the wee hours.

By morning, the fisherman had realized what was happening, but it was too late. All the crabs were dead. There was nothing left for him to fish. He couldn't work. He couldn't feed his family. No one in the village could, and they all had to leave. The seagulls, of course, are still there. One spring morning, mother seagull decided it was time to clean the nest. The babies were now teenagers and they never picked up after themselves. She felt sentimental about some of the junk that was lying around, but one thing was certain, she'd seen enough of that shiny, useless little ball. She flew away with the pearl and dropped it on the deck of one of the abandoned fishing boats.

— . . .

—What do you think?

—That's a really . . . sad story?

—It is, isn't it? Maybe it should have a happier ending. Maybe the seagulls are angry for being shot at and they start dropping things, little rocks, bombing the hell out of everyone. Then one of the baby seagulls can't find a small enough rock so he drops the pearl, right in the fisherman's hand. Is that better?

—I'm not sure . . . Is that all the help you're willing to give me?

—Help? I just thought you might like a story! You seemed a little on edge.

—I'm horrible with metaphors. I'm guessing we're the seagulls. Do the aliens think we stole Themis from them?

—Oh, I see. The pearl would be a metaphor for Themis. That's cute.

—Do they think we stole *anything* from them?

—No. They don't fish either, in case you were about to ask. I'm sure they'd like crab if they ever tried it, though.

—So we have alien beings who really don't like to interfere, but think they need to . . . somehow. The only thing I can get from your story is that they might be doing it for the wrong reason. Unless we're the crabs, and they're not trying to kill us at all. But who are the seagulls?

—Wow. I hope you realize you're talking to yourself now. I've already done a lot more than I should, so you'll have to go the rest of the way on your own. On the upside, you should find comfort in the fact that you'll "deserve" what success you may have. Ah! Our food's coming!

—Can I ask one more question?

—Is it a funny question?

—Are we . . . family?

—That *is* funny. Do we look like we're family?

—I mean, am I an alien? Part alien?

—What does that even mean?

—Am I like you? Your ancestors, a long, long time ago, they weren't from this planet, were they?

—And if they weren't, what would that make me? Better, or worse?

—I . . . I don't know how to answer that.

—You should. You really should.

FILE NO. 1600

PERSONAL LOG—VINCENT COUTURE, CONSULTANT, EDC AND EVA REYES

Location: Shadow Government Bunker, Lenexa, KS

—That's really nice, Eva. Did you draw that today?

—Last night. I couldn't sleep.

—Is that . . . ?

—Yes. That's you.

—That's me? When did my nose get so big?

—It's just a drawing.

—It's nice, Eva. You're really good, you know. And who's that one by your bed?

—That's my mom.

—Your—

—My Puerto Rican mom. Not—

—Her name's Kara.

—I know that.

— . . . You said you couldn't sleep. Nightmares?

—Mm-hmm.

—Me too.

—And I hate it here. This bed sucks, and—

—And what?

—Nothing. It's silly.

—You can tell me.

— . . .

—Come on!

—I had this—

—Yes . . .

—I had a plush turtle. I told you it was stupid.

—And it helped you sleep, and now it's gone.

—They wouldn't let me take anything. The people who—

—Would a beat-up gopher do the trick?

—What?

—It's a plush . . . gopher, about this big.

—No! My mom gave me that turtle!

—That one's also . . . It belonged to Kara. I don't know the story behind it, but she kept it in a box with some other stuff. It's missing an eye and it's ripped in a few places, but it's . . . Well, it's a gopher. It's yours if you want it.

— . . .

—Well, think about it. Can I ask how? Inside Themis . . . How did you know Kara was your . . . biological mother?

—I wasn't sure. I thought she might be. She looked like . . . like I imagined my mother would.

—How did you know the people who raised you in Puerto Rico weren't your real parents?

—They *were* my real parents!

—I'm sorry. Your *biological* parents.

—My mother was Puerto Rican. My father was from Belize. I'm . . . superwhite. But I didn't know. When I was seven, I broke my best friend's arm for saying bad things about my mother. It wasn't just her. All the kids, they kept saying my mom was sleeping around. I even believed them for a while. My parents explained it to me after I sent my friend to the hospital. I didn't understand. I'd seen pictures of my mom pregnant, pictures of my birth. I didn't know you could make babies that way.

— . . .

—What are you looking at?

—You have her eyes. Kara's.

— . . .

—I'm sorry Eva. I didn't mean to make you uncomfortable.

—Can I ask you something?

—Anything.

—What do you want?

—I just came to see how you were doing.

—I mean what do you want with me? You're not my "real" dad. You don't have to take care of me just because you gave a sample of your—

—Eva, I know you're upset. You have every right to be. You lost your parents. Then you met Kara, and she died too, but—

—I still have one left.

—One what?

—A mother. I still have one left.

—One mother? Who?

—Alyssa.

—Wh . . . Alyssa's not your mother. Who told you that?

—She made me, didn't she?

—I don't believe this. Who told you that?

—She did!

—When did you speak to Alyssa?

—She came to see me while you were away. She said she made me in a lab, so that I could pilot Themis if one of you died. She said you tried to stop her.

—Let me get this straight. Alyssa came to see you and she told you that she made you?

—Yes.

— . . .

—It's true, isn't it?

—It's . . . It's more complicated than that.

—Would you have told me?

—Would I have told you? Not now! Someday, maybe. I'm so sorry you had to hear any of this.

—I'm not. She's the only one who didn't lie to me.

—Look, Eva, I'm not sure what you think you know—

—I know you and Kara didn't want me.

—Kara didn't want Alyssa to knock her unconscious, strap her to a table, and remove her eggs without her consent. That doesn't mean she didn't want you. She had no idea you even existed. No one did, except for Alyssa. The minute she heard about you, Kara was gone. She went against orders to go get you! There were a lot of bad things going on, people dying, but she went to get you. Do you know where I was when she left?

—Where?

—I was missing. I was stuck with Themis at the bottom of the ocean and no one knew where I was. But she left anyway because she thought you might be in danger. Do you understand what I'm saying? There was no one more important to her. She'd never met you in her *life*, not once, and you were the most important thing in the world to her.

—She didn't care about me. She wanted a pilot for Themis.

—Kara died so you could live, you ungrateful little brat! Show some respect.

—I saw her die.

—I saw her die too.

—I mean *before*. I saw her die before, in my dreams. I saw a metal woman, like Themis, but now I know it was her. I thought she was falling upwards into the clouds. It didn't make any sense. I had that same dream all the time. They thought there was something wrong with me. They thought I was crazy.

—Did you see her face? In your dreams?

—Not really. It was . . . it was different, but I know it was her.

—Well, let me tell you something Eva. I saw her fall in my head too, over and over again. I still see her. She's falling backwards, her arms spread, and she disappears into a sea of white. That's what you saw, right?

—Yes.

—Me too. It's all I could see. *Over*, and *over*, and *over*. Then last night it hit me. Kara left *everything* to find you. She left her work, she left me, she left everything when the world needed her the most because she wanted to make sure nothing happened to you. She would have given anything, sacrificed anything to save you. And she did, she gave her life, and she saved you. That was the most important thing to her. So when she closed that hatch and fell backwards into a sea of white smoke, I *know* she had a smile on her face. She died happy, and she died proud. Close your eyes.

—I don't want to.

—Close your eyes! I want you to see her. Kara. Your mother. See her fall with a huge grin on her face. She won. She took on Russian mercenaries, giant alien robots. She took on the entire universe and she won. She did what she set out to do. Your mom was a badass motherfucker. I know you didn't get to know her, but Kara had the most beautiful smile when she was proud of herself. Smug, like you wouldn't believe. Made you want to punch her in the face, but it was beautiful.

—Do you hate me?

—Why would I hate you?

—You said Kara died to save me. It's OK if you hate me.

—I don't hate you, Eva. Kara would've lived if I'd been faster. She'd still be alive if I were as brave as the two of you. It's not your fault, believe me. Besides, you don't know Kara like I do. She'd come back from the dead if she thought I was angry at you. She'd claw her way out of the grave just to slap me around.

—I'm sorry she's dead.

—Me too.

—Was there a funeral?

—No. They wouldn't send a team to UN headquarters until this morning. They called me an hour ago when they found her body.

—Where will you bury her?

—I won't bury her. I'd like to. I'd like to have a place to visit her, but she didn't want to be buried. She thought it was creepy. She wouldn't watch zombie movies with me either.

—You can keep her ashes. My friend Angie had her sister's in her room.

—Nah. She'd hate it. She'd want me to scatter her ashes and have a party. Will you do that with me?

—Scatter her ashes?

—Yeah. I'll get someone to fly us over Detroit on a helicopter. Seems fitting.

—I've never been in a helicopter.

—Me neither. I'm afraid of heights, remember. So it's settled then. Just you and me, and a helicopter pilot, I guess.

— . . .

—Look, I don't know how to do this any more than you do, but I'm trying.

— . . .

—Is that a yes, Eva?

—OK.

—Good. We'll do that before we leave.

—Where are we going?

—I don't know. I haven't figured that out yet. Somewhere safe.

—But when will I start training?

—Training for what?

—Themis! When do I start training to pilot Themis? That's what you need me for, isn't it?

—What are you talking about? I don't want you to do anything!

—You don't understand! It's OK. I *want* to do it.

—Eva . . . I know you want to help, but—

—That's what I'm supposed to do!

—Eva, you're ten years old!

—But it's what I was made for! That's why Alyssa made me. I'm . . . I'm a tool. That's my purpose.

—I . . . First of all, Alyssa didn't "make" you, stop saying that. She spent all of twenty minutes in a lab. The woman who carried you inside her for nine months made you. Second, who gives a crap what Alyssa thought? Your mother d . . . Kara died so you could live. I wouldn't be much of a father if I put you in harm's way now. I'm not gonna let anything happen to you, Eva. I want you as far away from that robot as possible.

—People are gonna die if we don't do anything!

—People are gonna die anyway.

—You're just gonna let them die? You're not even gonna try?

—If it means keeping you safe, then yeah. I'm just gonna let them die. I'm your father, Eva.

—No you're not! You can't tell me what to do!

—Eva.

—Get out of my room!

—Eva, I—

—GET OUT!

FILE NO. 1603

STATION LOG—NATIONAL OCEANIC AND ATMOSPHERIC ADMINISTRATION (NOAA) SPACE WEATHER PREDICTION CENTER

Location: Silver Springs, MD

—Chief, can you come here a sec. We lost the sun.

—What?

—I lost the SXI.

—What do you mean, you lost it?

—What I just said. It's gone. I'm not getting anything from the Solar X-Ray Imager on GOES-13.

—There's no signal from the satellite?

—Nothing.

—Are you sure it's not your station?

—My station's fine. The satellite just stopped transmitting. Problem's up there, sir.

—Scoot over. I wanna check someth—What is it, Clara?

[*There's a problem.*]

OK, well, we're a little busy here. Go back to your station and I'll come see you when I'm done here.

[*I lost the signal from my satellite.*]

You lost . . . Which one do you have?

[*I'm on GOES-15. There's something wrong, sir.*]

No shit, there's something wrong. The problem's gotta be down here. Two satellites can't malfunction at the exact same time. Check the receiver.

—Sir, it's all of them. We're not receiving anything, from anywhere. Nothing on microwave. Nothing on VHF either.

—All of them? There you go. It's got to be our equipment.

—It's not. We're receiving. We're getting all kinds of static.

—This is nice. I've been here for a month! What am I supposed to do now?

—Hold on, sir—

—I don't know what I'm supposed to do.

—Hold on! NASA wants to know if we're getting JPSS data.

—Dammit! That doesn't make any sense. I'll check with Defense, see if they're still getting their feed.

—Europe is down too. They lost MetOp. No one is receiving any signal from orbit anymore. We're getting calls from *everybody*.

—Could it be solar flares?

—Space weather was fine a minute ago, sir.

[*Check this out!*]

—What is it this time, Clara?

[*That's a live stream from Mauna Kea.*]

The telescope?

[*Yeah. I asked them to track my satellite. Should be right here.*]

I don't see anything.

[*That's right.*]

Are you saying the satellite is physically gone?

[*I don't know, sir.*]

Well, can you see it or not?

[*I can't, but—*]

But what?

[*It's not the only thing we can't see.*]

What do you mean?

—Sir, she means the *stars* are missing. We can't see the stars.

FILE NO. 1604

INTERVIEW WITH EVA REYES
Location: Shadow Government Bunker, Lenexa, KS

—You asked to see me, Eva.

—Yes, Dr. Franklin.

—What can I do for you?

—I wanna do it. I want to pilot Themis.

—I don't think that's a good idea, Eva. Besides, this is something you should talk about with your father, not me. I know you haven't had a lot of time to get used to the idea but, technically, he is your dad, he's responsible for you.

—He won't do anything. He doesn't even want me to try.

—That sounds pretty reasonable to me, Eva. You're still a child, I'd want to keep you safe too if you were *my* child.

—You don't understand! He can't keep me safe. No one can. I'll be dead in a few days. You'll be dead too.

—I know you're afraid, Eva. We all are.

—I'm not afraid. I'm telling you, we'll all be dead soon.

—No one knows what'll happen, Eva. Things look pretty bad right now, but we're working really hard to find a way out of this.

—I know!

—How do you know, Eva?

—I just do. Just trust me, OK?

—You can tell me. How do you know?

—You'll just think I'm crazy.

—Eva, I don't know you well enough to make that kind of judgment. From what little I've seen, I think you're an extremely brave and intelligent young woman. Nothing you tell me will change that.

—I saw it.

—You . . . How?

—I see things. I saw Kara die.

—You s—

—Yes! I saw her die. Months ago. I saw this too. I saw it happen.

—Tell me.

—Rain. I saw black rain. It fell from the sky, not just here, everywhere, and we all died. I died.

—I'm sorry, Eva. There's—

—I told you you'd think I was crazy.

—I never said that. I just . . . Did you also see how to stop it from happening?

—No.

—Then how do you know things would be any different if I let you inside Themis?

—I . . . I don't. But—

—Like I said, Eva. It isn't up to me. You should talk to—

—He won't listen! He doesn't understand!

—He's your father.

—STOP SAYING THAT! You don't get it, do you?! He's gonna die too!

—Eva, come back . . .

FILE NO. 1605

INTERVIEW WITH BRIGADIER GENERAL EUGENE GOVENDER, COMMANDER, EARTH DEFENSE CORPS

Location: Shadow Government Bunker, Lenexa, KS

—Goddammit, Rose! It's three in the morning!

—You need to see this, sir.

—I'm tired. I'm jet-lagged. Make this quick.

—We lost all signals coming from orbit. We're not getting data from our satellites. No one is. It's a complete blackout.

—They're not transmitting?

—Maybe they are. But something's blocking it.

—Like a jamming signal?

—It's not jammed, it's blocked. We can't hear anything from up there. Take a look at these.

—What am I looking at?

—These are from telescopes all over. What do you see?

—I see . . . What's this dark spot over here?

—Exactly. There should be stars there. I think that's where it's coming from. Whatever is blocking our satellite signal, I think it's stronger there. It's blocking everything, including light.

—Where is it?

—It's . . . all over. We spotted eighteen of these dark spots so far, all around us. There could be more.

—How big are the dark spots?

—I don't know. Hundreds of miles . . . Thousands. Depends on how far they are.

—Any idea what's behind the black spots?

—Whatever it is, someone doesn't want us to see it.

—With everything that's happening, I think we can assume this isn't a naturally occurring phenomenon.

—It could be whatever brought the robots all the way here.

—It wasn't here before. Maybe it's . . . Goddammit!

—What?

—I think they brought in the big guns.

—Why? We weren't putting up much of a fight.

—No, Dr. Franklin, we weren't. But we're dying slow. I keep wondering why they'd send a dozen robots to wipe out a whole planet. It doesn't make sense to do it one small circle at a time. There's too much ground to cover. What they're doing, that feels more like a surgical strike, like they were looking for something. I thought: Maybe they just don't have anything better, but anyone who can build these things, make that gas . . . They'd have to be able to hit us a lot harder.

—The gas is denser than air. If they spread it around from high atmosphere, it would mix—

—It would be over pretty quick.

—Yes, sir.

—Any thoughts?

—I don't like it.

—Any thoughts on what we can do? We don't have anything we can fire at them.

—What would we fire at? We don't know what's there. We don't know how big or how far it is. I'm not sure there's anything we *can* do.

—Then, Dr. Franklin, I suggest you go back to bed. That's what I'm gonna do.

—I don't think we have a lot of time.

—When's the last time you slept?

— . . .

—That's what I thought. Go to bed, Rose. I'll have you meet some folks from the UN in the morning. They're working on plan B in case this all goes to hell.

—Can't you meet with them? I have a lot on my plate at the moment.

—I could . . . But then again, I'll be dead if it comes to that. The point is they'd like someone who'll survive the gas to be at that meeting. They wanna build some global infrastructure, so those who make it can get help, find other survivors. The first step is to create a network of two-way radios that can run on dynamos. We'd like to have some every couple miles across the country, help create pockets of survivors. They want to have some sort of blueprint people can follow to build communities. I'm sure they could use your thoughts on the matter.

—If we're all exposed to the gas, and the ratio of survivors stays the same, there'll be about 150,000 people left alive in the United States. That's one person per twenty-five square miles on average. They'll have to deal with over 300 million dead bodies decomposing everywhere, rats, bugs. Most people will be concentrated in urban areas, but so will the bodies. Disease will spread faster than people can imagine. First step has to be dealing with bodies, find medicine. Hospitals would be a good place to start a community from. There'll be food around for a while. We can worry about that later—

—Stop. Stop. Like I said, they can use your help. But you won't be useful to anyone if you don't sleep.

—Sir?

—Yes?

—I don't think I . . . I've seen enough death for two lifetimes. Apparently, I'm supposed to play a role in stopping this from happening. If I can't . . . If I fail, I'm not sure I have what it takes for what comes next.

—Well, I'm sorry the apocalypse isn't convenient for you. Now go to bed.

FILE NO. 1613

LETTER FROM CAPTAIN KARA RESNIK, EDC TO VINCENT COUTURE, CONSULTANT, EDC

Recovered on her body at EDC Headquarters, New York, NY

Hey Vincent!

I plan on destroying this letter when I get home so, if you're reading this, chances are things didn't go according to plan. I'm in Haiti. I know, I'm wondering how I ended up here myself. But I found her, I found our daughter. I should start from the beginning; you probably don't know about her yet.

Her name's Eva. They've been keeping her from us. That psycho Alyssa put our child inside another woman when we were in Puerto Rico. Another family had our baby. From what I saw, it was a good family, but they're dead now. Some very bad people killed them so they could get their hands on our daughter. The Russians think she can pilot Themis. I don't know that she can, but it doesn't matter. They have her now. They'll take her far away and they'll experiment on her. I don't even wanna think about it. I have to stop them. I have no idea how, but I'll come up with something. Doesn't matter how, I'm taking her with me. I'm bringing our daughter home.

That didn't take as long as I thought to explain. I was sort of hoping it would take all night. I'm sleeping—not sleeping, really—in the shittiest car you've ever seen. You'd like it. Everything holds together with duct tape. And it stinks! Like a dead animal. I smell like it now. I smell like roadkill. That and old, dirty engine oil.

That pretty much sums it up! Everyone lied to us. Alyssa cooked up a baby in a lab. Some other woman gave birth to our child. Russians are after her. I stink. I think you're up to speed.

That's a lot to digest, I know. We're parents! How scary is that? I know you'll be fine; you've always been good with children. But I'll have some adjusting to do. Somehow, I get the feeling taking down Russian mercenaries will be the easy part. Kicking and punching is something I'm good at. Meeting her first boyfriend . . . I'm not sure how well I can deal with that. You might have to stop me from punching his lights out for no reason. You know, like a vetting process. If he comes back, then he might be worthy. I know I'm getting ahead of myself. I'm not sure we can even adopt her. One thing I know: I'm not giving her up to *anyone*. She wouldn't be safe. They'll keep coming for her, Vincent. They'll chase her to the ends of the Earth. We have to keep her safe. Maybe, with everything that's happening, no one will give a shit about adoption laws. First things first. I have to make it out of here.

I keep forgetting if you're reading this, then it's a good bet I'm dead. It's hard to write as a dead person. What can I tell you? Hi! I'm dead! I hope you're not! Best, Kara.

When I left, you were missing with Themis. I hope you're OK. You have no idea how much I want you to be OK. I don't think I could live with myself. And I hope you don't hate me for leaving without you. I just didn't know what more I could do. You know I'm not good at sitting around. I couldn't help you, and I thought I could help her.

I sure wish you were here with me. I'm better with you around. You know when I'm about to do something dumb. You put your hand on my shoulder to stop me from doing it, or you don't and we do something even dumber together. Either way, I know everything'll be OK. I'd give anything to have you with me now. See if you'd put that hand on my shoulder or not. I'd feel a whole lot better if you were here to help me plan this thing.

The good news is Eva's safe for now. The Russians will kill me if they get the chance, but they won't hurt her unless they have to. So if I don't make it, then you have to find her. You have to find her and bring her home. Get help. The EDC, the US government, it doesn't matter. They'll wanna know if the helmets will turn on for her. I'm not sure how I feel about that, but they'll protect her. That's good. You have to promise me, Vincent Couture. You have to promise me you'll find her and keep her safe.

There's something else you need to promise me. When you find our daughter, I know you will, don't become someone you're not. I know your dad wasn't everything you wanted him to be. Don't let that change you. Don't try to be like him. Don't try to not be like him. Be you. Remember how unhappy I was awhile back? I didn't even know I was, but I was. It was because I thought I had to be someone else. It wasn't your fault. You never asked me to change anything. In fact, I'm pretty sure you weren't happy I did. I know I did it to myself. I guess what I'm saying is: Don't do what I did. Don't become something you're not because you think that's the right thing, or the "normal" thing to do. She has a good father. Let her get to know that man.

And don't be too hard on her. If she's anything like me, she might be a little rough on the edges. She might try to put you in your place every now and then. Good for her. You need it sometimes. And if she's anything like you . . . You're in for a sea of trouble if she's anything like you. She might not want you around. Don't take it personally. She had parents who probably loved her very much. They took care of her. They're her parents. She doesn't owe us. So be her friend if she's not ready for a dad just yet. Just be there for her.

Let her be what she wants to be. She might not have a long life ahead of her. The way things are looking, none of us have much of a future. Let her get through it on her own terms. Let her live. She deserves that. She's earned it, believe me.

Time to do something stupid. Hey! What am I saying? It will work. You'll be safe. I'll come home and surprise you in the lab, introduce you to your daughter, then I can throw out this letter. Easy as pie.

You know I love you, right? I don't tell you often because your ego would get even bigger and maybe implode and create a black hole. I don't want to destroy the universe. But I do. Love you, that is. You're a cocky, arrogant son of a bitch and I love you. You're also the bravest man I ever met. I'm not sure I ever told you that. We had fun, didn't we? Anyway, I did. I hope I haven't been too much of a pain in that Quebecois ass of yours.

You probably saw the other envelope. It's for Eva. Give it to her when the time comes. Not now. She's got enough to deal with, but someday. You'll know when it's time.

Be good. I'll see you on the flip side.

Kara

FILE NO. 1614

TRAINING LOG—VINCENT COUTURE, CONSULTANT, EDC AND EVA REYES

Location: Shawnee Mission Park, Lenexa, KS

[*Are you sure you want to do this, Eva?*]

—Yes, Dr. Franklin.

[*Call me Rose. Just don't try anything on your own. Listen to Vincent, OK?*]

OK!

—Eva. This is . . . this is your station.

—Are you OK, Vincent?

—Yeah. This is just—

—You're crying! Did I do something wrong?

—No! It's not you, Eva. It's just . . . harder than I thought it would be.

—Do you want me to leave?

—No! No! I'm good! . . . There! Hop on. I'll help you strap yourself in.

—What is this?

—That's a . . . It's a pedestal, so you can reach the controls.

—Is it a phone book?

—It's *two* phone books I duct taped together and glued to the floor. We can find you something prettier if this works. I'm pretty sure it's the right height.

—Are you sure I can do this?

—Nope. Absolutely not. That's what we're here to find out. The helmet might not work for you at all. Doesn't work for anyone else. Here, put this on like you would a jacket. See! Perfect height! Can you fit your fingers in there? Is it too tight? Too loose? I think the gloves fit you better than they did Kara. I'm going to close these on your forearms. This big thing here goes around your chest. There! How do you feel?

—I'm OK.

—Try to move a little. Move your arms. All the way up. Try to bend down. How far can you go? . . . What is it?

—Can I ask you something, Vincent? Is it OK if I keep calling you Vincent? I'm not—

—Oh yes. I'm not ready for that either. Let's take this slow. What did you want to ask me?

[*Are you guys OK up there?*]

Yeah, Rose. Just give us a minute. Go ahead Eva, she can't hear us now.

—What happens if I can't do it?

—Nothing. Well, we'll probably fall first, then nothing. It doesn't matter.

—Yes it matters! People are dying.

—Eva, I don't think either of us can make much of a difference at this point. But I'm with you, Eva, win or lose.

—What if I make a mistake?

—Trust me, kid, even if you completely sucked at this, you couldn't *possibly* do as much damage as Kara and I did when we first started.

For now, there aren't even any skills involved. Either the helmet turns on or it doesn't. You can't will it to work for you.

—Thank you, for changing your mind.

—Don't thank me. I'm a horrible father. I'm letting my ten-year-old girl pilot a humongous war machine. I'm going straight to hell, maybe to jail first, if child services ever hears about this. And I'll be honest with you, I'm hoping the helmet won't work. Then we'll know. We can let the world know. They'll leave you alone and you can have a normal life, whatever that is.

—And if it works?

—If it works . . . your life will get more complicated than it already is, probably a lot more.

[*Guys? What's going on up there?*]

What do you say, Eva? Are you ready to try this?

—Yes.

—OK, Rose! We're ready. I'm putting the helmet on her head now. Eva, put your arms straight so Themis doesn't move if this works. I'm not at my station, so I can't keep her balanced. Ready? Here we go.

[*Is it working?*]

Eva, is it working? Eva?

—What?

—Is the helmet working?

—I don't know, you told me not to move. I'm just looking at Dr. Franklin.

—You're looking at . . . You can see outside?

—Yes. Can't you?

[*Hello? Is everything OK?*]

Yes, Rose, we're fine. The helmet turned on for her.

—You mean it's working?

—Yes, Eva, it's working. You're your mother's daughter all right. Don't move! I want you to stand still until I get to my station. Then we're gonna try some very simple things, OK?

—OK. This is cool!

—Isn't it? Don't move, now! I'm gonna bounce around this place like a pinball if we fall before I'm strapped in.

—I'm not moving.

—Don't move! I'm almost there!

—I'm not moving!

—All right. I'm good. We're gonna try taking one step. I know this'll sound silly, but I want you to think about how you walk. When you lift one foot, you start turning your shoulders in the opposite direction. When you lift your right foot, you turn to the left. That transfers the weight of your body to your left leg. When you lift your left leg, you turn your shoulders to the right, keep the weight squarely on your right leg. Try it now, pretend you're walking.

—Will we fall?

—Probably later when we try walking for real. For now, I'm not moving my legs. It doesn't matter if you move yours, and I can shift my weight to keep the balance. Go ahead.

—Like that?

—I can't feel the weight shifting from side to side. You have to exaggerate a little. Pretend you're modeling. Walk the runway.

—That doesn't help.

—Hmmm. Pretend you're walking with something really heavy in your hands. Yes! There you go!

—Can we walk for real!

—Not today. Baby steps.

—Please!

— . . .

—*Please!*

—What the hell. Rose? Can you go back inside? We're gonna try walking a little. I don't wanna squish you.

[*Are you sure you want to do this? It took you months to learn how to walk with Kara.*]

I couldn't hold the weight back then. And no, I'm really not sure, hence the: "Go back inside. I don't wanna squish you." There're plenty of trees around. That should break the fall a little. Maybe not. Eva, this isn't such a good idea.

—Are you afraid?

—Are you really trying to pull a Marty McFly on me?

—Who's Marty McFly?

—Some guy who . . . Never mind. We'll watch the movie together sometime. I'd never do anything if I waited for good ideas. Are you ready to fall hard, get hurt, watch me break my nose on the console, blood gushing everywhere?

—Yes!

—Fair enough. We'll take a few steps. Let's start with one. You have to watch me move. Watch my legs, watch my shoulders. Watch me shift my weight before I lift a leg. You have to move *with* me, not after me. By then it'll be too late and we'll fall.

—Got it!

—Here we go.

—Like this?

—Nope. Not like this . . . Aaaand . . . we're falling. Put your hands up!

—AAAAAH!

—UGH! Damn, that hurts. Are you OK?

—I can't move my arms!! They're stuck to my chest!

—It's OK! That's Themis's weight pushing against you. It'll loosen up when your helmet's off. Let's get out of here while she's lying down.

—That was your fault! I wasn't ready!

—It's OK, Eva. We can try this again.

—I CAN'T MOVE! Get me out of here!

—One sec. I need to get out of my station first.

—GET ME OUT!

—I'm here. You're shaking like a leaf.

—I can't do this. I'm not good enough.

—Eva, it's OK. You couldn't expect to get this right the first time. We'll try again tomorrow if you want.

—This is stupid.

—It's up to you Eva. You don't *have* to do this if you don't want to.

—You don't understand. They all died for nothing if I can't do it!

FILE NO. 1617

INTERVIEW WITH DR. ALYSSA PAPANTONIOU
Location: Shadow Government Bunker,
Lenexa, KS

—Good morning, Doct . . . Dr. Franklin. I thought we were done with the gu . . . guards.

—We're not done with the guards. They'll be with you everywhere you go. You can go from here to your room, to here. That's all. I don't want you anywhere near Eva, or Vincent, ever again. What possessed you to go talk to that child?

—She has a right to know.

—You had no right to tell her. She's been through enough.

—I had no right? I mmm . . . I made her! I have *every* right to tell her. When were you gonna do it?

—When the time was right.

—Wh . . . when?! When things sss . . . settle down? When everything is OK again? We don't have that kind of time. She has a right to know what she is.

—She's a child! That's what she is!

—She's our best hope of saving the world! You w . . . wouldn't have that without me.

—You told her you were her mother!

—I told her I cr . . . created her. I never said I was her mother. She can ca . . . call me that if she wants to.

—You're insane! You're a psychopath, Alyssa!

—Insulting me doesn't make me wr . . . wrong.

—I don't wanna hear what you think is right, Alyssa. I just care about the science. If I had my way, you'd be locked up in some jail cell, somewhere hot and humid.

—That doesn't sound like you at all. You should leave the empty threats to him.

—Well, he's not here anymore, and I'm a fast learner. Believe me, when I make threats, there will be nothing empty about them.

—He's the one who brought me here. You should t . . . trust his judgment.

—He didn't trust you! He thought you could help, but he never trusted you. I don't either. I'll turn you over to the government the minute this is over.

—Then why keep me here? What mmmm . . . what makes you think I'll help if I know you'll have me locked up afff . . . terwards?

—Because I trust your sick, twisted ego to always have the better of you. I know that you wanna be the one to solve this. You wanna be the one who saves the world, not because you care, but so you can feel justified, vindicated. I don't think it matters to you at all whether you spend the rest of your life rotting in a cell.

—That is still him talking.

—I told you I'm a quick study. What do you say we stop wasting each other's time and you tell me what you've been up to these past few days?

—He had me com . . . pare DNA from the London survivors to genetic material from the alien b . . . bodies.

—Did you?

—Yes and no. Their ge . . . genetics is so different, none of my tests will w . . . work on them. I can't know how it would recombine with ours, *if* . . . it would recombine at all. I'd need live sss . . . specimens to go any fffurther. It doesn't matter, I know I won't find what he was looking for. He thought the survivors—

—He thought they were descendants of aliens who lived here three thousand years ago.

—He thought wrong.

—Are you sure?

—Yes.

—You're absolutely sure, Alyssa? Why?

—It makes no sense. It's t . . . too long ago. Everyone was your ancestor three thou . . . sand years ago.

—What do you mean?

—People look at fff . . . family trees the wrong way. They think you start with someone, then you branch down to their ch . . . children, then their grandchildren, and the tree gets bigger going down. It d . . . d . . . doesn't. It grows upwards.

—How does that have anything to do with the survivors?

—Think of it like this. You have two p . . . parents. You have four grandparents. You have eight great-grandparents, sixteen great-great-grandparents. That's about one hundred years ago. Twenty-five years, thirty years p . . . per generation on average. Two hundred years ago, you're looking at about two thousand ancestors. Ffffive hundred years ago, that's . . . fifty . . . million.

—How many going back three thousand years?

—Just keep d . . . doubling every thirty years. You get to a billion very fast. By t . . . twelve hundred years, you reach a trillion. Three thou . . . three thousand years ago . . . It doesn't matter what the number is. It's t . . . too big.

—That makes no sense. There weren't a trillion people on Earth twelve hundred years ago. There aren't close to a trillion now!

—That's because the same p . . . people appear mmm . . . many times on your family tree. Your twenty-fifth great-grandfather is also your distant cousin. Mmm . . . most people will appear hundreds, thousands of times in your ge . . . genealogy. The farther back in time you go, the fewer people there are on Earth, and the more branches there are in your family tree. Soon, you need . . . all of them, to fill the b . . . br . . . branches.

—I'm not sure I under—

—If you lived on Earth back then, either your line died out and you have nnn. . . . no descendants at all, or you're an ancestor to everyone alive . . . t . . . today. Everyone who lived a couple thousand years ago, and whose line didn't di . . . disappear, is your ancestor, and mine, and everyone else's.

— . . .

—Dr. Franklin?

—That's it, isn't it?

—That is wh . . . what?

—If aliens roamed the planet three thousand years ago, they couldn't have just a handful of descendants alive today. They'd either have none—and we know that's not true, I met one yesterday—or . . .

—Are you saying . . . ?

—That's exactly what I'm saying. Or they'd be a distant ancestor to everyone alive. I didn't survive because I have alien DNA, I'm alive because I'm one of the few people who doesn't. We're all aliens, part alien anyway. Every single person on Earth—well, 99.95 percent of them—has alien genetics.

—That's cr . . . crazy.

—Thank you, Alyssa. Your services won't be required anymore. These gentlemen will escort you out and take you . . . well, we'll figure that part out soon enough. Goodbye, Alyssa.

PART FIVE

IN THE BLOOD

FILE NO. 1619

INTERVIEW WITH MR. BURNS, OCCUPATION UNKNOWN

Location: New Dynasty Chinese Restaurant, Dupont Circle, Washington, DC

—They came for you, didn't they?

—What? No hello? No "it's nice to see you again"?

—They're here to kill you, not us!

—Fine, then. No hello.

—They made that gas so it would kill anyone who shared genetic material with them. They came here to wipe you out. They probably thought there were only a handful of you. But we all started dying, and they realized everyone on Earth—almost everyone—has alien genes. That's why they stopped.

—Bingo! I told you you were smart enough! Just enough.

—You lied to us! Everything you told us . . . Everything you told him, it was all a lie!

—First, I only told him a story. I never said it was the truth. Besides, everything I've said *is* true, more or less. I may have omitted certain parts of the story, but I didn't lie. A few millennia ago, they sent a dozen of these robots to Earth because they feared an attack from one of their enemies. Nasty people, or so I was told. A couple thousand years went by, no one came, so they went home.

—You said they left Themis behind so we could defend ourselves.

—Yes! They did, for a while. They also left pilots with her. You wouldn't have been able to use Themis otherwise.

—Because of our anatomy.

—I'm sure they never thought you'd be crazy enough to mutilate your own legs, but there's a much simpler reason. The controls wouldn't work for humans. They shouldn't. Even now, there are only a few people with the right DNA.

—Vincent and Kara.

—Among others. Why do you think we sent them to you?

—You sent them to me?

—Is it true they had a daughter?

—They did. Her name's Eva.

—Such a great name!

—You seem genuinely happy.

—Why wouldn't I be? I love children. How is she? Is she OK?

—She's fine. What do you mean?

—That was a simple question. Never mind.

—No, not never mind. What do you mean, is she OK?

—Does she see things?

—She does. How do you know about it?

—Just a guess. Her parents had more of our DNA than most. Their child could be . . . closer to people like me than most humans. Our people sometimes have some sorts of . . . episodes, visions.

—They can see the future?

—Not really. They get . . . glimpses into what might be. Some of it will happen, some of it won't. Not all of us see things. I never did.

Those who do sometimes have a hard time adjusting. Without the proper guidance, it might be a bit . . . overwhelming at times.

—You could call it that. The poor child is scared to death.

—She'll get over it. Children are more resilient than we give them credit for. I was saying something, wasn't I?

—I don't remember.

—Oh yes! Pilots! My point was, back then, you couldn't control Themis, so they left behind a small group of people who could.

—Your ancestors.

—No! My ancestors had chosen to mate with humans. They were dead by the time the robots left, but their children were alive. There were a dozen or so families. The pure aliens were instructed to protect the bloodline.

—What does that mean?

—They were told to slaughter them, and their children, and their children's children. Then they were to return home.

—With Themis?

—Of course. What would you do with her? So they went on their mission, probably thinking the half-humans wouldn't put up much of a fight. But they did, they protected their families. They killed all the aliens. Then they dismantled Themis, buried her pieces all over the world so she wouldn't be discovered.

—And the people who sent Themis didn't notice that she never came back?

—I'm sure they noticed. They knew something happened to her. It's a big universe. A lot of things can go wrong. My ancestors tried to make sure they wouldn't think *that* happened.

—What did they do then?

—Who?

—Your ancestors.

—Oh, nothing. They tried to stay out of history's way as much as they could. They were instructed to mate only within the group, to avoid . . . well, to avoid exactly what happened. They were very strict about it. But over the centuries, a few people ran away. And here we are!

—Why did they run away?

—I imagine they fell in love. People will do the craziest things out of love. That includes refusing to marry your cousin. Maybe theirs weren't attractive enough. Do you find your cousins attractive?

—But the chamber I fell in, it was left for us to discover, wasn't it?

—Indeed it was. When you were evolved enough, they wanted you to learn about them. But it wasn't a hand you were supposed to find.

—What was it?

—A communication device. It could send a message to their world. It could also reorganize matter, so that, in time, you could transport yourselves and visit. It's a big round thing with light in the middle. There's one of these very things inside each robot.

—That's how Themis can teleport herself.

—Yes! My ancestors took the device, replaced it with a hand so you'd have something to find. They used it to scatter the body parts all over the world. We used that same device to re-create you, so that you and I could be having this conversation when the time came.

—How did the aliens find out?

—You found Themis! You found Themis and you used her. Finding her was one thing, but you shouldn't have been able to do anything with her. They knew something was up. They probably figured out what happened to their pilots way back then and they came to finish the mission they started three thousand years ago.

—Then we all died and they realized their own genetics were now part of ours.

—Exactly. To them, that's a tragedy. It's the worst kind of interference. They don't want to kill you all, because . . . because that's bad, and it's also interfering. But the alternative is to deny you the future you were supposed to have! They believe that they have, however unwillingly, robbed you of your destiny.

—So they stopped killing us. Now what?

—Now they're looking for a reason not to finish the job. Like I said, they don't like to interfere. They'll do it if they think you wouldn't be where you are without them. They'll remove their genetic footprint from mankind's. You'll get a do-over.

—They'll kill everyone but those of us without any alien genes.

—Exactly. You get to rebuild an Earth all on your own, free of anyone's influence.

—What about you?

—Oh, my people die no matter what. We're criminals by birth. Our very existence is a capital offense. There's no changing that.

—You won't even try?

—I didn't say that—

—So how do we stop them? You said they're looking for a reason not to finish the job.

—You show them you could have gotten here all on your own.

—Could we have?

—How could I possibly know that? Does it even matter? It's possible. That's all that matters. Their DNA only makes a tiny fraction of yours. The point is, you have to convince them, give them an excuse to let you continue on your journey. They believe that, had we not contaminated human genetics, you might not have evolved this far, reached this level of technology, that you might not have fiddled with atoms and discovered what they left behind. All you have to do is show them they could be wrong. They won't wipe out an entire civilization without being one hundred percent sure.

—Reasonable doubt.

—If that's what you wanna call it—

—How can we show them something we don't even know is true?

—Show them what you're made of. Show them that pure humans can be better than they think.

—You mean me. That's why I'm here, isn't it? You brought me back because I'm still one hundred percent human.

—Still? You're not the way you are because you somehow magically escaped three thousand years of genetic changes. Your parents probably had alien DNA. It's just luck that brought you here. But here you are. Now you just need to show them how formidable you can be.

—But how?

—Defeat them.

—I can't defeat them! We couldn't beat them with all the armies in the world. How can I do anything on my own? We don't have the technology.

—Even if you did, that technology was created by people with alien genes. It's . . . tainted.

—Really? So you're telling me that I need to defeat these giant machines without using anything that was invented in the last three thousand years?

—Well, you can assume it took my ancestors a few centuries to spread their gene pool around, but yes, that's the general idea.

—But we had nothing three thousand years ago! Nothing! The wheel, early steelwork. We certainly didn't have anything that can destroy these robots.

—Then I'd say you're in some trouble, young lady.

—I don't understand. Why not tell me what I need to do? You've told me everything else. Why won't you save us?

—I haven't told you anything you couldn't have figured out on your own.

—Why not?

—Because if they think I . . . if they think my people helped you, they'll kill every living thing on this planet, alien DNA or not, and let you evolve from unicellular organisms.

—There's more than that. In some weird way, you agree with them, don't you?

—Agree with what?

—That we shouldn't be allowed to live if we've been . . . tampered with.

—Forgive me. It must be hard for you to understand. That noninterference thing isn't just a slogan. It is ingrained in our culture. It's something everyone on their world is taught from birth. That belief survived even here. The apple doesn't fall far from the tree, as you can see.

—Even after all this time? Even if they're trying to kill you in the process?

—I don't wanna die, if that's what you're asking. But I understand why they think I should.

—What about us? Do you think we should die?

—I wouldn't be . . . guiding you if I did.

—But you understand why they'd want us to.

—I understand why they think they'd be doing you a favor.

—What difference does it make whether I have DNA from another species or not? How does that make me better or worse than anyone else?

—Now you understand the problem. For them, it's not a question of better or worse, it's about you being what you're *supposed* to be. In their mind, humans aren't what they were meant to be. You, Rose Franklin, are. That means they'll pay attention to you.

—How is your ancestors coming here any different, any less "natural" than whatever accidental events led to life on Earth, than whatever mutations turned us into what we are? Who's to say we're not *supposed* to be part alien?

—They are! I don't know if they're right or not, but that is precisely what they're saying. And you better hurry. I don't think you have much time.

—How long do I have?

—I don't know. A day, maybe two. You know what's orbiting the Earth, don't you?

—General Govender thinks they brought in heavy artillery.

—He's a smart man.

—You know what all of that reminds me of?

—I don't, but I have a feeling it's something bad.

—Interracial-marriage laws. We had them until the late sixties.

—I know. I was there. They called them antimiscegenation laws.

—Whites weren't allowed to marry or have sex with blacks. It was considered a felony. In some states, it was even illegal to perform the ceremony.

—Louisiana banned marriage between Native Americans and African Americans. Maryland didn't allow marriage between blacks and Filipinos. I see what you're getting at, but these laws were based on the assumption that some races were superior to others.

—And that's not what's going on now?

—They believe there is a purpose to life, and that no one should interfere with that purpose—that things should be the way they should be.

—I'm pretty sure they used that argument in Louisiana and Maryland. I'd say anyone who feels they have the right to dictate what someone else's genetics should look like is feeling pretty superior.

—And what if they are?

—I don't think it matters. I don't think ants should do whatever cats want them to do. I don't think fish should obey dolphins. I don't think humans should dictate the behavior of every other species on Earth.

—Humans sometimes do make decisions that affect other species.

—Yes. Look how well that turned out.

FILE NO. 1620

UHF SATCOM COMMUNICATION

BALLISTIC SUBMARINE USS *JIMMY CARTER,* DESIGNATED SSN-23

Location: Bering Sea

ORDERS 774627-53N

SSN-23—Rooke, Demetrius, CAPT. 225-48-1627

Abort current mission. Return to US waters immediately. Hold position at 48.498682, -125.143043 off Vancouver Island.

Alert Status—Gamma Five. Maintain readiness for SLBM launch on domestic target. Stand by for orders.

FILE NO. 1622

TRAINING LOG—VINCENT COUTURE, CONSULTANT, EDC AND EVA REYES
Location: Shawnee Mission Park, Lenexa, KS

[. . .]

—You're doing it, Eva! You're doing it!

—We're walking!

—Yes we are. And now we're going to fall.

—What? NO! What are you doing? NO! NO! NO! AARGH! That hurt!

—You say that every time.

—What's wrong with you? It was working. I didn't make us fall! I never got it right until now.

—I know! Do you know what else you never did?

—What?

—Get back up. Every time we fell, you never even tried to get up again. That's the part that really matters. Now if you want to walk again, we need to get up. I gotta warn you, getting up is hard. Think you can do it?

—I'll try.

—There is no try.

—What?

—Just do it.

—I will if you stop talking!

—Don't push me, Eva, or I'll leave you here with your hands glued to your chest like a bunny.

OK. Getting up 101. I'm gonna crouch. There's no weight on Themis's legs, so she'll just bring her knees up. You have to push up a little with your elbows and bend down at the same time so Themis ends up with her legs in a ball.

—Like that?

—Yes! There you go! Push with your hands all the way up. Push hard! Push! OK, just stay like that. Now for the tricky part. I'm gonna extend my legs. That'll bring us up, but you have to straighten your back at the same time. Not too early, not too late, or we'll just lunge forward and break a bunch of trees.

—Yes! Yes! Do it now. My arms hurt!

—Here we GO! Whoa! Shit! We're up. Don't move. Don't do anything.

—That was fun.

—Oh, you liked that, didn't you? What do you say we call it a day? We can try and *really* hurt ourselves tomorrow.

—OK.

—OK? That's all you have to say?

—I'm hungry.

—Me too, now that you mention it. OK. Let's get her down!

—Down?

—Yeah down! We need Themis to lie down if we want to get out.

—You mean fall again?

—No. I'm crouching, just keep the balance a bit. I'll make us fall forward now. You have to bend backwards a little and catch us with your hands. Like that. Now bend forward, lift her butt up and I can . . . stretch my legs. Stand straight, and she's . . . down for the night. Just stay put. I'll unstrap myself and come take your helmet off.

—I can do it!

—No, don't! It makes Themis look like an idiot.

—What? How?

—She's still moving with you. She'll turn off with her hands around her head, makes her look like she's pulling her hair or something. Let me do it, keep her dignity intact.

There. Let's get you out of your straitjacket.

—Can I ask you something?

—Why do you do that? Ask if you can ask a question? Has anyone ever said no?

—I—

—Just ask!

—You never told me what made you change your mind.

—About what?

—About my trying on the controls.

—Your mom did. I mean Kara. That, and Luke.

—Who?

—Skywalker . . . Never mind. I was hoping we could sit down for this. Have a cup of . . . whatever it is you ten-year-olds drink.

—Can we talk about it now?

—OK then. Kara, she sent me a letter when . . . I guess it was the night before you met her. She wasn't sure she was gonna make it out of there alive, and she asked me to promise a few things in case she didn't. It's a shitty thing to do to anyone in a letter, but I would have lost that argument anyway if she'd been around. Anyway, she asked me to . . . to let you figure things out for yourself, to let you be what you wanted to be.

I was fine with it. I was fine with it until you told me you wanted to pilot Themis. That was just . . . wrong, on so many levels. First, Kara also made me promise to keep you safe. There's nothing safe about being in here. This has to be one of the least safe places, anywhere. And it's *her* place. Kara and I got together at that station, right where you're standing . . . without the phone books. To let *anyone* take her place . . . I don't know, that meant letting her go. I don't want to let her go.

—You don't have to.

—I wasn't finished. There's also *why* you wanted to get in here in the first place. You said that's what Alyssa made you for. You said you were a tool. That got me angry. It seemed so . . . cruel. You . . . You're not a toaster, or a screwdriver. You're not just a means to an end. *You* get to decide what you are. You're my kid! You're not a tool!

One morning, I was in the shower and I flipped my knees—I do it from time to time or it'll hurt like hell when I *have* to do it. I was feeling the metal in my kneecap with my fingers, running my hand up and down my shin. My whole legs are metal. All the bones, all the joints. I . . . I felt like Luke staring at his mechanical hand after he cut Darth Vader's with his lightsaber. I'm a tool too. I'm someone's handiwork.

I don't know if I ever really had much of a choice, but I like to think I did. And I chose that. I chose to do what they made me for, serve my purpose. They made me into a screwdriver, and I chose to drive screws. It just seemed hypocritical for me to deny you that same choice. I would be saying "you can be what you wanna be, except what you were made for."

You were right. You're a tool. You're someone else's handiwork. *This* is why you were created. But you're more than that, Eva. So much more. You're a bright kid, with some serious but not insurmountable emotional issues. You do have a choice. You can choose to be . . . You can join the Army, or be a musician. You can be a scientist, a chef, a ballerina. You were made for a particular purpose, but you can be anything you want. *Anything*, including that.

I wish you could deal with all this ten years from now, but we might not have ten years. So if you choose to be a ballerina, we'd better get going on those dance lessons.

FILE NO. 1623

PERSONAL JOURNAL ENTRY—DR. ROSE FRANKLIN, HEAD OF SCIENCE DIVISION, EARTH DEFENSE CORPS

I'm important, "useful" is what he said. That's why I'm alive. I'm supposed to do something. I don't know what that is, but given our circumstances, it has to be something like saving the world. That's what I was told. That's right. Someone told me that. He told me the same way he said it might be too early for kung pao chicken. How does one process that kind of information? Did I need to know? Would I not have done it otherwise? Will knowing stop me from doing it?

I'd love to believe it. I'd love to be special. But I'm not. I'm not important. I'm not a savior. I wish I were. The only thing that stopped me from taking my own life is that people were dying by the millions. I thought I could . . . do something. I thought I could help. I never thought I could do it on my own, but that's why I stayed. I thought . . . I hoped I might be important.

I wanted to save everyone. I wanted it so bad. Maybe it's because no matter how much I try, I can't shake the thought that they're dying because of me. I fell on a hand and I brought the world to the brink of war. They brought me back to life and a hundred million people died. I am the harbinger of death.

Now I'm staring at my computer. I'm looking at every piece of data we have on the alien robots and I don't know where to start. I don't know what I'm supposed to do. If there's a reason for me to be here, there's a good chance it has to do with what I'm good at. So I'm focusing on the metal, its composition, waiting for the answer to jump out of the screen. It's entirely possible that what I'm supposed to achieve has nothing to do with physics. I could be wasting what little time I have trying to convince myself I'm a good scientist. Now I'm overanalyzing everything, wasting time thinking about wasting time.

And what if they're right? What if wiping us out of history is the right thing to do? I can't claim to have any objectivity on the matter. Everyone I care about would die in the process and I'd be left to live the most horrible life I can imagine, so my bias is obvious. But these aliens are evidently more evolved than we are. Their technology is incredibly more advanced. It's at least possible that their understanding of everything else is also leaps and bounds ahead of ours. Maybe they know what's best.

I feel so alone. I don't do well on my own. I need people to guide me. I need . . . I need Kara. I need someone I can talk to about anything, anything but this. I need someone who won't judge me based on whether or not I can save the world. I suppose no one really does judge me that way, but Kara was the only one who made me feel like I could just . . . be.

I need you, my nameless friend. Would you be OK with my calling you friend? You died with your arm around me, that has to count for something. Still, you'd probably be uncomfortable with the idea. Talking about you, I realize I'm still angry at you. I can forgive Kara, but you . . . You had no right to die. You had no right to leave me behind. What would you say if you were here? Something caustic, like: **Are you talking to yourself, Dr. Franklin?**

Yeah, I'm talking to myself . . . There's no one else to talk to. Everyone's dead. What would you do? What would you say to make me see? You weren't a scientist, but you'd have made a good one. You were detached, methodical. You could see this problem for what it is. I can only see . . . nonsense. How can I—me, alone—defeat giant alien robots that can withstand a nuclear explosion, without using anything that was invented in the last three thousand years? What can I do without any technology whatsoever? I can't even go near them. What would you say to that? You'd probably ask: **Do you believe you can defeat them by conversing with the recently deceased?**

Probably not. But I'm . . . *allowed* to talk to an imaginary friend. It's in the rules. They had crazy people three thousand years ago. There was nothing else around, though. Nothing but rocks, and dirt, and bugs. I'm sure I wouldn't like what you'd have to say now. It would be dry, bordering on insulting, but somehow supportive, in your own twisted way.

I know: **If that is true, Dr. Franklin, I suggest you stop talking to the dead and find a way to defeat these robots with rocks, dirt, and/or bugs.**

I'm losing my mind—**I believe that was the general idea that I was trying to convey.**

Why does that sentence ring a bell? Rocks, dirt, and/or bugs. What can I do with that? Rocks . . . Dirt . . . Bugs . . . I can throw rocks at them . . . Maybe they'll take pity on me, decide we're not that evolved after all. Think, Rose. Think . . .

Rocks . . .

Dirt . . .

Bugs . . .

Rocks, and dirt, and . . .

I think . . . I think I've got it.

Thank you. I don't believe in the afterlife, but thank you, wherever you are.

FILE NO. 1626

INTERVIEW WITH BRIGADIER GENERAL EUGENE GOVENDER, COMMANDER, EARTH DEFENSE CORPS

Location: Shadow Government Bunker, Lenexa, KS

—You can sit down, Dr. Franklin. You're stressing me out.

—Thank you, General.

—The Quebecois said you have a plan.

—I do. Half of one anyway.

—That's a half more than what we had an hour ago.

—I suppose so.

—Well? What are you waiting for? We don't have all day!

—Yes, sir. You know I've been going through everything we learned about the metal these robots are made of. There are slight differences, but it's essentially the same material they built Themis with. It's an alloy, mostly iridium, and it has a bunch of properties we can't explain but that we're beginning to understand. For example, we know it's able to store energy. We don't really know how it works, but we can make things with similar properties. We can make metal that stores solar energy and releases it when we want it to. We turn ruthenium into fulvalene diruthenium. That will store reasonably large amounts of solar energy that can be released using a catalyst.

—Ruthenium . . . Isn't there some of that in the metal that makes up Themis?

—There is, but in very minute quantities. Nothing that could explain what it does. And the metal in Themis actually prefers nuclear energy. It can store a phenomenal amount of power. The closest thing we have is something like uranium. We can't make it do what the metal in Themis does, but uranium does store energy and releases it over time. It's slow if you don't do anything to it, but it's enough to keep the Earth cooking. About half of the heat inside the planet comes from radioactive decay. We have little control over the amount of energy uranium releases and the speed at which it does, but if we create a fission chain reaction—in a nuclear reactor, for example—we can release a lot more energy, and a lot faster.

Anyway, I decided to think of it as uranium, see where it would lead.

—And?

—It gave me an idea. There's this special kind of bacteria, *Geobacter*. They have tiny wires on them—they're called pili—that insulate them from the toxic environment they live in, and they're able to transfer electrons to radioactive metal and change its properties. Basically, they can clean up radioactive waste, turn radioactive metal into a mineral by changing its molecular structure. It's a slow process, though, way too slow. Takes years for these things to eat just a tiny bit of radioactive waste.

There's a lab at Michigan State—it's run by a Dr. Lina Texera. They play with a particular kind of these bacteria, *Geobacter sulfurreducens*. They were able to increase the strength of the pili and make them more efficient. Basically, they added armor to the bacteria, made them more resistant so that they can mineralize uranium a lot faster.

It sounded promising. Even with some superarmor, it would take forever for these things to colonize something as big as the alien robots, but I thought it was worth a shot. Anyway, I called her. Nice woman. She called me Rose, said we met at a conference before—must have been before I died. I had her send over a sample by helicopter.

It's really disgusting, green, gooey stuff. I wasn't sure what to do with it. Anyway, I put on two pairs of gloves, one on top of the other, I took the little shard we had chipped off one of the panels and rubbed some of that goo on it with a Q-tip. The plan was to expose it to radiation and see if it would take longer to saturate and discharge, maybe release less energy, something. I let it rest on a block of plutonium for a good hour, I couldn't get it to release anything at all. The last time I had tried that, it took only ten minutes to destroy half my lab.

I tried a few drops of the mixture on one of the panels. Nothing happened. I put some of it under the microscope and all the bacteria were dead. So I took the whole thing—about a cupful of it—and just poured it on the panel. It didn't do anything at first, as I expected. I figured I'd come back later during the day. I turned off the light on my way out, then I noticed that the turquoise light in the symbols was wavering. Just a bit at first, then a little more. After about five minutes, the panel went completely dark. That was two hours ago and it hasn't turned back on.

Whatever makes that metal do the things it does, it must be a very fragile equilibrium. I think the bacteria just throws it off balance, enough to make it stop functioning.

—So that's your plan? Throw some green goo at the robot—

—At one of them, yes.

—When you got back from Washington, you told me you believe these aliens are waiting for us to demonstrate that we could be just as evolved if they hadn't messed with our gene pool.

—Yes. I could be wrong, of course.

—So the idea is to beat them without using anything that didn't exist before they showed up thousands of years ago.

—That's what I'm running with.

—But you said these bacteria have some kind of body armor that makes them better at eating up metal. Isn't that . . . cheating? I mean, I don't know the first thing about any of this, but this sounds like cutting-edge shit. Seems to me you wouldn't have these superbugs without modern science.

—I wouldn't have the regular kind either. These things have been on Earth for millions of years, but we've only just discovered them. If the aliens want to be literal about this, then we're screwed. I can't unlearn everything I know either. I'm hoping they're just looking for us to make a point. Like a . . . proof of concept.

—Sure. If you think it'll work.

—I don't know that it will. Even if it does, I can't be sure they'll get what we're doing.

—That's what I was gonna say. You wanna throw bugs at them. Aren't you worried you'll just piss them off?

—I don't think we have much of a choice. If Mr. Burns is telling the truth, there might be about three million people left on this planet by this time tomorrow. Vincent and Eva will die first. Then everyone else who doesn't have my crappy DNA.

—Lucky you. What do you need me for? I don't know the first thing about bacteria.

—I need more. I need a lot more. Dr. Texera is sending me what she has, but it's not much, and there's no time to grow enough of them there. She said there's a lab in Dalian, China, where they've been growing the same bacteria for about a year to run some experiments in a wastewater-treatment plant. I'd like you to send Themis to get it.

—With Eva?

—Yes. They can be back in a couple hours. I don't wanna waste a day having it flown here.

—I can order Vincent to go, but I can't send a goddamn child against her will.

—Just ask. I think they'll want to go. If Vincent doesn't think she's ready, he'll tell you.

—I suppose if the world's gonna end in the next twenty-four hours, she's as ready as she's ever gonna be. I'll talk to her.

—Thank you. She was playing outside a few minutes ago.

—I have *one* more question about that half plan of yours.

—Go ahead.

—How are you gonna get the goo *on* the bad guys if you can't touch them? You've shown me birds dropping down a good foot away from the robots. Kara and Vincent fired lightning bolts at one of them and they couldn't hit anything either. Your superbugs are gonna get zapped by the robot's energy field before they can do their thing.

—Yes, that's . . . the other half of the plan, the one I don't have. I have no idea how to get around their energy field. I thought about building something that could go through it. I don't know what force could be used to build an energy field that stops solid objects, but if it's anything like electromagnetism, something made of superconducting material might make the energy field flow around it. I don't know. In any case, superconductors have to be kept insanely cold. We don't have anything I could just carry around. And even if we did, I couldn't test it. Besides, we don't have that kind of time. I'm betting on something much simpler. I don't believe their shield extends all the way to the ground. I think the bottoms of their feet are exposed, maybe the first few inches from the ground.

—Achilles' heel? That's your plan!? That sounds a little . . . convenient, don't you think?

—It would be *extremely* convenient if I could figure out how to reach under their feet. I don't think a few inches of bacterial culture around their feet will be enough to power down something that size. I'll need more surface for the bacteria to survive. The whole bottom of a foot might be enough, but I doubt they'll cooperate and stand on one leg.

—Maybe you can bring it a giant treat, teach it to give paw. Don't take this the wrong way, Dr. Franklin, but that has to be the dumbest, most ill-conceived plan I have ever heard! And believe me, I'm in the military, I've heard a lot of dumb plans.

—If I could make it walk . . . You're right. I have no idea how to do this. But it has to happen today, so I'll just have to improvise if I can't come up with anything before Vincent and Eva come back with the bacteria. I'll bring a shovel.

—Seven billion lives on the line, and you'll *improvise*—

—I wish I had something better, I—

—Dr. Franklin.

—Yes?

—Good luck.

FILE NO. 1629

MISSION REPORT—VINCENT COUTURE, CONSULTANT, EDC AND EVA REYES

Location: Shadow Government Bunker, Lenexa, KS

—This is Vincent Couture. I'm with Eva Reyes, back at the base. We had a lovely trip to China. They said they needed an extra couple hours to get the bacteria ready for transport. They had put it in a refrigerated container that wasn't gonna fit through our hatch, so . . . I asked Eva what was on her bucket list, and she said she'd like to see the pyramids. We crossed that one off. We were only there for five minutes, but she was happy. You were, Eva! You looked happy, anyway. She's smiling. Eva was a champ. We didn't even fall once, and she didn't freak out—OK, maybe a little—when we were at the bottom of the sea. We made it to Dalian just in time. We loaded the cargo and headed home. Total duration of our Chinese escapade: two hours, forty-seven minutes.

Dr. Franklin left for New York with the bacterial culture about an hour ago. At least I hope that was bacterial culture. It might have been beer. The friendly folks at the Dalian University of Technology gave us three kegs. For real, regular college-kid drink-from-the-tap-until-you-pass-out kegs. So, if Rose can't save humanity with what's in there, there's at least hope for a decent end-of-the-world party. Not for you, Eva, but we'll find you some Army-issued apple juice somewhere.

—Hey!

—OK. Maybe a sip. I could use a beer right about now. Dr. Franklin is probably there already. General Govender and the rest of the staff are in the control room. They have a bunch of drones up there— really cool quadcopters, they won't let me play with them—so they can see from different angles. It's like a football game. Eva . . . I think Eva was scared a little. She didn't wanna go, but she's racking up the nerves as we speak. I guess we'll—

—It won't work.

—I'm sorry, what'd you say?

—IT WON'T WORK!

—What are you talking about, Eva?

—Rose! Her plan. It won't work!

—How do you know?

—I . . . I just know.

—You saw something, didn't you?

—Yes.

—What did you see?

—She'll get stepped on. She'll die.

—Why do they step on her?

—I don't know! Maybe it's an accident. Maybe they just don't see her. All I know is she'll die. She gets crushed into the ground. Her body—

—OK, that's enough! Rose said that your visions are . . . possible futures, that what you see might not happen at all.

—She'll die! Don't try to make me feel better. I'm telling you, she'll die.

— . . .

—Vincent, please!

—We'll die if we go, Eva. You'll die!

—We'll all die if we don't. Please trust me.

— . . .

—Say something!

—Crap.

—What does that mean?

—That means . . . That means crap! Grab your gear! We can't just let her die, now can we? Hell, I've lived a good life. You got to see the pyramids, and Kansas, eat MREs three times a day. What else is there, really?

—Thank you.

—Ha! This might be the greatest mistake anyone has ever made in the history of the human race. You're just lucky there aren't any adults left around to make responsible decisions.

—Should we tell the General?

—Not if you don't want to be locked up in this room with half a dozen guards at the door.

—You think so?

—They've been planning this all day with just about everyone from the Army to the Coast Guard. I don't think they'll be really impressed when we tell them we wanna crash the party because the ten-year-old with a chip on her shoulder had a vision, while watching the *Walking Dead,* I might add.

—I was just asking. There's no need to be mean.

—I'm sorry.

—It's OK.

—I mean, I'm sorry that this is your life. You should be playing with dolls or something.

—I hate dolls.

FILE NO. 1631

MISSION LOG—BRIGADIER GENERAL EUGENE GOVENDER, COMMANDER, EARTH DEFENSE CORPS

Location: Shadow Government Bunker, Lenexa, KS

—We're missing someone. Where's Jamie?

[*He went to the bathroom, General. Here he is.*]

Nice of you to join us. Anything else you need to do, or can we get started?

[*Sorry, sir. Won't happen again.*]

Damn right it won't. All right, folks. Let's get this show on the road. We have a full room today. As you know, we have no satellite capabilities. These boys in the white shirts over here are on loan from the Federal Bureau of Investigation, UAS division. They are our eyes and ears. Fellows, welcome to the EDC. How many drones do we have?

[*Four, sir. One tracking your vehicle. Three standing by at Riverside Park.*]

Get them in the air now. I want drones at the northern corners of the park, the other one on the 102nd Street crossing. I want the robot on every screen in this room before Dr. Franklin gets within two miles of that thing. How are we doing on the ground?

[*Special Forces are in position at Bellevue Hospital. We also have an STS team standing by in case we need air evac.*]

That was Lieutenant General Alan A. Simms, visiting us from Fort Bragg. He is in command of our extraction team. Thank you for joining us.

[*Happy to serve, General.*]

We couldn't find anyone from special ops with the genetic makeup to survive a gas attack so these men will keep their distance. We did find one NYPD officer with the right DNA. I forget his name. Jamie?

[*Officer . . . something.*]

Thank you . . . Jamie. Thank you so much . . . Officer . . . something . . . is standing . . .

[*Langdon!*]

Dammit, Jamie! Officer Langdon is standing by at . . . Park and 110th. He can get Dr. Franklin out of there if this turns into a smoke fest.

Speaking of . . . Dr. Franklin flew to Davison Army Airfield in Virginia earlier today. She left for New York on a UH-72 and landed at Bellevue Hospital about twenty minutes ago. She is driving the rest of the way, alone. Plan is: She'll approach the robot on foot. We want them to see her. She'll spray bacteria on whatever section of the robot she can reach. If she's right, that should disable it within a few minutes. If she's not . . . Let's just hope she's right. Is that her on number four?

[*Yes, sir.*]

Put her on the big screen. She'll get off the FDR at 96th . . . there . . . she'll enter Central Park at 97th. Put her on audio. Dr. Franklin, you're with us?

{*Yes, sir. Had to go around a few abandoned cars, but I'll make it. Two minutes.*}

Good. We have you onscreen. Let us know when you get there.

All right people! You heard the lady. Two minutes! Remember, this is her show. If she asks for something, don't look at me, just do it. You see anything, you let her know.

{*General, I'm entering Central Park.*}

Roger that. We're ready when you are.

   Everyone. Stay sharp. I wanna know if that robot so much as farts in her general direction.

{*I'm getting off here, General.*}

Very well. Rescue team is standing by. Holler if you need anything.

{*Thank you. Wish me luck.*}

Luck is believing you're lucky. Go get 'em.

   She's having a hard time getting the containers out of the car. Jamie, how much does this bacteria stuff weigh?

[*About 160 pounds.*]

Thank you . . . How the hell do you know?

[*That's how much a beer keg weighs. I figured, they're both liquids . . .*]

We're lucky to have you. All right, she's moving towards the robot. Any sign of movement?

[*No, sir. Nothing on infra—*]

Goddammit! What's Themis doing there? Gimme that radio! Couture, is that you?

<*Yes, sir. Me and Eva.*>

You goddamn son of a bitch! Get your dumb ass out of there before you get her killed.

<*Eva! Raise your arm! I can't talk, sir. Bye . . .* >

Don't you hang up on me, son! Don't you *dare* hang up on me! Jamie, get him back.

[*General, the alien robot is firing on Themis.*]

Yes, I can see that! Come on, Vincent, the shield! Dammit, put your shield up! Good boy! They're gonna get slaughtered. Dr. Franklin. You need to get out of there!

{*Yes, General! That's what I'm trying to do!*}

They're getting pounded. Does the kid even know how to fire the weapon?

[*Not as far as I know, sir. They only practiced walking.*]

Goddamn, that was stupid! Why is Dr. Franklin still there? No! No! Leave the damn keg!

[*She's running now, sir.*]

It's about time.

[*Themis is up.*]

What the hell are they doing?

[*What are they doing, sir?*]

Is there an echo in this room? They're . . . They're giving it a bear hug! Dammit, Couture! They'll never be able to hold on with a ten-year-old controlling the arms.

   Jamie, tell Officer Langdon to drive north as fast as he can, I have a bad feeling about this.

[*I'm on it, sir. He'll be—*]

What just happened?

[*Sir, we lost video, communications—*]

Goddamn! Everyone listen! We're deaf and we're blind. That is unacceptable. Jamie, call Dr. Franklin on her cell. FBI, can you get more drones in the air?

[*Ten minutes.*]

We don't have ten minutes. This will be over in two. Jamie! How about that call?

[*It goes straight to voicemail. Cell towers must be down near the park.*]

Keep trying. General, is there a camera on that chopper of yours?

[*There's one with STS, but it transmits via satellite.*]

Get it airborne anyway. One of your men must have a cellphone with a camera. They couldn't have knocked out every cell tower in Manhattan. Jamie, can you get a video call on the big screen?

[*In the next minute, no. I can show it on my laptop. It's in my locker.*]

Then what the hell are you still doing here! Gentlemen, I want eyes on in two minutes. Two minutes!

I'll call the president.

FILE NO. 1632

MISSION LOG—VINCENT COUTURE, CONSULTANT, EDC AND EVA REYES
Location: Somewhere in Missouri

—Vincent! What are you doing?

—What does it look like I'm doing? I'm getting us to New York so we can do . . . *God knows what* and save Rose.

—We keep reappearing on the same highway.

—Well, yeah . . . We don't have GPS anymore. If I transport us somewhere far, then . . . well, then we'll be far, and we won't know where we are. We can't exactly stop for directions, you know. So I'm following the highway.

—Won't that take forever?

—I'm jumping about two miles every three seconds. We're not exactly standing still.

—I don't think we have enough time.

—Not enough . . . That's twenty-four hundred miles an hour! We'll be there in thirty minutes.

—We need to go faster.

—How do you know? Do these visions of yours come with a time stamp or something?

—Please!

—You wanna go faster? How about . . . this?

—AAAAH! Where are we?

—We are . . . in the Atlantic Ocean. I just jumped twelve hundred miles due east. If I'm correct, we're off the coast, somewhere near Atlantic City. If not, then I don't know. But I got the water part right. We're definitely in the ocean.

—I can't see anything! I'm—

—You're a little freaked-out, aren't you?

—Can you get us out of here?

—Sure . . . Pretty sure.

—Please! Please! Go!

—Hey! You're the one who wanted to go faster! I was perfectly fine on the highway, but you thought three times the speed of sound was too . . . leisurely.

—GET US OUT OF HERE!

—OK! OK! I'm turning us around! There! We're moving again!

—We're still underwater!

—Now! There we are. Well, that's not Atlantic City, but it's the shore and we're south of where we're going. We'll just follow the coast to New York. Here. Enjoy the view. You'll be able to see New York in a couple jumps . . . Look! Over there. That's Manhattan.

—Where are we?

—New Jersey. The highlands. That island over there is Sandy Hook.

—You've been there?

—No, but I saw brochures when I was a kid. Maybe a year or two younger than you are. My mother always wanted us to go. We never did. But I liked the brochures. Let's see if I can eyeball us across that bay. Meh. Second time's a charm. We'll stay in the Hudson River until we get as far north as Central Park.

—We won't see anything!

—Sure we'll see. It's shallow. Look! Our *ass* is above water. It won't get deeper than that. We're almost there, anyway.

—Can we walk the rest of the way?

—I'd rather not. God knows what's down there. There are at least a couple tunnels in the Hudson between here and where we're going. Here's one. And . . . I think we missed one. What do you think? Think we're far enough?

—I don't know! Why don't we walk on land . . . like normal people?

—Normal people can walk without tearing down every electrical wire. We can't fit anywhere in the city. We'll get stuck, destroy things. I'm gonna try and jump straight into the park. Google maps say it's about five thousand feet from the river. If we're in the right spot—

—You've been looking at your phone all along?

—Did *you* bring a map, Eva? Didn't think so. Let's do this. Are you ready?

—Go! Go!

—And . . . we're there. Err . . . Maybe not.

—We're in a river again.

—More or less. I think we're on what's left of a bridge. We're in Harlem, we must have gone too far. I'll turn us around. One more jump and we're there, for real. Ready?

—You can stop asking. Just go . . . Holy shit! We're right behind him!

—Damn! That guy is *huge*!

—Back up, Vincent! Back up!

—I am! Rose! Are you there? It won't work! You need to turn around!

[*Vincent! What are you doing here?*]

Eva saw it. It won't work! Get out of the way!

[*Get out of here, Vincent! They'll kill you!*]

I said it first, Rose. Go! Run!

—Vincent. He's turning around! Back off! Back off!

{*Couture, is that you?*}

—Yes, sir. Me and Eva.

{*You goddamn son of a bitch! Get your dumb ass out of there before you get her killed.*}

—Vincent! He's gonna hit us. What do I do? Vincent?!

—Eva! Raise your arm! I can't talk, sir. Bye . . . I'll give you the shield. Raise your left arm, Eva. Like you're . . . Yes, like that!

—AAARRGH!!

—That asshole knocked us on our ass again. Eva, you OK?

—It hurts! Make him stop! Can we leave?

—Not with the shield on. But let's see if we can return the favor. Raise your right arm. Point it at . . . You're good at this! Firing! Again! Again!

—It's not doing anything! Vincent!

—We're not done yet. Rose! We're gonna try to knock his shield off for you with an energy burst, like we did in Denver. Do you understand?

[*Wh . . . I need more time!*]

No can do. Get as far away from us as you can. Eva, keep the shield up! When I tell you, push us off the ground with your right arm. I'll get us up.

—What are we doing?

—Something your mother and I did once.

—Did it work?

—Well, we killed Rose. Now! Push! OK, we're up. I'm running at him.

—We're gonna hit him!

—Exactly. Wrap your arms around him and hold on!

—Like that? I'm scared, Vincent!

—Just hold on to him, Eva!

—I can't!

—You have to! Just a bit longer!

—I CAN'T! He's too strong! What are you doing?!

—I'm taking my helmet off. I'm coming to help you. Don't let go!

—Who'll control the legs?!

—We don't need to use our legs. We just need to hold on. Themis will do the rest.

—Hurry! My arms are—

—We're gonna die if you let go, Eva. I'm almost out. Pretend you're in a storm at sea, and he's the only thing you can hold on to.

—I'm not strong enough! I'm sorr—

—I'm here! I'm here, Eva! I'm gonna wrap my arms around you and we'll hold on together.

—I can't see with you standing in front of me.

—It's OK. You don't need to see him. Just look at me. Look at me, Eva. There. Biggest hug in history.

—What's that noise?

—That's Themis getting angry. She's absorbing power from his energy field. That hiss means she's about to overload. Rose! Ready or not! Close your eyes, Eva. It's gonna get really bright.

—AAAAAHH! What just happened?

—His shield is out. Keep your arms around him while I get back to my station, then we'll kick his ass.

—No! Don't go! I can't . . . He's out! Vincent! He's out! He's grabbing us! He's gonna throw us down! I can't stop him!

—AAAAAARRRGGHHHH!

—Vincent! Vincent, are you OK? Answer me!

—I'm . . . not OK. I flew into the wall when we hit the ground. My shoulder . . . I think I broke my arm. My right leg's all . . . bent. It won't move at all. Roll us on our back, will you? I can't see anything.

—How do I do that? OK, I got it.

—I'll get to the console and turn on the shield again. He's coming at us.

—Can you get us up?

—No. I can't get into the controls. Let me get my helmet on . . . He looks like he's about to punch us in the face. He is punching us in the . . . AAARGH! *Calver!* Can you hit him too?

— . . .

—Eva! I know this is scary but you need to snap out of it. Can you hit him?

—Our left arm is pinned under his foot. I can hit him with the right.

—Hit him in the gut.

—I can't reach his gut.

—Doesn't matter, I'll fire when you get close. Now! Ha! That hurt, didn't it?

—Keep firing, Vincent! Again!

—That's my kid kicking your ass! You messed with the wrong ten-year-old!

—Again! Again! Again! . . . Again! Vincent, keep firing! He's still up!

—I'm—

—What?

—We're out of juice. We discharged, and now we've drained whatever was left. She won't fire.

—Themis won't move with me anymore.

—I know. We can't move. We can't do anything.

—Then what?

—Then . . . I guess we wait.

—For how long?

—I don't know. We've never drained her bef—

—He's coming back! He's coming back! Vincent, there's a . . . it looks like a disc of light in his hand.

—Shit.

—What is it?

—I'm pretty sure that's what erased half of London.

—Do something!

—I can't!

—Are we gonna die?

—Eva, I—

—I don't wanna die . . . I wanna get out!

—Eva!

—HOW DO I GET OUT?

—EVA!

—GET ME OUT OF THIS THING!

—EVA, STOP!

— . . .

—You're a good kid, Eva. I'm glad I got to meet you.

—Can you hold me again?

—I wish I could, Eva. You can't imagine how much I want to, but I can't get to you. Look at me.

— . . .

—I'm right here, Eva. Look at me.

—Dad . . .

— . . . Yes?

—I'm sorry.

—There's nothing to—

—LOOK! He's turning away from us!

—I can't see. I took my helmet off.

—He's looking at . . . There's a pickup truck coming!

—Does he still have his disc thing in his hand?

—I don't think so. Someone's getting out of the truck. I think it's Dr. Franklin.

—WAY TO GO, ROSE!

—There's white gas coming out of . . . somewhere, everywhere.

—What do you see?

— . . .

—Eva! What do you see?!

—I see nothing. Nothing but white.

FILE NO. 1633

MISSION LOG—DR. ROSE FRANKLIN, HEAD OF SCIENCE DIVISION, EARTH DEFENSE CORPS
Location: Central Park, New York, NY

—General, I'm entering Central Park.

[*Roger that. We're ready when you are.*]

This is awful. There are people lying on the grass . . . everywhere. It looks like they're taking a nap. Cyclists on the side of the road. Someone should take care of them. I'll stop here. I think that's close enough. I must be . . . a thousand feet from the robot.

General, I'm getting off here.

[*Very well. Rescue team is standing by. Holler if you need anything.*]

Thank you. Wish me luck.

[*Luck is believing you're lucky. Go get 'em.*]

I believe. I believe. So . . . I'm out of the vehicle. The robot is standing right in front of me. It is facing me but I don't know if they've seen me or not. I must look like an ant from where they're sitting. I'm getting the bacteria out of the vehicle. One . . . The containers are . . . really . . . heavy. I'll have to carry them one at the time with the . . . dolly. Two . . . The pump and the hose are in my backpack. I also . . . brought . . . a small Army shovel. And that's three.

I'm making my way towards the robot. I'll turn on my projector in a second. I don't know how they'll react but I have to make sure they see me. They have to know that I'm responsible for whatever is happening to them, if anything happens. Shit. The robot's feet are on East Drive. Part of the right foot is on the grass, but only for five or six feet. The rest is on asphalt. So much for my shovel. I hope there's enough of a gap in the shield above ground for me to . . .

What the . . . ? Themis just appeared a hundred feet behind the alien robot.

{*Rose! Are you there? It won't work! You need to turn around!*}

Vincent! What are you doing here?!

{*Eva saw it. It won't work! Get out of the way!*}

Get out of here, Vincent! They'll kill you!

{*I said it first, Rose. Go! Run!*}

The robot is turning away from me. I don't know what to do . . . They're firing! I'm heading back to the vehicle.

[*Dr. Franklin. You need to get out of there!*]

Yes, General! That's what I'm trying to do! I can't . . . run with this. . . . I can't hold the dolly. Shit . . . I lost the container. It fell off and it's rolling away. . . . Got it . . . I'm bringing . . . it . . . back—

{*Rose! We're gonna try to knock his shield off for you with an energy burst, like we did in Denver. Do you understand?*}

Wh . . . I need more time!

{*No can do. Get as far away from us as you can.*}

Shit! Shit! . . . I'm leaving the container behind. I'm almost there. OK, I am back in the vehicle. Where did I . . . ? In the ignition. I'm turning around . . . Heading back south the way I came. I'm driving by the baseball fields now. I need to put at least half a mile between me and Themis before she discharges . . . Jesus Christ! Someone fired at the road ahead of me. A good chunk of it just . . . disappeared. I almost drove straight into it. I just crossed 97th, still heading south on East Drive.

{*Rose! Ready or not!*}

No! Not yet! Arrrghh!

. . .

God, that hurts. Everything went . . . white. I . . . I hit a car. The air bag . . . I . . . I think it broke my nose. My Jeep's dead. I'm trying to get out of here. If I can just reach the handle . . . Yesss! I'm out. Wow. The road behind me is . . . gone. The pulse missed me by about a hundred feet. I can't see Themis. Just the other robot pounding at the ground on the edge of the crater. It must be them.

General, tell them to teleport out of here. You have to get them out! General? General, can you hear me? Anyone? I have to get back. I hit an abandoned pickup truck. Let's see if the keys are in it. Yes! I'll just grab one of the containers . . . Put it . . . in the back . . .

Vincent, can you hear me! I'm coming!

I need to get their attention. I'm heading inside the crater. High beam, low beam. Fog lights! Yes! I hope they can hear the horn. The robot is standing above Themis. She's not moving. I see some light in the alien robot's left hand. Some sort of disc. I think it's about to do what it did in London the first time. Faster! Here! I'm here! Come on! *Come on!* Look at me! There you go! That's it! Turn around!

It's looking right at me. I'm getting out of the truck. I'm roughly two hundred feet away. I'm taking the container out of the back. Getting the hose out of my backpack and . . . plugging it in. I think that's how it goes. Now all I need is to . . . drag . . . this . . . thing . . . two hundred feet . . . in the dirt. The robot is just staring at me. I think . . . Yes, the light on him is getting brighter. It's . . . it's releasing gas. I can't see where it's coming from. It's as if it's forming *around* it. It doesn't seem to be coming out of anything. The gas will reach me in about five seconds. I hope it's the same thing it sent out before. We'll know soon enough . . . That's it. I'm completely surrounded. I can't see. I can't see my own feet.

That container's so heavy . . . I'll just . . . stop . . . sit for a minute . . . I can taste the blood running into my mouth. That iron taste . . . We're . . . We're all made of the same thing.

The gas is dissipating. I can see the sky again. I can see the light of the robot seeping through. I can see my feet. Soon they will see me too. Time to get up.

I'm about halfway there. It's really . . . heavy. I . . . I wonder what they're thinking. They're probably wondering who this crazy woman is, dragging a beer keg in the dirt. At least, now they know I'm . . . not like them. There's only a bit of gas left on the ground, like dry ice onstage at a rock concert. My feet are dragging through it, creating small currents in the mist. It's really pretty . . . The keg doesn't feel as heavy anymore. It must be the adrenaline. Those feet are gigantic when you're standing next to them. I'm there. I can . . . I can touch it. The shield is gone. It's . . . It's cold. Even where there's light, it's cold.

I'm ready. Holding the hose. I'm pumping . . . It's working. I can reach . . . maybe fifteen feet high. I can cover the whole foot, the ankle. I feel like a dog urinating on a lamppost. I'm afraid they'll just kick me away. This side is pretty well covered. I'm dragging the container to the other side. The robot's feet are fairly close to one another. If I stand here, I can probably . . . Bad idea. I have to get closer. I'm running out of solution already. That's it. I'm all out. I'll just give it a minute or two.

Slowly stepping away. I'm walking backwards the way I came so they can see me. So far nothing. It might not be enough. That container looked big until I was standing inches away from the alien robot. It's like painting a building. I should have brought the other container. I can always go back to get it if this doesn't work.

I'm beginning to doubt this entire plan. If they were looking for us to make a statement, my spreading green goo all over their feet seems a little . . . understated. I don't even know if that's what they're looking for. I don't know if they're looking for anything. This might be a complete waste . . . Wait . . . Wait . . .

It's hard to see in daylight, but I think the light in the right foot is beginning to flicker. Maybe I'm just imagining things. No . . . The light went off for half a second or so. Again . . . Again . . . The lights went off on the entire foot now. I wonder it that'll be enough to . . . Now the lower leg is dark. The left foot is flickering. I barely sprayed anything on that one. I think they've lost power on the entire right . . . I . . .

I barely got out of the way. The lower leg just fell off. It's now standing on one leg, and that one is losing power as well. I think it's about to fall on its—I don't even know how to call these—the upper knee. I have nowhere to run but straight ahead. There are trees everywhere. I'm running as fast as I can, but I'm not sure I can outrun a twenty-story building. I can hear it crumbling down behind me.

The bacteria must have thrown off the molecular structure on the entire robot! It's coming down. I can see its shadow stretching in front of me. I don't think I'll . . . AAAAAARRRRGGHHHH!

Something caught my leg. A rock, maybe. I don't think it's a piece of the robot. I can see its head to my left. I think it was a large rock. My knee . . . My leg is . . . I can see the bone sticking out. I think I'm gonna faint. Take a deep breath, Rose. The worst is over. I made it. I don't know if that's what they were looking for, but it worked. That robot is done for. My leg . . . Can anyone hear me? Vincent? Vincent, can you hear me? General? I need help. I need a doctor. Hello? Is anyone list . . . ? OH GOD!

One. Two. Three. Four. . . . Five. Six, seven, eight. They're . . . I think they're all here now. The alien robots, they . . . they just appeared, all of them. AAAHHH! One more . . . It just materialized, maybe one hundred feet in front of me. I can't move . . . I can't run away . . . Can anyone help me?

It's . . . It's magnificent . . . They're just looking at me, all of them. It's like . . . Times Square, the first time you see it. It's like an army of gods, each with its own color. It must mean something to them. The one closest to me is orange. It's Hyperion. What's it doing? It's crouching. It's putting its hand down on the ground, maybe thirty feet to my right. His head . . . His head is coming down over me. God help me. It's . . . It's right above me. I can almost touch it . . .

I'm . . . I'm so sorry. Please forgive me . . .

Where did it go? It was staring at me, then it vanished. Another one . . . They're all disappearing, one at a time.

I'm alone . . . It's over.

EPILOGUE

FILE NO. 1641

PARTY LOG—EVA REYES

Location: Inside Themis, EDC Headquarters, New York, NY

—This is Eva Reyes. We're on board Themis, celebrating. I'm with my dad, Dr. Franklin, and General Govender. I . . . I don't know what I'm supposed to say! Hey Vincent?

[*Yes, Eva?*]

Why do I have to wear the headset?

[*Because we're recording this. Rose likes to record everything.*]

I know that, but why me? Why can't any of you wear it?

[*Let's see. I have a broken shoulder and a bent-up leg. Rose has a broken tibia.*]

It's a headset. It goes on your head.

[*You can move around more than we can. Stop complaining, will you?*]

The General could wear it.

[*The General is slightly inebriated.*]

{*I heard that, Couture!*}

[*Sorry, sir. I meant to say you're drunk as a skunk.*]

{*It's that damn champagne. Why can't I get a real drink? And why is it so dark in here? I can barely see my glass!*}

That's the other thing I wanted to ask about. Why am I the only one drinking juice?

[*So you can do the recording. Oh, that and you're ten.*]

Come on, Vincent! I just kicked some giant robot's ass. I just want one glass of champagne.

[*Technically, Rose kicked his ass—*]

<*Come here, Eva. I'll give you a glass. A small one!*>

Thank you, Dr. Franklin.

<*I told you to call me Rose.*>

I'm not sure I—

<*Vincent does it. If you don't, I'll start calling you Ms. Reyes.*>

Ok, then, Rose. How does it feel?

<*Champagne? It's—*>

No, I meant you were right. Your plan worked.

<*I guess it did. Why are you making that face, General?*>

{*Show the aliens we could be just as tough without them messing with our DNA, by shooting some green goo full of bacteria out of a keg—*}

What are you saying, General?

{*I'm saying . . . What was I saying?*}

<*The General was saying he didn't think my plan had any chance of success.*>

Is that right, General?

{*Not a chance in hell.*}

Haha! What about you, Vincent? Did you think it would work?

[*Me? I—*]

<You thought it was stupid. Come on, Vincent! You can say it!>

[No, Rose! I understood the logic behind it. I just wasn't sure that, even if the bacteria worked, the aliens were gonna get the right message.]

<We don't know that they did.>

How can you say that, Dr. Franklin? They left, didn't they?

<It's Rose, remember? We don't know why they left. We don't know if that's what they really wanted us to do. This is just what Mr. Burns told me. He knows more about them than we do, but he hasn't talked to them. He was probably guessing as much as we were.>

Why else would they have left?

{Because Dr. Franklin sprayed them with some goddamn goo!}

[General, maybe you should try some of Eva's juice.]

It's apple juice.

{Shut up, Couture! That's an order!}

Seriously, Rose. Why else would they leave?

<Your father can guess. Ask him!>

Vincent?

[I don't know! I think, maybe, they could have been scared by the bacteria. What if all their robots, their ships, maybe their homes, are made using the same technology. Imagine for a second what would happen if some of that bacteria made it to their world.]

. . .

What was that?

[I can't remember what I was saying. Did the light just get brighter?]

Maybe.

[I think Themis just powered up.]

<Without any of the helmets on?>

Can she do that?

{I don't know! I've never been in this damn robot of yours.}

Vincent?

[*The console is lit up. Eva, get up there and put your helmet on.*]

Sure. But we're in a garage! What do you expect me to see?

[*I don't know, Eva. It's just a hunch.*]

I'm putting it on. I . . . I don't think—

[*What is it, Eva?*]

<Eva?>

{*Goddammit, kid! What do you see?*}

Guys? I don't think we're on Earth anymore . . .

ACKNOWLEDGMENTS

One of the things you learn as a debut author is that you're basically one book behind in your acknowledgments. You write them a good year (a year and a half in the case of *Sleeping Giants*) before your book goes on sale and you don't yet realize that about thirty thousand people will work on it before it hits the shelves.

So, for this book and the last. Thank you, Seth. You're a superhero. Theo keeps asking me for pictures of you. Thank you, Will Roberts and Rebecca Gardner for getting my books translated in more languages than Themis has body parts, and for challenging me to expand my whisky collection. *Seventeen* languages as I'm writing this. That's crazy! Thank you, Mark Tavani for believing in this book. To my new, awesome, alien-butt-kicking editor, Mike Braff: you are the best. So glad to be working with you on this, and I hope we get to pilot many more giant robot adventures together. So many people to thank at Del Rey: Keith, David, Tricia: you are as amazing as you are tireless. To Emily, Ashley, Erika, Alexandra: Wow! Thank you for the best promotion any author could ever dream of. Oh! Erich! I wrote *Star Wars* canon because of you. *Star Wars!* Canon! Thank you! I know I'm forgetting a million people who worked on this: copy editors, graphic designers, etc. Even if your name is not on this page, believe me when I say, I'm grateful.

Thank you, Sheila at Random House Canada for all the work on our side of the border (and for sending me to Space). Thank you, Emad, Huw, and everyone at Michael Joseph for your amazing work in the UK. I hope you don't live in one of the neighborhoods I obliterated. To all the voice actors on the audiobook: Andy Secombe, Charlie Anson, Christopher Ragland, Eric Meyers, Laurel Lefkow, Liza Ross, William Hope, Adna Sablylich, Katharine Mangold. Bravo! I don't know the names of everyone who worked behind the scenes on the audio but you created something special.

Thank you to all the reviewers, journalists, and book bloggers who featured *Sleeping Giants* and helped promote this book. Booksellers! I love you all! I was looking for a good metaphor, but I don't need one. You sell books! How cool is that? I owe you a debt of gratitude, and a beer.

To the people close to me: friends and family who have given me their love and support, group hug.

And you! Yes, you! I've been blessed with the most amazing readers from the start. All of this would be meaningless without you. There's really no way to express how grateful I am for your interest, your time, your emails, your tweets, your letters. This has been one big crazy trip for me, and I'm so glad you came along for the ride.

He just wanted a decent book to read ...

Not too much to ask, is it? It was in 1935 when Allen Lane, Managing Director of Bodley Head Publishers, stood on a platform at Exeter railway station looking for something good to read on his journey back to London. His choice was limited to popular magazines and poor-quality paperbacks – the same choice faced every day by the vast majority of readers, few of whom could afford hardbacks. Lane's disappointment and subsequent anger at the range of books generally available led him to found a company – and change the world.

'We believed in the existence in this country of a vast reading public for intelligent books at a low price, and staked everything on it'
Sir Allen Lane, 1902–1970, founder of Penguin Books

The quality paperback had arrived – and not just in bookshops. Lane was adamant that his Penguins should appear in chain stores and tobacconists, and should cost no more than a packet of cigarettes.

Reading habits (and cigarette prices) have changed since 1935, but Penguin still believes in publishing the best books for everybody to enjoy. We still believe that good design costs no more than bad design, and we still believe that quality books published passionately and responsibly make the world a better place.

So wherever you see the little bird – whether it's on a piece of prize-winning literary fiction or a celebrity autobiography, political tour de force or historical masterpiece, a serial-killer thriller, reference book, world classic or a piece of pure escapism – you can bet that it represents the very best that the genre has to offer.

Whatever you like to read – trust Penguin.